Novels by
William F. Buckley, Jr.

STAINED GLASS
SAVING THE QUEEN

Published by
WARNER BOOKS

William F. Buckley, Jr.
teams his CIA hero Blackford Oakes
with the Russian KGB in a "mission
impossible" adventure
to stop World War III.

"Buckley executes the international thriller as well as nearly anyone . . . There's a lightness of touch and a facileness of invention that suggests that even if he is dead serious about the ingredients of his novel, he is having nothing but fun in putting them together."
—Christopher Lehmann-Haupt, *New York Times*

"An elegant and engaging tale of East-West skullduggery."

—*Saturday Review*

"With admirable versatility, he combines tantalizing intellectual conundrums with wildly improbable, hilarious action. Even for confirmed liberals, this is several hours of superb diversion."
—*St. Louis Post-Dispatch*

"Buckley's main purpose is to entertain; he's erudite and stylish and witty and sly, and so is this caper."

—*The Village Voice*

"Buckley's superb command of the language, his rapier wit, his flair for intrigue and depiction of political chicanery add up to literate escapism . . . fun."

—*South Bend Tribune*

STAINED GLASS

"An abundance of wit . . . He has substantial talents as a storyteller."

—*Wall Street Journal*

"A brilliantly tantalizing plot to tickle one's brain power."

—*Cleveland Press*

"Delightfully suspenseful . . . enough style and unexpected angles to transcend the formula. It is, one might say, a work of vulpine scrivening."

—*People* magazine

"A bright, entertaining novel written with sophisticated wit and eloquence."

—*Fort Wayne Journal-Gazette*

"An engrossing story, wrought with verve and intelligence. For it, Buckley deserves a low bow, a toast raised high, and many appreciative readers."

—*Nashville Banner*

"Prepare yourself to be caught up totally for a few heart-stopping hours in intrigue, danger, romance, atmosphere, intellectual challenge, geographical evocation and fun."

—*Monterey Peninsula Herald*

"Delightful light reading . . . contains a satisfactory amount of bloodshed, intrigue, sex and sardonic wit."

—*Cleveland Plain Dealer*

STAINED GLASS

William F. Buckley, Jr.

WARNER BOOKS

A Warner Communications Company

For Gerhart Niemeyer

Prologue

Although a mere deputy, Colonel Dmitri looked up from his high-backed chair and whispered to his superior, "Sir, should I perhaps open the window?"

General Wassily Lestovich Mishkin, Hero of the Soviet Union, twice decorated with the Order of Lenin, chief of staff of the armed services of the Union of Soviet Socialist Republics, gazed at him wordlessly, his eyebrows contracting, the compressed sweat catching the light of the huge log fire obstinately, copiously fed by an orderly, maintaining a temperature in the smoky, airless, fur-covered anteroom of—Dmitri estimated—90 degrees. Mishkin returned to staring at the fire, and Dmitri returned to his stiff uprightness, looking across at the two other deputies, and, seated on the little sofa opposite the general, Admiral Nicolai Stepovich Fechitov, chief of Soviet naval intelligence, the sweat staining the armholes of his crisp light-blue jacket; and so they waited for the reappearance of the man who, invoking the august name just after eleven in the evening—three agonizing hours ago—had summoned them from their apartment to drive with him to Trionoshka, the dacha that sheltered the omnipotent, omniscient, omnicompetent leader and patron of them all.

Reaching it, they were escorted by Captain Gektor Glazunov, personal aide to the Marshal, into this anteroom, lit by a small lamp at one corner, and by the firelight. They were stunned by the heat, a wrenching contrast to the creaky-snow-cold they experienced during the short silent walk from their limousines into the dacha. General Mishkin looked over to Ilyich, who had brought them here, chief of the KGB, responsible for the internal security of the Soviet Union and for intelligence operations worldwide, and whispered,

"The heat?"

General Mishkin had never before been summoned to Trionoshka, where, in progressive isolation, the Marshal was now spending practically all his time.

"He does that." Pyotr Ivanovich Ilyich had paid a dozen visits to Trionoshka since the days when it was gradually transformed from an occasional country lodging into a semipermanent residence. He had often been summoned at midnight, been kept waiting in this room an hour, even two, before being called by Glazunov into the windowless bedroom-study. When the anteroom was hot, it always followed that so was the temper of the overseer of Trionoshka, and of the Soviet empire. Moreover, the little lamp gave off insufficient light to read by, so there was no means of distracting oneself, even if it were possible to focus on other matters than what to be prepared to say in reply to whatever it was that the leader would ask about, hint at, or command.

But moments after the general, the admiral, the KGB chief and their deputies sat down, occupying six of the eight seats in the room—two sofas and four heavy wooden chairs—the shaded door at the other end opened, and Glazunov came back into the room. A youngish man with thinning blond hair and spectacles, his cheeks, normally a steady pale, were flushed. He went directly to Ilyich.

"The Marshal will see you."

Ilyich stood, cleared his throat, and followed Glazunov, who closed the door quietly behind them."

Instinctively Admiral Fechitov looked at his watch. It was twenty minutes past two.

He stole a look at it when Ilyich reappeared fifty-five minutes later.

Ilyich took the unoccupied stiff-backed chair and drew it up to the perimeter of the semicircle around which the men were seated.

"The Marshal"—he cleared his throat, and by great force succeeded in controlling it—"the Marshal is very . . . *upset* . . . over the develop-

ment in Germany. He finds it . . . *inconceivable*
. . . that that . . . *young fascist* . . . should be . . .
countenanced. He wishes to know why the . . .
friends of democracy . . . in the area have not
asserted themselves and silenced him. He is . . .
impatient . . . with the suggestion that this person is only a flash-in-the-pan. He does not wish to
listen to such . . . *subversive gibberish*. He does
not want to listen to it from me . . . *a notorious
bungler*. He does not want to listen to it from . . .
stupid . . . chiefs of staff. He does not want to
hear it from . . . *lazy and ineffectual* . . . admirals
who are . . . *allegedly* . . . exercising their responsibilities. He directs me to arrange for the
immediate trial for treason of the editor of *Pravda*, who wrote the article saying that the count is
merely a 'hot-headed college debater' He is a
college debater in the same way that Hitler was a
. . . *paperhanger*. He wishes to know why Americans have succeeded in maneuvering the agent
Oakes into the picture while we . . . *dolts, buf-
foons, incompetents* . . . have yet to move . . .

There was silence. Finally General Mishkin
spoke.

"What concretely does he desire us to do, Pyotr
Ivanovich?"

"He declines to say."

Admiral Fechitov said in a hoarse whisper,
"Does he intend to speak to us directly?"

"I don't know," said Ilyich.

"Is he through with *you*?"

"I don't know that either."

"Does he"—Mishkin asked—"habitually fail
to advise you when he is through with you?"

"He does not say. Glazunov tells you."

"What do we do now?"

"We sit here, until we are summoned, or until we are dismissed."

1

At first, they were saying about him, Oh my God, it's Hitler all over again! That was back in the days of the Berlin blockade, when this dismayingly young man gave the speech at Heidelberg declaring that it was the German people who must open the roadway to Berlin blocked by the Russians. A middle-aged veteran in the audience got up and, achieving the speaker's attention, delivered the Nazi salute. There was pandemonium, and the heckler was finally dragged out by two campus police, after they were roused from their game of chess at the gatehouse and went at a run to the student union building. But that disturbance wasn't the sensation of the evening.

It was the speaker. This was not the bluster

of one of those sulky veterans boozed up on nationalism. Axel Wintergrin spoke with a moderation quite un-Prussian. It made the experience of him all the more vivid. The crowds—there were crowds now, everywhere—would listen, and *cheer*. And the cheers had in their full-throatedness that resonance that is missing from responses to spellbinding oratory when, in the back of the crowd's mind, the speech is seen as resting, finally, on rhetorical orchestration, vocal fury, bombast. "It's the kind of satisfaction," Blackford Oakes wrote to his superior in the first dispatch, "that Socrates must have given his students after completing one of his syllogisms." The distinctive enthusiasm aroused by a mobilizing analytical demonstration, rather than by a mere call to action to appease tonight's restless glands—his was a call to a fundamental reorientation.

Axel Wintergrin managed this by any number of elaborations on two central themes. The first was that life under the Soviet domination was intolerable. "That isn't the correct word for it," he said on one occasion, pausing to make one of those mid-speech distinctions which no professor of rhetoric would have thought, well, tolerable, in a declamatory situation "—no, if it were *intolerable*, then people would not tolerate it. But people *do* tolerate it. Just as"—and here was the kind of thing his critics, more properly his enemies, could not forgive him for—"just as the German people *tolerated* Adolf Hitler. It is *insufferable*," he went on, "that a people presumed to have been liberated in 1945 should have been instantly enslaved in 1945. It is worse than insufferable that the brothers of those enslaved people—you, my friends, I, all of us in what they call 'West Germany'—should apparently acquiesce in their enslavement." He had called for a German militia "to enforce the terms of an agreement that has clearly been violated," and everywhere units of young and middle-aged Germans were spontaneously forming when, suddenly, the Russians relented, ending the blockade.

His second theme, as he developed it later, touched America. (He had a way of simply ignoring the other NATO powers, as if they were vermiform appendages. This greatly irritated western European leaders, to say nothing of his second cousin, Queen Caroline of England.) America, he would explain, was a country of decent people who insisted resolutely on their own freedom and had made great exertions to bring freedom to others, and to liberate Germany and East Europe from tyranny. But before their effort was consummated, the will failed; and the result was not only the satellite empire of the Soviet Union but a divided Germany. The thing about America, he said, is that it is engrossed in its own pursuits. Its NATO enterprise is purely defensive. This was the line he was now taking, in 1952, four years after the Berlin blockade. When John Foster Dulles, during the presidential primary campaign that spring, had made the wispiest noises about the liberation of East Europe, he had been roundly denounced as a warmonger, said Wintergrin, and it was plain to see from the hasty retreat of candidate Eisenhower that the good and kindly general believed his

Crusade for Europe was ended. It was also quite clear that General Eisenhower had no appetite for reopening that which, however "infelicitously" (the young count's sarcasm was strangely unabrasive), had been settled at the diplomatic conferences of 1945. Under the circumstances, America was of very little tactical use to freedom-seeking Germans. But Germans could find comfort in this. Wintergrin would tell his audiences: Just as American troops in Europe were less than anxious to take on the Russians, neither were they anxious to take on Germans determined to effect their own liberation. And he, Axel Wintergrin, had a plan, which in due course he would divulge.

Whereupon Stalin, who in the early days had himself made something of a joke of Wintergrin —oh yes, they tell jokes in the Kremlin!—became obsessed by the young phenomenon. Orders went out to do something about him.

This, Blackford wrote in a long dispatch one week after arriving in Germany in September, when he became an extension, however attenuated, of Stalin's will, was not going to be easy to do; indeed, all the routine things to control or moderate Wintergrin had been tried now for four years—ever since Heidelberg—and simply hadn't worked. There was the initial setback in 1949.

2

Wintergrin was twenty years old when Hitler
marched into Poland. A first lieutenant in the
lead reconnaissance battalion, he reached Warsaw ahead of the shock troops that would crush
the city. Twenty-four hours after he was in Warsaw, Lieutenant Axel von Euchen Wintergrin
disappeared.

For a few months the relevant people tried
to find out what had happened to him, but notwithstanding the diligence of German record-
keepers, interest waned, and it was supposed that
Axel Wintergrin, the gifted young Count of St.
Anselm, was the casualty of a Polish sniper, or
that he had been kidnaped and killed. After six
months, during which the German prisoners held

by the Poles were liberated or killed as the resistance movement was smashed, Wintergrin was officially reported Missing in Action and Presumed Dead, and his widowed mother was sent a decoration of sorts which she hung around the photograph of her son but only after prying from the medal the disfiguring swastika. The absence of it was noticed by the mayor of St. Anselm's on the feast day of St. Anselm, when the countess, observing tradition, entertained local officials at the castle; and the countess, her graying hair in perfect trim, her leathery face handsome and resourceful, sipped her tea, then said Yes, decorative swastikas are not safe these days when the patriotic fever causes them to be so greatly coveted. She would not be surprised to see it materialize on the charm bracelet of her silly little maid, Nona.

Did the countess—the subject could now safely be raised without opening the year-old wound—have any private opinion what might have happened to her son? Yes, she said, she did have a private notion, but it was so ridiculous, she did not really want to share it. We are old friends, said the mayor: Confide in me. The countess leaned over to him and pointed to the little gray kitten, asleep near the fireplace, and whispered: "Do you believe in reincarnation?" The mayor changed the subject, and went gladly back to the village to resume the war. The countess, a lifelong clairvoyant, knew Axel was alive, though no word from him or of him had reached her. Moreover, she was sure that he was well;

and altogether certain that—wherever he was
—he was risking his life in the fight against the
Nazis.

It had been, in fact, a very near thing. Axel
was roughly treated when, in civilian clothes tak-
en from a corpse, he presented himself to a Polish captain in command of a rearguard outpost.
Axel understood only enough Polish to gather
that the captain had calmly given orders to take
this German lad out somewhere and shoot him.
But he had anticipated some such possibility, and
accordingly had memorized the Polish words necessary to communicate a willingness to mark on
the map the two major repositories in Warsaw of
Nazi ammunition laid up by foreign commercial
agents before the invasion began, one of them in
a part of the city as yet unoccupied. It took less
than three hours to verify this, and from the ju-
bilation Wintergrin briefly wondered whether he
would be made to stick around and serve as
grand marshal of the Pulaski Day Parade. What
he wanted was to be escorted out of the country.
The Polish captain promised to guide him to So-
pot whence, assuming Nazi airplanes did not
completely close off the traffic in the Bay of Dan-
zig during the next two or three days, he could be
infiltrated by ferry into Sweden, whereafter he
would become a Swedish problem. Axel's guide,
Zinka, was a woman who spoke no German, and
after the first two days of walking and bicycling
north toward Olsztyn, his vocabulary failed him,
he ran out of variations on hidden ammunition
dumps, and so they walked (and sometimes ran),

and ate, in silence, the stocky forty-year-old gym teacher from Warsaw, and the angular twenty-year-old Westphalian aristocrat.

Approaching Malbork, Zinka suddenly motioned Axel into a barn when she spotted the checkpoint down the road. The uniforms were Polish but confused reports, snatched here and there from overheard talk, from fragments of broadcasts on municipal radios blaring the grim news into village squares, suggested to Zinka the possibility that units of Polish troops had been conscripted by their captors. The word was that no one carrying papers unfranked by the Gestapo would be permitted to travel, and that anyone without papers of any sort would be detained. Zinka, alone, ran toward the two soldiers. Axel strained to discern what was happening but succeeded only in seeing the indistinct figures apparently in commotion, and then both soldiers racing in their motorcycles up the road over which he and Zinka had just bicycled. The girl motioned Axel to come on, and as the motorcyclists disappeared, he did so, and she described, miming rather more graphically than Axel required in order to catch the gist of her story, her complaint to the patrol that five kilometers back, a young German in soldier's uniform, jumping her from the side of the road, had raped her. Axel wondered whether the chivalrous pair of Polish soldiers was prepared to challenge the entire Nazi Army, rape being the sport in which, at this point, he assumed the German Army to be substantially engaged. He even considered the possibility that *he* would be apprehended and hanged as a rapist.

So they left the main road and traveled cross-country. As they came closer to the coast Axel's well-disciplined face brightened, even as Zinka's grew pensive and sad. *He* was moving away from the Nazis, *she* would return to their most recently occupied European capital. At the garage near the commercial pier she extended her hand, but her eyes looked down. Axel took it, bent his head formally, touching his lips to her graying hair, and, in English, said, "Goodbye, Zinka. I will never forget you."

Axel made his way through Sweden to Norway, where he presented himself to Norwegian intelligence. After the Nazi invasion of Norway he joined the resistance. For five years he made no effort to be in touch with his mother or any other relatives in Germany or England: he would not risk retribution against his family. When the war was over he received from the Norwegian monarch the highest decoration for bravery in a simple ceremony to honor all the surviving heroes of the resistance. "Like lining up for food stamps," one veteran grumbled. Axel returned to Germany with an undetailed story of detention in Sweden, whither he said he had escaped after a brief period of captivity in Poland and where he was held incommunicado. The story was routinely, indeed listlessly, accepted by a society crushed under the events of recent months. In such a season Marco Polo could not have commanded an audience of six people to hear out his exploits.

Axel resumed his studies, pursuing philosophy at Heidelberg under Karl Jaspers, and receiving an advanced degree after three years, working long days in the library and long afternoons in the gymnasium, where he boxed with some success as a middleweight. He was serious, but not fanatical or even obsessive in his pursuits, and though he led an apparently carefree life it was true—as later was widely remarked when every commentator in Europe undertook the definitive portrait of Axel Wintergrin—that strain was etched into a face otherwise that of a healthy twenty-eight-year-old: the calling card of Gestapo torturers in Norway who, pity the poor innocents, never even discovered that the man they were mutilating was a German. But he could smile through his calcified sadness, though nobody could quite remember when last Axel had been seen laughing. This is a very serious world, he told his closest friend Roland Himmelfarb, who as one of the few surviving German Jews—he sat out the holocaust in the strangest, strongest sanctuary of them all, serving undetected in the records department of the Gestapo in Berlin—hardly needed advertisement of the fact. Indeed, in his circle no one disagreed with him, because no one applied to Axel the conventional criteria. It was not expected of Count Wintergrin that he should join in beer-drinking contests or take his turn entertaining his associates with accounts of bawdy adventures or attend the games to cheer on his university team. Even as a boxer, he fought with a certain detachment. Although he was first-rate, adversaries and acute spectators got the impression he had a disinterested concern with the sport: often he eschewed the opportunity to cripple his opponent after maneuvering to do so—rather like throwing back into the stream the trout you have labored so hard to land. And after the match, though always affable and sportsmanlike, he would leave rather than stay on to see the other matches or join the team at refreshments. He would return to his studies, or write a letter to his mother or a friend, or write in his journal, which he never shared with anyone. His desultory romantic life was of concern to his mother, since Axel was her only child, and heir to the huge landed estate of his father. At first he obligingly escorted the ladies proffered by his mother for his attention: the neighboring blue bloods. Then others came from remoter parts of Germany. When he traveled with his mother to England in 1946, he saw for the first time, since graduating from Greyburn in 1938 after six years of English public-school life, his second cousin Caroline, herself first cousin to the reigning monarch, whom she succeeded as queen a few years later after the fatal accident. Caroline was imperious by nature and undertook to find the perfect girl for her glamorous, studious, wealthy, driven German cousin. Axel obligingly affected to be quite taken by the three girls (beautiful, literate, witty, in differing mixes) he escorted during the summer, all of whom were deeply attracted to him (Lady Leinsford in particular, though it had not amused Axel when she said to him, sighing in his arms, "For you, Axel, I'd even become a Nazi"). Axel's treatment was perfunctorily ardent. He would systematically contrive to seduce them (four days, three days, eleven days respectively), and then with much tenderness announce that he had to get back to his work, the nature of which he never specified.

"Has it ever occurred to you, Axel," Lady Caroline once said, "that it isn't absolutely clear whether you are a nice man? I mean, I love you very much—you know that, Axel—but you are very distracted. And your interest in people seems, somehow . . . abstract." She searched his eyes. "But I am certain you are going to do great things in European politics. If you don't mind, Axel, when you take over Europe could you please leave this little island to its own idolatrous pleasures? Don't forget now, Axel. That can be your bread-and-butter present to me on leaving Stamford House." Axel smiled—and then actually appeared to . . . think about it. ("I do believe," Queen Caroline said, recalling the incident in 1952 when Axel Wintergrin announced the foundation of his political party, "I do believe," she repeated, "that when I made that flippant—that ludicrous— 'request' of Axel, back when he was a mere child [Axel had been a mere child of twenty-six], he hesitated *precisely* because he was trying to decide whether to *grant* it!") Back home, after two months' summer indolence in England, Axel drove himself in his studies, adjourning altogether that part of his romantic activity that could be said to be oriented toward a possible marriage. "All in due course, Mother," he comforted the countess.

After submitting his thesis and taking his degree, he spent his time traveling throughout Germany. He would know, on arriving in a city or town he had never been to, just where to go:

always he would find the man, or woman, who shared his obsession. And—always—in a matter of days he had made fast friends, who as often as not became disciples. As his movement grew it became easier for him because he would come to town, check in at a hotel, and there he would be reached by those who had word of his coming. They would seek him out, sometimes a single man or woman, more often two, three, or a half-dozen people, and talk with him. He would be asked to speak to a gathering, but always he stipulated that not more than a roomful should be there. He was not ready to address large audiences.

He spoke quietly about the genuine idealism of the German people who had become united less than a hundred years earlier, and now were sundered by a consortium of powers, one partner in which had designs on human liberty everywhere, while the other partner, fatigued by a war that had roused its people from a hemispheric torpor which they once thought of as a part of the American patrimony—an American right, so to speak—was confused now and disillusioned by the ambiguous results of so heroic an effort. The Americans saw a Europe largely enslaved by Allied victory—and unconcerned about Germany. No, never count on allies beyond a certain point, he said: only Germans can reshape their own destiny. Only Germans can come, would come, to the aid of their brothers in the East. Faced with such resolve, the Russians would necessarily yield; even as, eventually, the Nazis had yielded.

Always the questions were practical, always

he gave the same answer: How, in the absence of
armed help from the West, could he effect the
liberation of East Germany? Always he answered:
by spiritual mobilization.

Did he mean the satyagraha preached by
Gandhi?

Spiritual mobilization, Axel said, means the
mobilization of all one's strength. Foremost is the
will to live as free men. Any means appropriate
to the realization of that end are licit—from
peaceful resistance to ultimate weaponry.

Would he be more explicit?

In due course, he would say, and his smile
was without smugness, without affectation,
though he would then fasten or unfasten (his
only mannerism) the two bottom buttons of his
rusty-green tweed jacket, a perfect cut on his tall
frame, and his light-brown hair would respond
sluggishly as he shook his head to the right, his
lightly chiseled, sensitive features, and sad eyes,
struggling in coordination with his thoughts to
frame the answer in a way so many of his followers sought.

All in good time, he answered, as if to say:
Allow me to trouble myself, on your behalf, on
these technical matters. I shall not let you down.

When he rose at his alma mater to announce
that if the Occupation Forces would not deliver
an ultimatum to the Russians to reopen the road
to Berlin, the German people should do so, he
was suddenly a conspicuous figure on the European scene, a man not yet thirty years old. Until then no national notice of him had been taken,
only here and there a character piece in a local

newspaper about the aristocratic curio who dreamed of irredentism and talked as if he would smash the Red Army with the might of his left fist, trained at the gymnasium at Heidelberg. These efforts at caricature failed when undertaken by reporters who went to hear him talk. They could no longer bring off conventional ideological denigration. ("Count Wintergrin seems to have forgotten the horror of war . . .") But after Heidelberg, all the major papers in Europe suddenly began to take notice of Axel Wintergrin and his—his what? they asked themselves. Here was someone who, biologically, could have been the grandson of Adenauer, the *de facto* leader of the country (with his Christian Democratic Union, serving as chancellor under the authority of the joint occupation command). And when direct elections came in November 1952, Adenauer would surely win—with the Social Democrats under Erich Ollenhauer taking perhaps one-third of the seats. Germany's future would be a generation's oscillation of power between these two parties, the analysts joined in predicting. There was no room for the so-called "Reunification" Party of this Wintergrin. Why so much fuss over a quixotic Heidelberg Manifesto? Why had groups in every major city in Germany suddenly invited the young count to address them: elated veterans' organizations, cynical student associations, inquisitive business associations, wary labor unions—even, here and there, always discreetly, organizations of civil servants . . . why the fascination with him?

The disciplined left, and of course the papers

in East Germany, had the ready answer. Wintergrin was this season's Hitler!

In late December 1949 *Neues Deutschland* ran a large feature section triumphantly announcing that a search in Sweden revealed that there was no record that Axel Wintergrin had been detained in a Swedish concentration camp. The article suggested he had feigned opposition to Hitler for the sole purpose of sparing himself the rigors of military life and the dangers of service on the eastern front, and had spent the war years in Swedish dissipation. The story, given wide circulation everywhere in Europe, and intensively circulated within West Germany, brought a tide of curiosity and evolved quickly into dismay in his camp. Wintergrin's failure during that heavy week to answer questions about the sensational charges caused apprehension among even his closest followers, though those who knew him did their best to reassure everyone that he would be vindicated, as they firmly believed, somehow, he would be.

Finally he scheduled a press conference—and limited attendance to six journalists. What he had to say—he gave out in a general release—was not easily said in the hectic circumstances of a general press conference. ("Shee-yit!" the dumbstruck, excluded New York *Times* correspondent in Bonn reacted, on receiving the notice. "Who does this young kraut think he is? Immanuel Kant calling a press conference to explain his *Critique of Pure Reason*?") But clearly there had been no political favoritism in making out the list—one was the correspondent of *Der Spiegel,* a journal whose hostility to Wintergrin was rancorous and sustained.

The meeting took place in a private dining room in the Rheinhotel Dreesen at Godesberg, where ten years earlier Hitler had talked Chamberlain out of hunks of Czechoslovakia. The reporters arrived on time, and there were a score of others outside the room, patiently but firmly denied entrance by Wintergrin's friend Roland Himmelfarb. One reporter-photographer from *L'Humanité* pressed for admittance, and three burly figures, manifestly at his service, added their pressure to the reporter's attempt at a forced entry. Surrounding photographers snapped pictures of the contest. Himmelfarb, holding the door, called out for the help of hotel personnel. Axel Wintergrin, disembarked from the small Mercedes driven by a student volunteer, entered the hotel lobby at the height of the commotion. An aide, rushing to relieve Himmelfarb, paused to brief Wintergrin in telegraphic bursts. "Communist bastard . . . *L'Humanité* . . . here with thugs . . ." Wintergrin reached out, collared the French reporter, and lifted him whole up on his toes, his nose within a few inches of Wintergrin's, holding him there silently until the noise abated. "Go back to your commissar in Paris. Or, better still, head that way"—Wintergrin pointed his nose to the east— "to the Soviet Union, and tell them that force in Germany will be used only *against* tyranny, not to promote it." He dropped the paunchy reporter, whose swagger had diminished as, one by one, his companions had been subdued by Wintergrin's partisans, and he fell almost

31

to the floor before salvaging what he could of his aplomb and, muttering something about how Nazis will always be Nazis, scurried out of the lobby, the most photographed photographer of the season. Wintergrin walked into the room and apologized to the press for detaining them.

Wordlessly he distributed a copy of the citation he had received from the King of Norway. He gave the names of three Norwegians with whom he had associated in the resistance. He would prefer, he said, to answer questions after the press had satisfied itself of the validity of his representation. The first questioner asked why had he not revealed his actual story, instead of saying that he had been detained in Sweden.

It was precisely because he had in fact been active in the anti-Nazi resistance, he said.

"What was there to hide then?"

"The German people know now that it was wrong to support Hitler. I did not want, in 1945, to lecture my countrymen, most of whom, after all, were Germans fighting under Nazism, not Nazis fighting under Hitler. Their punishment was heavy enough without adding to it the reproaches of a twenty-five-year-old."

"Are you then saying that Germany now, the Germany of 1949, is different from the Germany of 1945?"

"Even in 1945 the support for Hitler was largely inertial. If the war had ended, and Hitler had faced a free election, he would have lost. There is no significant nostalgia for Hitler today. Those unhappy Germans in the East who continue to live under tyranny do so because they have not—yet—been given another choice."

The meeting ended. In a matter of hours, Norwegian reporters tracked down the former resistance fighters. Olin Justsen was now a naval architect, living in Kristiansand, and he said to the reporter, Yes, he had known "Alec"—he knew him by no other name, but recognized him on seeing his photograph in the paper—and had participated with him in two missions.

"What were they?"

"Well," said Justsen, puffing on his pipe, his eyes glazed, his hand trembling slightly, "one of them required attaching an explosive to the hull of a freighter sent over by the Germans to take a load of heavy water to Germany. That mission was accomplished."

"What was the other?"

"The other," Justsen said, in measured accents—he had consulted his own conscience rigorously on this, anticipating the question—"involved the elimination of an individual."

"Who?" the reporter asked.

"We do not give out his name."

"What had he done?"

"We do not describe his crimes."

"Was he a German?"

"We do not give out his nationality."

Neither of the other two Norwegians questioned knew about the assassination. They had served with Wintergrin on other missions. Pooling their information, reporters counted two parachute jumps into German bases in Norway, three demolition jobs, two intelligence sorties into Nazi installations, plus the mysterious assassination. Rhitto Heitger, the grand old man of the resistance, would not talk except to say that from the time Wintergrin presented himself in 1939, occupying a desk in routine intelligence work, through the occupation, until liberation, he had refused no assignment except one that might take him to his native country, betraying his identity, and imperiling his mother.

The information, consolidated in the major newsrooms of Europe, was sulkily reported by the hostile press and, dispiritedly, the newsmen gave up that line of attack on Axel Wintergrin, which would have taken care of so many problems, if only *Neues Deutschland* had been right. When next Wintergrin spoke, on Wenceslaus Day in Frankfurt, he was given a standing ovation before he uttered a word. He received this by fastening the two bottom buttons on his coat, and smiling his half-distracted smile. His speech was on the usual themes, and later, at the press conference, he spoke the words, in answer to a question, that caused the phone to ring at the home of Pyotr Ivanovich Ilyich in Moscow, even though it was almost midnight there; and, in the United States, where it was late afternoon, caused an aide to walk right into the office of Allen Dulles. What, the reporter at Frankfort had asked, were Count Wintergrin's plans? Why, he said, his plans were to organize his movement into a political party to compete in the elections in November, which elections he was certain of winning.

Having won them, he would proceed to liberate East Germany.

3

After Blackford Oakes's mission in England was completed—his maiden mission, he mused—it was thought wise by his superior to immerse him in his trade in order to fortify his cover. "You've been posing as an engineer, Black. Maybe it's time to remind yourself that that's actually what you got your degree in at Yale." Black was listening at a safe house in London to his experienced, relaxed superior, Singer Callaway, the only American in England who knew that Blackford Oakes was a deep-cover agent of the CIA. "Figure out a convincing way to terminate your project here in the next couple of weeks—you can say the sponsoring foundation has run out of funds; or maybe that they're satisfied with what you've already submitted—figure out exactly what to tell your mother and your friends. Go back to Washington. Tell your mother you have to report to New York on the work you did: hell, Black, you attend to the details, then let me know what the story is and I'll get it coordinated with New York."

Blackford did so, and it did not prove difficult. No one knew enough about his arcane work, researching historic projects, to question him.

His mother gave a little farewell dinner for him at her house on Portland Place, and his sartorially overstuffed stepfather, dressed in velvet smoking jacket and gold-braided evening slippers, delivered an affectionate and prolonged toast. Black loved the unabashed orotundity of it. A couple of glasses of port, and Sir Alec Sharkey sounded like Mr. Micawber. While managing to look exaggeratedly, impossibly British, he nevertheless looked proudly in the direction of his stepson, as though they were one flesh and blood. Blackford, at twenty-six, six months a resident of London, was by then experienced in the celebrated amenities of upper-class British life. He rose to his feet, said soothing things about British engineering technology, and—as was always expected of him—made genial references to British ways and institutions. Ah, dear old England, Blackford thought, while his lips were going through the motions: But what can the rest of the world reasonably expect of you, after all you have been through? At least you have yourself a first-rate queen, who cares . . . . "And so, on my leave-taking, I wish to thank Sir Alec for all his patience and goodness during the past months, and to thank all his friends—and my friends—who have been so kind to me. And of course, to toast, with suppressed emotions on the subject of her expatriation from our native land, my beloved mother, Lady Sharkey." His mother rose with tears in her eyes, and Blackford took his seat, the object of universal admiration: the ladies loved his stunning good looks, his fair hair and inquisitive blue eyes, and easy manner; the men were taken by his slouchy informality, which managed just the necessary ration of deference owed by the young to their elders, without any suggestion of sycophancy, or any presumptive commitment to the bizarre notion that because he was young, he was any less competent, in his own disciplines, than they in theirs. Blackford had the American republican's innate aversion to servility. Even as a schoolboy at Greyburn he would say "sir" once, to confirm his understanding of an axiomatic hierarchy. But he would never repeat the word in the same conversation. At age sixteen he got into serious trouble for a libertine application of his code. At twenty-six his amiable self-assurance set him slightly apart: the young man, bright, inquisitive, courteous . . . to whom, however, condescension would have been inconceivable.

Sir Alec had a friend, Lord Brougham, who was beloved by all until the third drink of the evening, at which point His Lordship would begin to talk about his most recent pheasant shoot —usually that morning—as if all the world hungered to hear the details and savor every step of the chronology. (*The Day Lord Brougham Shot the Pheasant,* by Jim Bishop, one survivor of an evening had suggested as an appropriate title and author for a book.) Mostly his friends coped with him by the simple expedient of avoiding his company after 7 P.M. or the second drink, whichever came first. On the occasions when they found themselves trapped in his company at a dinner party, they would sweatily engage other members of the party—*any* other member of the party—in concentrated, often nonsensical, discussions, for so long as they hovered as possible targets of Lord Brougham's narrative compulsion. It happened to Blackford early on during his stay in London, and he was unprepared as Lord Brougham, scotch and soda in hand, began to tell Blackford what had been the situation in the field that morning at nine-fifteen. When, fifteen minutes later, Lord Brougham was describing the situation in the field that morning at nine-thirty, Blackford summoned his training as a scientist to project that at such a rate Lord Brougham, having spent all day hunting, would be done with the account of his hunt at approximately 2 A.M. He thought fleetingly of interrupting His Lordship to tell him about the review of *Parsifal,* which his father delivered on the lone occasion when he had been dragged by Blackford's mother to the Metropolitan, so far from his chosen world of airplane work, airplane talk, airplane testing, airplane jokes. "*Parsifal* is the opera that begins at five-thirty and when you look at your watch three hours later, it is only five forty-five." But Oakes's sense of occasion stopped him. Instead, he put his arm firmly on Brougham's shoulder and, winning the admiration of all experienced martyrs in the room, said to him in mock earnestness: "Lord Brougham, I'm too young to stand the suspense. Unless you shoot that bird in the next"—Blackford looked at his wristwatch—"sixty seconds, I'm going to have to ask the butler for some saltpeter." This was said with such high good humor that Lord Brougham, who didn't really understand exactly what it was Blacky said, actually stopped talking and laughed —which sound, Blacky later told his mother, would certainly have scared away the birds.

On the plane home he opened the letter from Sally, scooped up in the valedictory probe of his mailbox on his way out to the taxi, lugging bags and briefcases. He had waited deliberately until he was in the Constellation before opening it.

"Dear Blacky:

"Has it ever occurred to you that I am a *professional* student of English and that I ought to be *paid* for writing you letters, which take me away from the pleasures of pursuing my inquiry into Geof. Chaucer? It isn't as though my letters were responses to your own, since I have written you six times since the first of January. That was the day you made The Resolution. I'll quote it to you. I am in the mood to quote Blackford Oakes, my darling, to Blackford Oakes, that crud. 'Dearest Sally: It is New Year's Day, and though distracted in London (I am going to Buckingham Palace to a party for Margaret Truman), you are as always first in my thoughts, on the first of

39

January. I am a very methodical feller, Sally, as you probably never realized, since you concern yourself with odes to Westminster Bridge, while I concern myself with building Westminster Bridge. Anyway, my vow tonight, for my darling, is to write you twice a week, come rain or come shine, even if at Buckingham Palace I find myself having to say to the Chief American-Watcher: "Where is the nearest desk?" I've really got to go.' Very funny, Oakes. That was twelve weeks and three letters ago. I'm glad people don't have to drive their cars over bridges built on your promises.

"So, how do I retaliate? It would serve you right if I wrote to you about what we have recently learned about Chaucer's Middle English. Or in Middle English. But just to show I'm a Christian prepared to turn the other cheek, and knowing your vulgar concern with politics, here are a few of this season's leads, as I get them in the graduate school from such as Professors Cecil Driver and Willmoore Kendall (who hate each other, needless to say, both being terribly bright).

"The smart money is on Eisenhower. He'll probably take Taft in New Hampshire, and erode his base. He's got to be pretty truculently anti-Communist, and he's already let it be known that J. F. Dulles will be his Secretary of State if elected. Since we're supposed to have a bipartisan foreign policy, it doesn't hurt that Foster's brother Allen is head of the CIA. Do you know *anybody* in the CIA? The only one I know is Cord Meyer, I met him—remember?—when I was a World Federalist at Smith, and he was top dog and debated at Yale with Arnold Wolfers. You said after it was over that Cord would need to retire, and sure enough he did. The pros are saying Ike's charisma (the word comes in from Mac Weber, and it's sweeping the country, along with 'expertise') will being him in, on the assumption that he will be able to end the Korean War. Meanwhile the Democrats are taking an awful beating. Joe McCarthy's attacks on the 'Red Dean' (poor old Dean Acheson, the original Establishmentarian, son of a preacher, trustee of Yale!) have convinced a lot of people he's a subversive, and even though he's Secretary of State, he's pretty much ignored by his fellow Democrats, though most people are finally agreed at least that Stalin *is* subversive, though only J. F. Dulles ever says anything about liberating the liberated territories, but he says that mincingly.

"Suddenly I'm bored writing to you, Oakes. If you come back to the States, ring my secretary and make an appointment. I divide my time about equally between New Haven, Washington, Athens, and Caracas. How are you, darling? —Sally."

Blackford leaned his seat back all the way and closed his eyes, and worked out how many hours, minutes, and demisemiquavers separated him from Sally.

If Singer Callaway in London had no idea what Blackford would be assigned to do, in Washington his superior, "Mr. Lamb," was not at all vague: Oakes was to penetrate the new move-

41

ment in Germany headed by this Axel Winter-grin. He should count on staying in America at least three months, as many as six, depending on his progress in learning German. He would be briefed extensively the next day by a specialist who would know Oakes only by his code name of Geoffrey Truax. That specialist— "Mr. Munch" —would direct Oakes up until his departure for Germany, at which point the name of his superior there would be disclosed, together with instructions on how to effect contact. Meanwhile, immediate thought must be given to his cover while in America. Any creative ideas Oakes had should be discussed with Mr. Munch the next morning (the meeting would take place at 10:03 A.M. in room 708, Wardman Park Hotel). Oakes should give some thought to the requirements: 1) he must reserve five hours a day for the study of German; 2) he must live in either Washington, Boston, or Palo Alto, where the agency had suitable arrangements for him to study German at the maximum speed; 3) he must study those aspects of engineering and architecture that would qualify him to deal expertly with the reconstruction of a thirteenth-century church.

Blackford had had only one earlier experience with "Mr. Lamb"—who had told him eight months earlier that he must go to England. When Mr. Lamb was done, Black remembered, he simply stopped talking. He did not supply a coda of any sort, from which one might deduce that the interview had terminated. At their last meeting, this resulted in Blackford's staying in his chair while Mr. Lamb stayed in his, neither of them uttering a word; accordingly, after waiting a full three minutes, Black rose, shook hands, and left.

He had taken the precaution not to advise Sally when he would arrive. She would want to know his plans, and these were unformulated. By the same token he did not feel free to call any of his friends in Washington, who would also be curious. He indulged himself the fantasy of convening "Tom," "Harry," "Alan," "Rudolph," and "Alistair," the pseudonymous instructors during his training period in Washington, and having a dinner party for the purpose of telling the boys what he had done in London since last seeing them. He smiled at the sheer impiety of the thought, and comforted himself that The Firm protected itself against any such mad compulsions by the simple expedient of making it impossible to find one's old associates. He reflected. If at this very moment he desired to be in touch with everyone he knew in the Central Intelligence Agency, he would be good for: 1) one telephone number in London, attached to one employee; 2) Anthony Trust, who had recruited him—a man Oakes had known since he was a schoolboy; and 3) the telephone number of Mr. Lamb. Amazing, he thought, that only two months earlier the resources of the Agency had worked to concert, through him, an extensive operation; extensive intromission, he smiled, lecherously, thinking of one bedroom in particular. But if his life had depended on it, he would not know how to be directly in touch with Singer Callaway, for instance, let alone the august Rufus—not a

single one of his instructors, let alone the whole
platoon.

Without having any very clear idea how he
would spend the balmy spring evening, he walked
out of the Hay-Adams Hotel in the late afternoon
and crossed Lafayette Park toward the White
House. He wondered idly which of the park
benches Bernard Baruch occupied when coaching
American Presidents. Presumably the one closest
to the big House. So he walked south toward the
bench, passing the bureaucrats coming out of the
Executive Office Building, fanning out to cars
and buses. Two children were playing in the park,
and their dog, held in leash by their mother, was
howling in empathic excitement at their game.
Blackford sat and stared at the White House, recalling the giddy evening he had spent there
dancing with Sally after going through the receiving line for the Shah of Sinrah. It would have
a fresh occupant this time next year, Blackford
reflected, turning his head abruptly as if to express his ignorance of who it would be. A man
was reading a paper, seated two benches down:
middle-sized, hirsute, wearing horn-rimmed
glasses, dressed in a heavy, etiolated, brown, winter suit. The suit seemed out of place in the spring
heat of Washington. Then he remembered. That
morning. Coming in from the airport in the air-
line limousine, waiting with his briefcase in the
choked aisle to step down into the street: the
man who stayed seated. The man in the winter
suit. THAT MAN IS FOLLOWING ME Blackford was suddenly as certain of this as that the
building across the street was the White House. A

pang of stomach chill seized him. What's going on? He sought to calm himself.

In the first place, there is no reason *to believe this superstitious conviction of mine that that man is following me. In the second place, if he is, conceivably it is someone from the Agency, checking on me. In the third place, if it is one of theirs, what kind of danger am I in? A hundred yards from the White House! A half mile from the headquarters of the Federal Bureau of Investigation!*—He let his mind run on: *One mile from the Smithsonian Institution, which has Lindbergh's* Spirit of St. Louis *which I could certainly, as a qualified jet navy pilot, fly away in, if somebody could be got to gas it up. Twenty miles from the Aberdeen Proving Grounds, where they could give me a blowgun with mysterious poisons that would make the man in the winter suit drop quite dead.*

He derailed the runaway train of thought, and forced himself to analyze exactly the causes of his apprehension. No one of *theirs* was supposed to have any cause to follow Blackford Oakes around—his cover discipline had been very scrupulously adhered to. So didn't it have to be one of ours who, knowing Oakes's affiliation, was checking on his off-duty activity?

First things first: I must establish whether my suspicion is well founded.

So he kept his eyes trained on the White House, away from the man with the winter suit. Summoning his instructors' teachings of the previous summer, he laid out his plan. He would in due course rise, walk across the street and

over to the guard at the west gate of the White
House, and ask him a routine question: "Where
does the line form for visitors to the White
House?" In asking that question he would have
reason to face east, reacting to the direction in
which he knew the guard would point. If the
man in the winter suit had left his bench but was
still visible, Blackford would prolong the conversation with the guard while tracking the man's
movements. If the man stayed seated on the
bench, Blackford would thank the guard and
walk west along Pennsylvania Avenue, cross the
street, and duck in at number 1750 to pick up a
hot dog at the little stand inside the perimeter of
the big entranceway to the massive office building. He would soon know if he was being followed.

He rose and crossed the street. The guards
that season were not talkative. Not long ago,
Puerto Rican terrorists had assaulted Blair House,
attempting to kill President Truman. The guard
pointed impatiently to the east, and advised
Blackford in hortatory accents that loitering was
not permitted outside the White House. Notwithstanding the abbreviation of his encounter,
Blackford had time to notice that the man in the
winter suit remained seated, his newspaper
raised to cover his face. Blackford walked in a
casual gait toward number 1750, in one of whose
upper rooms he had studied a year ago under
"Rudolph." He ducked in and stood by the quick-
food counter, cutting the angle of vision from
the street to twenty yards. In thirty-six seconds

the man in the winter suit emerged. He too
turned abruptly into the building, but walked
to the newsstand opposite, bought a newspaper
and a magazine, turned back toward the street,
never looking to his left at the food counter,
hailed a taxi and went off. Blackford, hot dog in
hand, stared at the disappearing cab. *What goes
on?*

Blackford meditated now whether to report
so inconclusive an experience to Mr. Lamb. He
would think about it, and meanwhile be especially attentive. What if it had been a CIA agent,
doing a routine check? Would they own up?
What were they looking out for?

Blackford looked haphazardly at the movie
page of the *Times Herald* left open on the counter
and decided impetuously to go to the late-after-
noon showing of *The Caine Mutiny*, thereby
avoiding the long lines he had read about. He
walked to Seventeenth and E streets, bought a
ticket and some popcorn, walked into the theater,
spotted an empty seat near the aisle, and slithered by the knees of the man squatted on the end
seat. Eyes adjusted to the light, he focused on the
movie and the deeply interesting question of
whether Van Johnson really was entitled to take
over Humphrey Bogart's ship. It wasn't open and
shut, no more than the hanging of Billy Budd or
—come to think of it—the conviction of Galileo.
The presumption in favor of stipulated authority's right to exercise his authority is very heavy in
an orderly society. Blackford knew that, in part
because by temperament he was anti-authority.

So he had tried for years since analyzing his natural inclinations to compensate for them—by collecting intellectual arguments in favor of the presumptions.

He finished, regretfully, his popcorn. In the sequence on the screen where the younger officer imitates Queeg, the man next to him on the aisle, like everyone else in the movie house, laughed. It was a vaguely familiar laugh, and Blackford glanced briefly over to his right, to discern the unmistakable profile of Senator Joseph McCarthy, also with popcorn in hand, happily whiling away two hours during which probably every reporter in the world was trying to find him, he being the major pursuit of the press in the spring of 1952. Blackford reached into his jacket and pulled out a small notepad. In the dark he scratched out four words, and folded the piece of paper. The movie over except for the final music and the credits, Blackford slid back toward the aisle, and as he did so inserted the paper silently into the senator's comatose right hand, and walked gleefully out into the street. He had written: SENATOR: INVESTIGATE ALLEN DULLES!"

Late the following afternoon he found himself reaching for his suitcase almost immediately after the train had left Bridgeport, though he knew from one hundred experiences that another fifteen minutes would pass before the New Haven stop. It was good in any case to remove himself from the car, so thick with fetid tobacco smoke. So he stood in the rattling, twisting, noise-making connecting chamber, leaning his head out of doors where the conductor had neglected to secure the panel. The spring air, even with all the grit from the industrial activity in the area, was bracing after the five-hour ride from Washington, and he found himself not merely excited, but truly happy at the prospect of seeing Sally: who was there, peering anxiously at each of the exiting vestibules of the forward cars as they slid by her, until she spotted him. He hoped she had not changed her simple hair style, and indeed had devoted one of his three most recent letters to the theme. She hadn't; it was straight, curling out at her neck, and her eyes were alight, as transparent as her mouth with the thin, lightly touched-up lips, stretched now with pleasure as he jumped down and hugged her. They walked together to her little Volkswagen, saying only the utterly conventional things to each other, as if he had come in from a neighboring college on a blind date.

They reached her Volkswagen, and Blackford drew up abruptly.

"I don't believe it."

"You don't believe what?"

"I mean, how do you see out the back window?"

"I don't. I've given up seeing out of the back window for the duration of the campaign. Besides, that's how Republicans do things—looking backward."

"How does sealing the entire back window of the car with Stevenson posters help Adlai Stevenson become President?"

"It demonstrates the total devotion of the younger generation to Adlai Stevenson."

"In the first place, since they can't see through the window, how will anyone ever know the driver of the car is a member of the younger generation?"

"I'll drive so slowly, everyone will have to pass me."

He laughed, wedging his suitcase in the back. "Shall I drive?"

"Sure," Sally said, handing him the keys. "Only remember, sir, over here we drive on the right-hand side."

He felt he was home again, and they drove to the apartment she shared with another graduate student, her dear friend Sheila, obligingly absent for the weekend.

He went to wash up and returned to find Sally with an apron over her skirt.

"We're going to eat here, and don't contradict me. Anyway it's too late. I turned on the oven two hours ago."

"Darling, I'll do anything you say. I'll even pretend I like your cooking. But I could have taken you out. Still, I suppose it's easier here to tell you about all my exciting architectural discoveries in London."

He thus teased her about her scientific illiteracy, and her adamant disinclination to correct it. "Then, after that, you can tell me about

Chaucer. And how if Chaucer were alive, he would be campaigning for Adlai Stevenson. Without a backward glance."

A scotch in his hand, he hovered about her as she tinkered with the salad and the duck and the orange gook she ruined it with, he opened the two wine bottles and the deep-frozen cake, and they talked through the dinner hour, and impulsively he asked if she wanted to drive to Zeta Psi for a nightcap, and she said yes, and ten minutes later they stopped in the driveway between the *Yale Daily News* and the fraternity house. Blackford made rather a point of asking Sally to stand outside to direct him as he slid the Volkswagen backward into the crack between two squalid American cars—"because I can't see through Adlai. Nor can most Democrats," he chortled. "Hey, you know what I just committed?" he said, twisting the wheel as she instructed.

"What?" she shouted, to overcome the motor noise.

"I said, 'Do you know what I just committed in that sentence,' 'cause if you don't, I'll report you to your English teachers, and you won't get your degree!"

"Ass. You mean the see-through-Adlai bit? You 'committed,' as you put it, a zeugma. Even the *New York Times* doesn't know what that is. Should we suspend operations so I can congratulate you?"

Black was chagrined, completed the parking, and took Sally by the arm, wondering vaguely for the first time what rights alumni had to use their old fraternities: he could not remember if he had received a bill of any sort for post-graduate membership.

But it was most of the old crowd, and he was welcomed warmly by the bartender, and gravitated to the corner, where he had first taken Sally when she came as his date to the Junior Prom two years ago. A thousand years ago.

She sipped at a menthe frappé, he at a bottle of beer, and she said to him, "Blacky, what *are* you up to?"

"Well, the foundation is winding up the business I went to England for—I gave them six books full of drawings, notes, ideas—and now there's some talk of getting me involved in a restoration."

"A restoration of what?"

"I won't have the details until after I go to New York. It's a Marshall Plan project, some devastated cathedral or something in Germany."

"Why do you want to take it on?"

"I don't know. I've flown over Germany shooting at other airplanes, but I've never been *in* Germany. It kind of intrigues me. I don't feel like going back to graduate school. Not right now, anyway."

"Do you feel like being a whole continent away from me?"

"Darling, obviously I don't *feel* like being a whole continent away from you. Or continent with you. But don't give me those feminizations. They don't become you." He looked at her. She was cocking her head ever so slightly, as she had always done, looking in the dim light as desirable as he had ever seen her. "You know that. But you're totally absorbed, and you have one more year to go. Meanwhile, I'm picking up some useful experience. Besides, there isn't anything here to reconstruct. I mean, unless you count the town of New Haven."

"I see." And in fact she did see, Blackford knew, which was one reason why he loved her so dearly. She saw, even, that his epistolary neglect didn't mean anything.

"In return for your understanding, I'll listen to you talk about Adlai Stevenson."

Which she did. She talked about hearing him give a speech at Princeton, about its startling literacy, about the allusions to great diplomatic and historical figures, and, above all, about the necessity always to read books. "It was the most stunning speech by a political figure I ever heard."

"I can believe it," Blackford said. "He'll stun the majority of the American people right into the Republican camp."

"That," her voice rose a bit, "is sheer cynicism. I predict he will win. If he does, I shall propose to him that you be made general-in-chief of the Corps of Engineers. Is that what they call him?"

"Something like that. Let's go, darling." And they drove home, talking to each other happily, tilting their vats of stored knowledge, jokes, reminiscences, experiences steeper and steeper, in their anxiety to catch up. And so it was through the evening, with only the absolutely necessary interruptions. Blackford resolved there and then to agitate to take his training in Boston, and settle down to commuting to New Haven.

He succeeded.

4

Blackford Oakes had been advised that he was
expected at the Palace of St. Anselm at five to
take tea with the Countess Wintergrin and her
son Axel. The letter, hand-delivered to his quarters at the local inn, two kilometers up the road
at St. Anselm's village, indicated that following
the refreshment he would go off to the library
and discuss with Count Wintergrin the plans for
the reconstruction of the celebrated chapel.

It had been designed by Meister Gerard, the
great architect who had also done the renowned
cathedral at Cologne, a hundred kilometers west
of St. Anselm. "Count Wintergrin takes this opportunity, on behalf of the people of St. Anselm's, and of the international community who

venerate the small masterwork of Meister Gerard, to thank the people of the United States who, through the instrument of Marshall Aid, have undertaken to finance the reconstruction of a chapel which, although damaged by American artillery, is properly the concern of the Germans who were responsible for the outbreak of hostilities between our peoples. Upon completion of the work, the people of St. Anselm's will send a token of their appreciation to the President of the United States as a permanent reminder of their gratitude." The communication was not signed by Wintergrin, but, on his behalf, by "R. Himmelfarb, Sekretär."

The evening before, Oakes dined at the Westfalenkrug, the restaurant across the street from their inn, the Rittensgasthof, with Jimmy Overstreet, on loan from the Corps of Engineers for the St. Anselm project. The corps was engaged in rebuilding a number of monuments destroyed during the war. St. Anselm's, being small and privately owned, was off the beaten path. But it had been approved by a committee of Congress with considerable dispatch at the discreet urging of Mr. Acheson, who when apprised of the unwonted speed with which his request had been honored, remarked acidly to an aide that if the rebuilding of gutted churches was all he had to do as Secretary of State, he would be getting on better with the Congress. Blackford Oakes, a young graduate of Yale University with honors in engineering, highly recommended for the post by a powerful senator on the Appropriations

Committee, was given the job of chief engineer. His assistant James Overstreet, age forty, had been building things since, at age fourteen, he apprenticed as a bricklayer in Austin, Texas. Jimmy Overstreet contrived to get a job in a construction unit during the Depression by volunteering to work in the Panama Canal Zone. It was remarkable that with a background in construction, he had actually been used for construction projects by the army when the war came—"After Pearl Harbor," he chatted to Blackford, sounding like every cynical G.I, "they were using engineers to teach Japanese, and Japanese linguists to sit in concentration camps in Nevada making sand castles." Accompanying an American technical mission to the Soviet Union, Overstreet visited Leningrad and saw there the painstaking work the Russians were doing to restore the devastated palaces and museums in the area. He was impressed, and determined now to use his ingenuity to make St. Anselm's whole. "Anything that can be built, we can reproduce," he said, appropriately affecting the Texas drawl he had all but lost since childhood.

Oakes's other principal assistant was an Italian-American, Arturo Conditti, borrowed from the fine arts department of the University of Rochester. Conditti's father was an Italian-Jewish professor of Renaissance art, student of Bernard Berenson, who came to New York with his family in 1937 and worked as a waiter at Mamma Leone's. Arturo was eighteen the day the Japanese surrendered, and so was unmolested by the draft. He took his doctorate in 1950. His dissertation, on the construction techniques of the gothic masters of the thirteenth century, had been accepted for publication, and he was excited at the prospect of getting practical experience. Overstreet and Conditti both accepted Oakes's authority without surprise, taking him to be a political appointment, which in ways neither of them knew was exactly the case. On meeting him when, coming in from different parts of the United States, they converged on St. Anselm's, both were agreeably surprised.

"Come to think of it," Overstreet said to Conditti, "I suppose there's no reason why you shouldn't be able to learn something about engineering at Yale University."

"I hadn't thought about it," Conditti replied. "He's bright. I don't know yet whether he has a good eye. He's definitely not a bureaucrat. Whoever his patron in government is, he might have made a mistake, selecting Oakes. Seems like the kind of guy who gets things done. But I wonder how patient he'll be with me when I get around to telling him it might take me six months just to get the right mix in the stained glass."

"As a matter of fact," Overstreet said, "that count fella may turn out to be the real boss. The agreement says he's got to approve *everything*. I wonder why he goes to all the trouble. The way they tell it, if he becomes Germany's boss there'll be another war. Then they'll bomb the church all over again." He smiled at Conditti. "Oh well . . . I guess that's one way of providing employment. For your kids."

The Schloss St. Anselm is a walled compound, four acres in all, surrounded by what was once a functioning moat. At the western end, looking haughtily over the Westphalian plains, the castle itself stands, two turrets, built in different centuries, with a third piggybacking on the first two and reaching a height of one hundred and twenty-five feet above the Schlosshof, the courtyard. The living quarters elbow out from the collection of turrets, dark cold rooms, some crowded with medieval artifacts, others decorated by mural paintings stretching right around, doorknob to doorknob, and one huge banquet room, with the usual regimental standards, and iron battle dress surrounding a heavy oak table around which fifty people can sit, and often did before the death of Axel's father, who was gregarious, and something of a gourmand. "I say if you've got to live in a museum, live it up!" he had told his wife Eva after she had accidentally espied his food and wine bill for the preceding month.

But there was an austere side to his character. Abutting the banquet hall in the second story was an extensive library. It was there—not in the banquet hall—that the eighteenth Count Wintergrin was found dead at age thirty-eight, the cause of death a swollen blood vessel, not a swollen liver. They found, among his papers, a complete history of Schloss St. Anselm, pronounced by university scholars a work of art as well as of scholarship. It was published with extensive illustrations in 1936. Axel read it when he was seventeen years old, and wept at his misperception of his father. He had loved him even as he was, but the studious, serious young Axel would carefully desist, during his holidays from Greyburn, from talking with his father about anything more exacting than horses, hounds, partridges, and weather, for fear of having to condescend to him. To think that while at Greyburn he was reading schoolboys' histories of the Middle Ages, his own father was composing a book on the period that would turn out to be something of a classic in the field. Axel's determination to reconstruct the chapel perfectly was partly a private act of homage to his underappreciated father.

Across the courtyard, along the southern end, were converted stables. By the account in the history, one hundred and twenty horses were once kept there. There were still horses, but only the four used by the family. The space had long since been given over for use by a half-dozen little shopkeepers who resided in the apartments upstairs. There were larger stores down the hill, and up the road at St. Anselm's village. But at "the courtyard," as the natives referred to the cobblestoned Schlosshof, one could find an all-purpose grocery store, a small restaurant and bar —the Anselmsklaus—an apothecary, and a little hardware store.

And then, at the eastern end, a hundred meters from the castle, the chapel. It was the Catholic church for the whole village, the churchgoing members of which came the two and one-half kilometers on foot, by bicycle, and increasingly by car and bus to attend Sunday services, weddings, funerals, and baptisms. During the final western offensive, the Nazis had installed a heavy mortar unit on the northern wall of the courtyard. On the first of April 1945, this outpost was manned by three remaining soldiers— the rest of the squad, seeing the end only a few days away, had deserted. The Americans, misreckoning it a massive resistance point, ordered up heavy artillery. The very first shell perforated the seven-hundred-year-old roof of the chapel and passed through a wooden trapdoor to the crypt, exploding beneath the level of the stone floor. The church was in one sense devastated: the eye could not travel a foot in any direction without coming on the fingerprints of the explosive. Yet its ghostly silhouette was unaltered. And after six weeks spent removing rubble—and segregating lovingly anything that might prove useful if ever the good Lord, having attended to more urgent matters such as Berlin and the cathedral of Cologne, got around to the painstaking job of piecing back together their beloved St. Anselm's chapel—the parishioners were attending divine services there again, sitting on makeshift benches, and using a borrowed table from the castle as an altar. They did not know (it was Overstreet who made the analysis for Blackford) that two critical timbers in the roof scaffolding had been pierced by the shrapnel. They stood in place "only by the grace of God and inertia," as Overstreet reported it. "One substantial vibe, coming in from any of a dozen parts of the wall, and that roof would come right down," killing, or wounding, potentially, the entire congregation of St. Anselm's. Mostly older men, women of all ages, and children.

Half the younger men had died in the war, yet no one was heard to express resentment when it transpired that their very own dashing count, young Axel, had—for all they knew—shot at their own sons, shot at his fellow villagers. The war (and indeed life itself) was so complicated. And since one wasn't any longer sure what to believe, wasn't it really safer to start all over again, and to believe in the transcendent wisdom and loyalty of their own count, whose ancestors had fought for their village, and for the rights of the people of their village since the beginning of history, or at any rate as much of history as the people of St. Anselm's were concerned with?

Blackford left his car in the courtyard, and as he walked into the huge archway, the small door embedded in the gate swung open, releasing a shaft of yellow light into the late-summer dusk. Someone had been waiting for him. He followed a creaky old man wearing a green vest over a white shirt, and an apron over his pants, through a cold hallway into a warm, chintzy living room, the fireplace crackling, over which a single crystal chandelier, its dozen candles lit, hung, illuminating the eight painted panels depicting the Borghese Gardens in midsummer. The countess was there in her drawing room and rose to greet him, a warm but formal smile on her high-boned face. Did he mind if she spoke to him in German? It had been *so* long since she had practiced the

English she had learned as a girl, and in any case she had reports that Mr. Oakes's German was— she raised her hand, thumb and forefinger touching—"perfect." Blackford smiled, and replied in a German that paid tribute to what he called the sadistic Huns who had taught him the language —after the first grueling day he had looked the two words up in his dictionary, and ever after so referred to the he-she German team retained by the agency to torment him five hours a day for five months in Boston. "My Axel will be here presently," she said, lifting her hand to signal the butler to bring in the tea. "Dear Axel, he is so busy these days. But he attaches such a high priority to the rebuilding of our little church. Do you have churches in America, Mr. Oakes? I mean, Mr. Oakes, do you have beautiful churches in America? I mean, Mr. Oakes, do you have . . ."

"Do we have any churches in America built during the thirteenth century? No, Countess, we don't. But we do have the Grand Canyon, and that was built even earlier." He smiled.

"Ah, yes, I have heard about it. Master craftsmen, those Indians. Tell me, Mr. Oakes— my, but you *are* handsome. What did you do during the war?"

"I fought on the same side as your son, Countess," he replied cautiously.

"Yes, of course, how silly. I mean, what did you *do* in the war? Really, it is so ironic. It would be ironic perfection if it happened that you were the artillery officer who fired on our chapel! But I suppose that would be just too much. But really, talking about the war is so depressing. And now some of my friends tell me there will be another war if Axel has his way, but I don't believe it, not for a minute. I tell them all the same thing: Axel is a peaceful young man. Even as a child he did not like to quarrel. But he *does* know his mind. Always did. When he was eleven he told us—came right to our bedroom, and told the count and me—that he could not put up one more day with his governess, Mlle. Lachaise, that we would be *forced"*—she laughed with evident pleasure at the recollection—"he told us that we would be forced to *choose* between *him,* our son, and *her,* his governess! Casper told him to go to bed, to say his prayers, and to wait another ten years or so before undertaking to superintend his own education.

"Well, Mr. Oakes, the next morning at breakfast-time Mlle. Lachaise reported that Axel was gone. No trace of him! Not even the groom knew where he was! It was two days before the police stopped him, all the way south at Eisenfeld. His father dealt most severely with him. But after Axel's tears had dried, he turned to his father—would you believe it, Mr. Oakes?—and said to him: 'Father, unless you get rid of Mlle. Lachaise, I shall have to run away again tomorrow.' That night the count and I conferred, and the next morning we dispatched Mlle. Lachaise. The alternative was to put Axel in the palace dungeon.

"Do you suppose, Mr. Oakes, that the Russians will deal that way with Axel? Will they decide they might as well let Axel *have* East Germany?"

Blackford reflected that nobody in Washington had trained him to deal with such as Countess Wintergrin. He mobilized himself to attempt a reply to her impossible question, then decided to sidestep it. Instead, he asked:

"Tell me, Countess. What *was* wrong with Mlle. Lachaise? She must have been a brute."

"Mlle. Lachaise? Now let me see. Which one was that? She was *not* Mlle. Bouchex. No. And she wasn't Mlle. Longueville. No. Mlle. Lachaise . . . I can't really remember. When Axel comes, we must ask him."

Blackford very nearly panicked. "No, no, thank you very much, Countess. It doesn't really matter. I'm sure Count Wintergrin had good reasons, whatever they were."

"Oh, indeed, Mr. Oakes. Axel *always* had good reasons. It's just that other people don't always know what those good reasons *are*. I'm sure that's true of you, Mr. Oakes. I am sure you have good reasons for being here."

Axel Wintergrin strode into the room, leaned over to give his mother a light kiss on the forehead, then extended his hand to the visitor. He was dressed in his favorite rust-colored tweed, and though the jacket was unbuttoned, the trimness of his body was evident. He took a biscuit absent-mindedly from the tray on the table and sat down, extending his long, thin hand to take the cup and saucer the butler handed him.

"It is very good to meet you, Mr. Oakes. Good evening, Mother."

"Good evening, darling."

"You are most welcome, Mr. Oakes"—he spoke in English. As fluent as Blackford's, though the accent was British. Not surprisingly, there was a trace there of the distinctive Greyburn slur.—"as I hope I have made clear. In due course we'd have attended to the church ourselves. But it would have been a long time. Perhaps ten or fifteen years from now. Even the Russians, who can conscript their laborers and their artists, are talking in terms of twenty-five years to rebuild all their palaces in Leningrad. It is irrelevant that the liquidation of the state as promised by Karl Marx will be delayed even longer. The gesture of your government, in any case, is greatly appreciated. You are familiar with my father's book?"

"Yes, I am. An admirable work. I trust one day it will be translated into English."

"You anticipate me, Mr. Oakes. It is my intention to subsidize a translation in a memorial edition dedicated to the American people when the rebuilding is done."

"Dear Axel"—the countess rose, upon which the two men followed suit—"forgive me. You have matters to discuss with Mr. Oakes. I have matters to discuss with my cook. So nice of you to come, Mr. Oakes." She extended her hand, but drew it back with that abruptness of the European who suddenly recalls that it will not be kissed, because the gentleman is American and doesn't . . . know; so don't embarrass him, and she smiled wholesomely through her lightly tinted lips, turned her tweedy presence to the door, and muttered something to the butler, who followed her out.

"We will stay here, since my mother has left us alone." Blackford had his first direct experience of the surefooted authoritativeness of Axel Wintergrin. (He hadn't said—important difference—"Shall we stay here, now that my mother is gone?") Black nodded, and Wintergrin began to talk.

"You know, Mr. Oakes—from my father's history book—that the building of St. Anselm's church coincided with the settlement of the village. When the church was consecrated, just after 1250, the first Baron of Wintergrin was charged by the bishop to maintain the church in its pristine mini-magnificence. Probably that is the single charge all my ancestors have taken seriously." He smiled. "Though that's not entirely fair. On the whole they have been a good lot, and the one who was executed for adultery simply lived at the wrong time: the German Catholics were especially anxious, at that period, to distinguish their own position on marital fidelity from that of the British king." Blackford smiled. Fancy. Royal adultery!

"I have, as you certainly know, undertaken the organization of a national political party to compete in the elections in November. This will require me to spend a great deal of time away from St. Anselm's. But I make every effort to get back here on Sundays and Mondays. I shall always be at your disposal to review your work and that of your assistants—I look forward to meeting them—to check every particular. The chapel must be authentic."

He paused, reflecting. "The supreme challenge is the stained glass. The colors were magnificent! Tomorrow I shall take you through my father's library, which has a complete collection of photographs of the church: every square inch, with careful colorwork and coding. My understanding is that you have made preliminary arrangements with carpenters, stonecutters, masons and glassmakers."

"That is correct."

"Splendid. Let me ask, how many men will be working on the project at the outset?"

Blackford said probably a half dozen, with an additional two or three coming in, as skilled craftsmen were located.

"It is a vulgar question. But *do* you have any idea how long it will take?"

"We've talked about it—Overstreet, Conditti, and I. Not less than a year. Say a year, if all goes well. Knock wood." This mundane appeal to superstition had the effect of prying his host loose from his preoccupation.

"A glass of wine? Or do you prefer beer? Whiskey?" Wintergrin rang the bell at his side, without waiting for an answer.

"Thank you, a glass of white wine."

"I understand you flew during the war. Do you still fly?"

"Not regularly," Blackford said. "I did fly the new American Saber at an exhibition in London recently. My father is the European salesman for Saber. You perhaps read about it: the British flier in the Hunter was killed."

Axel looked sharply at Blackford, and his voice went up a half tone.

"*Of course. It was you!* I was related to Viscount Kirk. And we were at school together. Greyburn." Wintergrin did not advertise that— like Kirk—he too was related to the Queen.

"I spent a few weeks in Greyburn myself." Oakes stepped forward. He had decided, in his dealings with Axel, that he would hide only what he had to hide.

"Indeed? When were you there?"

"From September, 1941, until December. I would tell you that I left on account of Pearl Harbor, and it's true that I'd have had to leave on account of Pearl Harbor, but in fact a couple of days before Pearl Harbor I ran away." Blackford was tempted to add that he did so because the headmaster declined to discharge Mlle. Lachaise.

Axel looked as if he would ask why Blackford had run away, thought better of it, and instead tilted the conversation to a slightly different course.

"We did not overlap, in that event. I was graduated in 1938. Kirk was a couple of years younger. A fine horseman, even then. An impressive war record."

Blackford sipped his wine. "Yes. And a fine flier. The whole thing was tragic and . . . inexplicable."

"Did they ever discover the cause of the accident?"

"No," said Blackford—and thought, God help me if ever they do.

Axel asked whether he had known this person, and that person. Whether he had had experience with this teacher, or that teacher. What was his opinion of the headmaster, Dr. Chase, who was still there? Blackford said he thought Chase a cold fish and a bully, but had never studied under him. Wintergrin said he had had fair treatment from Chase up until the Austrian Anschluss. "After that, he thought of me first as a young Nazi, only then as a student at his school."

"Were you"—Blackford's risk was calculated—"at that point a nationalist, er, a defender of German policies?"

"You are asking if I was identified with the Nazis?"

"I simply wondered, knowing Chase."

Axel trilled his fingers on his glass of wine—which, Blackford noticed, he had not touched. "I decided when I went first to Greyburn at age fourteen that I would answer no questions and involve myself in no discussions having to do with the policies of my government."

"I wish I had followed the same rule," Blackford said.

"No one who knew me at Greyburn would have had any grounds to know what was on my mind. That training proved useful. And during the holidays I avoided political discussions here in Germany, pleading that any involvement in them would make life difficult for me back in England where, after all, I was spending nine months of every year. When I left Greyburn and went to officers' school I was assigned to the Kavallerieschule in Hannover, where the traditions are very strict, very . . . venerable. There are no political discussions—for the simple reason that it is commonly accepted that everyone is entirely enthusiastic about every policy of the government."

Blackford decided to press his luck.

"When did you decide to defect?"

"I decided to defect after an incident at officers' school."

Blackford said nothing. He would let Wintergrin decide, without any pressure, whether to tell the story. Wintergrin said nothing. After a moment's pause, Blackford decided to take him off the hook:

"Perhaps one day you will write your story completely?"

"When my story is written," Axel said, "what I did or experienced as a nineteen-year-old will not greatly matter."

Again Blackford thought it wise to ease off.

"I hope they will find it appropriate to say about you, Count Wintergrin, that you always found time to give to the concerns of St. Anselm."

Axel rose. "Indeed."

The meeting was ended, without abrasion. On the contrary, Wintergrin had liked the American: his tone of voice reflected this. They walked to the door.

"Tomorrow, then, at ten, we shall go over to the library. I have meetings at nine and at twelve.

71

Perhaps you will bring your associates?" Blackford noticed that he stood slightly to one side as the door swung open, avoiding needless exposure. Outside, Blackford paused an instant, closing his eyes to adjust them to the night, whose blackness at first disguised the profile of his Fiat, even though it was the only car in the courtyard.

In the Anselmsklaus, the little eatery across the courtyard, the traveler with the trim beard ate perfunctorily, conjoining pieces of dry Westphalian ham and chunks of bread lackadaisically. He seemed distracted, staring out through the window at the entrance to the palace. When the door opened and the light streamed out, the figure that emerged, pausing slightly before walking to his car, could not be seen except in outline. Günther Matti did not need to see the face. He knew the figure of Blackford Oakes well enough. He could have picked him out if faced with the silhouettes of twenty men of approximately the same age and size. There was the trimness, the firmness of step combined with spontaneity of movement. And besides, there had been no effort at disguise. His car was right out there, and he walked right to it. All those tedious months, from mid-January until now, late August—London, Washington, Boston, New York, Bonn—finally, paydirt. Boris Andreyvich Bolgin would be very pleased. Most important of all, Stalin himself would perhaps smile. Not for long. Oh, how he would rage on assimilating the data. But meanwhile there would be a kind word for the technicians. That's all he was, Günther Matti reminded himself, turning now zestfully to his meat and wine, just a technician. He had done as much for the Nazis. But he would never betray his clients. He worked for cash, and on this job alone he would have earned enough to return to Switzerland and live a year with his family without thought to expenses. It had been tedious. Günther Matti had earned his keep.

5

Boris Andreyvich Bolgin looked wistfully at the cartoon hanging in the second floor of the Brighton Pavilion. Imagine, he thought. Just imagine. One hundred and thirty years ago, and the British press could even *then* write thus critically, derisively, about their own king! Their sovereign! Well, granted that Prince William wasn't technically yet king—but almost. And in the public press! Cartoons now preserved! Framed in a museum *belonging to the Crown!* . . . Here was Prince William, great-great-great-grandfather of Queen Caroline, *ridiculed*. Made to look like a pig! A lecher! An idiot! An imbecile! Why, in Russia, if one feature—just the bulbous nose, say, or the cauliflower ears, or the pig mouth—were affixed to a single picture of Joseph Stalin, what would happen? What? Boris Bolgin asked himself melodramatically.

Of course the artist would be arrested, tortured, and executed. That, of *course*. But then they would start coming, coming in droves. Bolgin knew. In his younger days, before reaching his present eminence, he had served among those droves. They would ask around about the cartoonist's family. About his associates. About his associates' associates. About his associates' associates' associates. Shall I go on? Bolgin thought to himself. Yes, he would go on. He was at the Brighton Pavilion, in Brighton, Sussex, England, and nobody in the world who saw him could know what he was thinking. So he would continue. He would think with *abandon*. Lasciviously. He would now resume . . . They would question his associates' associates' associates' (Bolgin was now counting on his fingers) associates, and send *them*—to Gulag.

Here was something he did *not* know. Once, way back (Bolgin was stunned, using his fingers once again, to reckon that it was only ten years ago, during the siege of Stalingrad), when he and Pyotr Ivanovich Ilyich were rising stars in the intelligence service, stationed in Finland, they had devoted an evening to the question: What was it that finally caused Stalin to stop to catch his breath? They thought the purge in 1937 was over. Until the purge of 1938 began. It had been so in 1933. The purges had no trace of rational justification. Stalin must have known that. Ilyich, who had once spoken with Stalin—poor Ilyich, head now of the KGB, had to speak with Stalin regularly, sometimes at two, three in the morning, returning to his apartment exhausted, relieved that he was still alive; wondering whether, imprisoned as he was by his circumstances, he could truly say he was glad to be alive—Ilyich had said that night in Helsinki that he figured Stalin called an end to purges only when he was personally surfeited with them. But there was never any way of knowing when this would happen, and pity the man who wrongly anticipated Stalin's surfeit! The current purge building up had all the earmarks of an eructation. Stalin eructates, Bolgin thought. Lesser phenomena, like volcanoes, merely erupt. There were literally millions of Russians who this very night would go to bed apprehensive. Because they felt the tremors. Ilyich's agents were already doing Stakhanovite duty, pounding on doors at night. Stalin himself kept out of sight these days. He never left his dacha, it was said. From there he caused all of Russia to writhe in pain and fear. His reach was everywhere—except Yugoslavia! How had Stalin managed to fail to bring Tito to heel? Bolgin thanked his venerable mother for not having brought him into the world to serve as Stalin's agent in Yugoslavia these last four years. Or, rather, one of Stalin's *late* agents in Yugoslavia—may they rest in peace.

But Bolgin had his own troubles. When the KGB was outwitted in London, Stalin turned his attention to the American spy responsible, Blackford Oakes. What job would he be assigned to? *Find out,* Ilyich had said. *And do not fail us.*

77

(He *always* said, *Do not fail us*.) (And he always meant it.)

"That cartoonist was greatly feared in England," the stranger at his side remarked.

Bolgin shook himself out of his trance, and returned the code. "He outlived Prince William."

Bolgin closed his guidebook and turned to the staircase, followed by Matti. On the street the two men—Bolgin wearing his fedora and his fur-lined Burberry raincoat, Günther Matti with his brownish heavy winter suit, carrying an umbrella and a newspaper—walked silently. At Colby's Tavern, two blocks down, they walked in, taking a table in the corner.

Bolgin had received, by code, an account of Blackford's arrival in Washington, and of his subsequent move to Boston. It had been several weeks before Matti was able to ascertain what Oakes did at the apartment in Cambridge to which he repaired every evening at five-thirty, leaving after ten. The tenants of the apartment sometimes stayed overnight, sometimes left it together or singly, usually a bit after Oakes did. One morning, after an exasperating week of conjecture, Matti followed the girl to a little store specializing in German books. The young man, on the other hand, worked during the day as a Mercedes mechanic. It wasn't until Matti finally bugged the apartment that he discovered that Oakes was spending five hours a night learning German. During the day Oakes's movements were irregular. Sometimes he would audit classes in engineering, sometimes he would go on to the library, disappearing in the stacks. Often he would spend time at a construction project. The foreman had befriended him, though it turned out he knew nothing about Blackford except that he was a graduate engineer interested in practical training. Weekends he would go to New Haven, dancing attendance on his girlfriend Sally Partridge, who—Matti expained in his methodic way—studied English literature at the summer session of the graduate school . . .

"Do get *on* with it," Bolgin interrupted. "I don't *care* what his girlfriend is studying."

"I almost lost him, Leonid my friend"—Matti persevered; he had never before laid eyes on "Leonid" before today, but his orders, through the cut-out agent, had always come from "Leonid."

"And don't tell me about your narrow escapes," Bolgin sighed. "Get on with it. *Where is he now? What is he doing?*"

Günther Matti was put off by the abrupt acceleration of his story. So he gave it out sulkily. "The night before last"—he looked at his watch—"at nineteen thirty-two, he left St. Anselm's castle, and the company of Count Axel Wintergrin."

Bolgin's heart stopped beating, the blood drained from his paunchy face, pockmarked by frostbite in Siberia. He whispered to himself: "Axel Wintergrin. Axel Wintergrin . . ." And then, "Go on, go on! Do you know what he was doing, talking to Wintergrin?"

"Yes," said Matti. "He heads a team of

79

Americans who are rebuilding the church at St. Anselm's, which was practically destroyed during the war."

The fried fish, tepid when served, were cold now. Bolgin drew Matti's newspaper toward himself and deftly inserted a thick envelope into it, as deftly retrieved by Matti and placed in his pocket. He called for the bill, muttered, made a few comments to Matti and walked out, hailing a cab to the railway station, where he caught the 4:57 express to London, reaching his apartment at 6:15, and his vodka at 6:21. On the train he had reflected that Ilyich could wait until the next morning to get the news.

6

"They gotta be nuts!"

"That's what I told them, though I didn't use that language."

"Those Russian bastards make me so . . . goddam mad. They're all the same. I used to think it was just Stalin. Hell, they're *all* like him. It doesn't matter what you do, what you tell 'em, what evidence you give 'em—we're backing Adenauer, not Wintergrin—*still* they won't believe you. Christ, they think *we* want a third world war?" He looked at the legend on his desk reading "THE BUCK STOPS HERE" and revised his formulation: "They think *I* want a third world war?"

"Sometimes you would think that, the way they talk."

"Sometimes I almost feel like shoving it to 'em. Strike that. I *could* call in that bastard ambassador and give him a piece of my mind."

"I wouldn't do that."

"Why not?"

"He'd think you were running the show yourself."

"Well, Christ, I can't think of any other show in town I should be running if not this one, if we're supposed to take the threats seriously."

"They haven't formulated their threats, but it's obvious what their ultimate threat is."

"Move in?"

"Move in."

The peppery man behind the august desk paused a moment, working his fingers on the paper pad in front of him. He spoke now more reflectively. "They think we'd just sit here and let 'em do it?"

"That's what we don't know. But they know they can get plenty out of us in return for pulling back from the brink."

"What do you figure they know about what we could do to them if it came to that?"

"We can't be sure. It's nice to feel we've got *some* secrets left. They know we can reach any of their facilities, all the population centers."

"What could we do in East Europe?"

"Report them to the Security Council."

"Christ."

"Almighty."

He paused again. "If Eisenhower wasn't so

goddam busy trying to be my successor, maybe he'd have left NATO in better shape."

"Actually, it isn't his fault. They've all got problems—Britain, France, the Low Countries. And anyway, nobody anticipated *this* problem."

"You offered to remove our feller out there?"

"The very first thing I suggested. It didn't stop him for a minute." The Secretary mimicked the ambassador's accent: " 'Removink one man vill not make Axel Wintergrin no less an American operation' is what he said. He wants something more, but he isn't willing to tell us what it is."

"Shit, are we supposed to *guess* what's on their minds? What's he want us to do, penetrate the Politburo to find out what *they* want us to do, so *we* can do it."

"They certainly want us to sweat over it."

"Well, go talk with Allen Dulles, and come back when you've got a proposal."

"All right, sir."

The Director of the Central Intelligence Agency left the State Department and returned to his own office, calling in his deputy. "Have them get out the folder on Blackford Oakes, O-a-k-e-s, and bring it in. We've got work to do."

In the subterranean repository where the files were kept, Colonel Bristol, aide to the deputy, presented himself. He showed his identification to the guard, who spoke through a microphone from his enclosed bullet- and gas-proof cylindrical booth. Colonel Bristol stepped through the steel doors that lifted at the command of the guard—promptly closing again, admitting the aide. Inside the enclosure Colonel Bristol, using a wall apparatus, dialed the code for that day, then gave his name into the receiver to the guard billeted inside the huge vault. In a moment the doors to the inner sanctum opened and as promptly closed. Only the archivist could open them, by tapping in a code on the controls. He inspected the document in Colonel Bristol's hand. Since it called for removal of a file, the authorization had to be personally authenticated by the deputy, whose private number he now dialed. "It says here, sir, to turn over the file on Oakes, Blackford, to Colonel Bristol." Satisfied, he put down the telephone and walked off to a remote part of the warren, coming back in a minute with a locked steel briefcase, which he routinely handcuffed to the extended wrist of Colonel Bristol. Outside both doors an armed marine was waiting to escort the colonel to the office of the deputy. It was all maximum security. Nobody knew that Blackford Oakes was a member of the Central Intelligence Agency at this point except the archivist, Colonel Bristol, the deputy, the Director and the Russians.

The Director spread the papers on his desk, and as he went over them one by one he handed them wordlessly to his deputy, Jim Sanderson. Then he said, "I remember this one, Jim. He cracked the big one in London last January. Came close to going down along with the Brit. Rufus's preference is always for not taking any chances. I personally authorized him to extricate Oakes. Here we are again, I guess you could say, up against the consequences of Western sentimentality. How the hell do you suppose they found out about him? None of the Brits have any idea he was our man. I know we aren't supposed to think the Commies are superhuman, but it beats me how they find out about some of these things. Now, Joseph Stalin, Secretary of the Communist Party of the Union of Soviet Socialist Republics, having discovered that one young Yalie, Oakes, CIA, is working at St. Anselm's rebuilding Wintergrin's church, has it all figured out: *"We're* behind Wintergrin! Never mind that we've been investing in Adenauer for seven years. So, the Soviet ambassador calls on the Secretary of State and chews and chews and chews his ass —sometimes I envy the ambassador, Jim—and says unless we 'take care of the situation,' Stalin will take care of the situation in his own way. Of course, he doesn't tell us what Stalin would do, and he doesn't tell us what *we're* supposed to do. It isn't as easy as recalling Oakes—the Secretary suggested that. No, sir, he wants much more. But he isn't willing to say what."

Knowing his boss, Jim Sanderson knew he was expected to give concentrated thought to what was being said; knew he wasn't supposed to comment until the Director's ruminative questions stopped being rhetorical. He did most of his thinking by soliloquy, preferably in the presence of one other person. Toward the end of his introverted trance, he would actually consult.

The Director leaned back and puffed on his

William F. Buckley, Jr.

pipe, which had lain unused on his table for ten
minutes, suggesting the gravity of the emergency.

"I tell you what let's do, Jim. Let's drive out
and see Rufus. He's the best; and he has the advantage of knowing this Oakes, in case the rec-
ommendation we come up with requires some
action at his end."

Rufus, yielding to the entreaties of his wife,
had finally agreed, after thirteen years abroad, to
repatriation. The war years had been spent in
England, the postwar years in France. Not given
to expressing his feelings, he hadn't told his wife
—hadn't succeeded, really, in informing himself
—just why he was averse to returning to America,
even for a visit. After the Oakes crisis in London
early in the year, he was ready to move back to
their cottage in the French countryside and resume the tending of his beloved roses. The night
after Viscount Kirk was killed, he took Muriel
to the theater, and on to dinner at the Con-
naught. He ordered a whiskey—his first drink
since taking on the case—and she drew courage
to ask, Wouldn't he now, nearing sixty, take her
back to America? They were childless, but her
sister lived in Baltimore, and Rufus had two very
old friends in Washington who always visited
him when they traveled in England and France,
giving him much pleasure. She asked why he resisted returning, and he forced himself to think
the question through. He was silent—Muriel was
no longer exasperated by this tic of her husband's, rooted in him, against which no force of

man or nature was effective: when Rufus was thinking, generals, prime ministers and wives simply sat there and waited. "I could have read through the novels of Jane Austen during Rufus's pauses between 1941 and 1945," the director of MI-5 complained to Churchill after the war. "If it hadn't been for Rufus," Churchill snapped back, "you would be reading Jane Austen in German."

An exaggeration, of course. Everything Churchill said was an exaggeration. But this one was as close to the simple truth as Churchill ever came. Eisenhower explained Rufus to a skeptic: "Look at it this way: He was the man who kept the atom bomb from Hitler. And the guy who told me it was safe to move into Normandy."

Eventually Rufus came out of it. He told Muriel, taking her hand under the table and pressing it, that during the war he had been responsible for saving a great many American lives.

"I know that, darling, I know that."

"But I was also responsible," he blurted out, "for killing Americans."

Muriel did not react, though her hand turned lifeless now.

"I am talking about *innocent* Americans, Muriel."

She knew that her role now was to supply the soothing background noises. Any attempt at moral analysis was not likely to advance what her husband had obviously already attempted; indeed, it would perhaps set him back to hear points he had already traversed analytical ages earlier. It was sufficient that he spoke now less emphatically than before about *not* returning. So all she said was what she felt she could safely say. "You tried to do not necessarily the right thing, but the better thing." He looked at her, his eyes widening. The formulation, though only a variant of the cliché about choosing the lesser of two evils, struck him as fresh and liberating in this conjugation of it. That evening Muriel wrote to her sister to say that, although the decision had not finally been made, she thought it safe to predict that they were at last coming home.

It was an hour and a half's drive to Westminister. Rufus had said over the telephone that he would have a light dinner waiting for them, after which they could go to his study while Muriel did the evening work at the nursery. On that understanding, Muriel went to the greenhouse, and Rufus washed the dishes, while Dulles and Sanderson dried.

"What do we know"—Rufus handed Dulles a wet saucer—"about the prospects for Wintergrin in November?"

"You ask the critical question, Rufus—as usual. We don't *know*. This is September, and anything can happen. His movement might collapse tomorrow. He hasn't been around long enough to be an 'established' national leader. There's so *much* that works against him. He is *thirty-one* years old. He has never run for elective office. There must be a lot of Germans who resent his having fought against Germany, never mind Hitler. He has given out no elaborated plan of what he will do if he achieves office. He's got people running for legislative office in every district. How many of *them* are going to risk associating themselves with the Reunification ticket?"

"That's one side of the picture," said Dulles. "Now—here Jim, your turn"—Dulles handed his deputy the wet coffee cup to dry. "The other is that he is becoming—has become—a national hero, and don't underestimate that. He apparently speaks with a quiet eloquence that leaves people . . . consecrated. Leaves them hungry for sacrifice, for a national effort—to free East Germany and unite the German people. He tells them only an act of *will* can bring this about. That history and 'right thinking'—I asked Father Avery what that meant, and he said it comes from '*recta ratio*,' medieval Catholic abracadabra for the basis for doing the right thing—"

"Is he a Catholic?" Rufus interrupted.

"Yes. And excepting the political left, and the people who believe that good old Adenauer ought to be rewarded by being the first elected chancellor, he doesn't *really* have any hard enemies. The free labor union people are suspicious, but not hostile. The students are fascinated by him—he's given them the first taste of idealism they've ever had. Remember that. All the Germans have had to engage them during the last seven years is the rebuilding of their country—that's kept their muscles busy. But aside from contrition over Hitler, there hasn't been anybody a around who's asked them to make a national sacrifice. And what a cause! To liberate their fellow Germans!"

"Have there been polls?"

"Until the treaty goes into effect next March, political polls are technically forbidden. That was one of McCloy's obscure precautions back in 1945. He didn't want any radical movement ignited by poll fever. We know some of the big publishers are going to defy this and take some polls, and it isn't clear whether the occupation authorities will go to court and try to get an injunction against them. Meanwhile we've taken our own poll, ostensibly a commercial poll testing German attitudes toward a number of economic products."

"How does he come out?"

"Twenty-one percent. And that was three days ago, Labor Day."

"How are the other two parties doing?"

"Neck and neck. Ollenhauer's SPD is logging thirty-three percent, Adenauer thirty-six percent."

They were seated now and Rufus continued his interrogation.

"Gromyko said *we* have to come up with something, but wouldn't say what?"

"That's right. And he wouldn't tell Acheson what Stalin would do if we didn't do whatever we're supposed to do, but he made it sound like the end of the world."

Rufus rocked slowly in his chair, and thought. Dulles and Sanderson were silent.

"It seems to me Gromyko isn't being all that difficult to understand."

"About what he wants us to do?"

"About what he wants us to do. He wants us to kill Axel Wintergrin."

7

Blackford was told the political strategem early in September, and instructed to try to get an idea what Wintergrin's countertactic might be. Under no circumstances was he to bring up the matter until it was public knowledge. After that, he should evaluate Wintergrin's reaction, and advise his contact in Bonn. Whether he would be able to get any reaction at all depended on the evolution of his relations with Wintergrin. Would their talk be confined to the church? Or would Wintergrin, committed to spending several hours per week with Oakes, digress to talk about other matters as well? If there were ways to do it, the CIA would have programmed Instant Friendship between Geoffrey Truax, a.k.a. Blackford Oakes, and Axel Wintergrin.

In fact it worked out. Although the day after they first met Wintergrin was formal at the rendezvous in his father's library, by the end of the three-hour session he was clearly relaxed with Blackford. In the chapel, seated in Blackford's makeshift little office, or in his father's office surrounded by drawings and photographs, or back in the chapel talking with the carpenters or masons, or seated at the chromoscope, Wintergrin was clearly taking his relaxation from the exigencies of a week planned from breakfast to midnight with speeches, meetings, interviews, broadcasts, always in the company of his staff, a week harnessed to the single objective of taking political power. Once a week he would meet with two men whose identity was not known to any member of the staff save Himmelfarb, who would set up the appointments at times and in places where the three men could meet unnoticed. The first, known to the staff only as "Herr Mahler," was a repatriated Jewish physicist at the University of Heidelberg whom Wintergrin had come to know during his college days, the second ("Herr Gottstein") a businessman in West Berlin. Apart from these very private meetings, Wintergrin was away from his staff only when with his mother in the castle—and with Blackford Oakes in the chapel.

By the following weekend, Wintergrin felt at ease with Blackford, to whom he would recount, when the mind wandered from the business of the chapel, something of the week's experiences. At first he judged Oakes to be the unique combination: someone entirely apolitical who was however interested enough in the drama of which Wintergrin was the protagonist to be engrossed in the narrative. Later he discovered that Oakes, too, was highly engaged in the Cold War, though this did not distract him from his work in the chapel. Wintergrin liked, too, the extraordinary self-confidence of Oakes, whose easygoing competence had instantly disposed of any problems with his staff arising out of his relative youth and inexperience. And, besides, Wintergrin had not really known any Americans, though he had read American journals and American authors, and seen the usual movies. At Greyburn there were no Americans when he was there. A planned visit to America in the summer of 1939 was put off for the obvious reasons. In Norway there were no Americans, save the occasional few who came down in the dead of night in parachutes. The handful of Americans who worked at the University of Heidelberg were not typical of the breed. He saw in Oakes the self-confidence America fleetingly exhibited in the postwar years, a brightness of spirit, an appealing social audacity and wit, unmannered, uncultivated—that and a seriousness of purpose. In two weeks, after five meetings, they were, in fact, friends.

The CIA plan was to amend the Constitution of the Federal Republic so as to make it unconstitutional for anyone to serve as chancellor before he was thirty-five.

The plan had the drawback of being a bill of

attainder not very different from a proposed constitutional amendment barring any chancellor with the initials A.W. As it stood, it had the virtue of simplicity, and a certain generic plausibility. What was so unreasonable about requiring that the principal executive officer of West Germany should be at least thirty-five? Wasn't there a provision in the United States Constitution—paradigm for the world!—that demanded exactly the same thing?

None of the abstract arguments was in the least objectionable. There was only one trouble with the idea: Nobody had thought of it before. Nobody even brought it up during the two laborious years dedicated to constructing a new constitution, which had been duly approved by the occupying powers and had gone out to the people, who in turn overwhelmingly approved it. Now an addition to that constitution was being proposed, the purpose of which was the disqualification of Axel Wintergrin. That criticism Washington had of course anticipated. "What they *don't* know," the Director said to the Secretary, "is that a bill of attainder against Count Wintergrin is a hell of a lot less personal than bumping Count Wintergrin off." (The Secretary had winced at the levity.) Following a protracted and argumentative ritual between the Secretary and the Soviet ambassador, in three acts over six days, in which the dialectic sometimes became so oblique that the Secretary at one point wondered what he had *himself* meant to imply by his last statement, it was agreed that an effort to abort the reunification movement via a constitutional

amendment would be made, and that the resources of both powers would be mobilized to
make the move succeed.

An endorsement of the amendment by Adenauer was not difficult to elicit, once the amendment was scheduled for a vote by the filing of the
requisite number of signatures—easily collected
by highly organized opponents of the Wintergrin
movement. The grand old man, after all, was living reproof of the impetuosities of the young who
had so thoroughly backed Hitler. Every line of
his corrugated face reminded one of the wisdom
that accumulates slowly, but ineluctably, like dust
on wine bottles which, emptied too early, give
only sullen satisfaction. At Wintergrin's age, Der
Alte was running for member of the diet of the
Rhine province.

Asked after his endorsement to explain the
provision as afterthought to the constitution,
Adenauer reminded the press that there had been
ten amendments to the United States Constitution
passed as afterthoughts—"the so-called Bill of
Rights."

Did he not see the amendment as designed
primarily to stop the movement headed by Count
Wintergrin?

Adenauer replied that the minimum-age requirement was, after all, statutory confirmation
of what is widely accepted: that effective government requires a measure of experience. If it was
indeed an oversight not to have written it into the
constitution at the time of the convention, what
better time to make amends than now? It would
concededly have the effect of holding back Win-

tergrin, said Adenauer, but since he was opposed to the movement of Count Wintergrin, why should it be surprising that he welcomed the incidental benefit of tabling Count Wintergrin's quixotic political campaign by means of an amendment that was intrinsically desirable? He doubted that Count Wintergrin, with the advantage of another five years' experience in politics, would renew undifferentiated and bellicose demands for the instant reunification of Germany, which goal he, Adenauer, and his party, the Christian Democrats, were pursuing in their own way, but with due regard for the realities.

The candidate Erich Ollenhauer, cautious about the popularity of Wintergrin with young voters whom he was himself wooing, conferred privately with his advisers and after several hours it was publicly announced that Herr Ollenhauer would not undertake, in a matter involving a constitutional amendment, to commit his party. The matter would be voted on at a special party conference the following week.

"They will of course vote in favor, but this way Ollenhauer will not appear himself to be casting aspersions on youth. That's what they call having your cookie and eating it too, eh, Oakes?" Wintergrin sat on the stool, bent over Conditti's hulky chromoscope—an ingenious device invented by Conditti's father which permitted the viewer, while looking through the viewing port, to vary the intensity of the light by manipulating a lever with the right hand, and, with the left, to darken the color by interposing one or more colorless screens over the crystal being examined.

The coordination of light and screening yielded a code number, translatable with considerable success by the crystallographers into glass of the desired quality. Sitting on the stool, head bent down, through the left viewing port Wintergrin inspected a shard of blue rescued from the north rose window. With his right eye he studied a diamond-shaped blue crystal, and adjusted the levers so as to attempt a perfect duplication. The blue, the magic solvent of the great stained windows, was always the root problem. "It isn't exactly 34-A, and not exactly 34-B. Is the shard perhaps too slender? Can we thicken it by adhering a second fragment?"

Blackford was taking notes.

"I'll check."

"No," said Wintergrin, bending down again over the viewing port and trying a finer tuning with the control levers. "Our friends are not going to get away with this. I don't mind telling you, Oakes, that I welcome this move. It appears to be a smart move, but it isn't."

"Oh?" said Oakes.

"Under the constitution, a proposed amendment is subjected to what they call the clarification process. If a clarification, with sufficient signatures, is deemed by the high court to be germane to the amendment, then the vote is on the original amendment *as clarified*.

"Next Monday, I will call on my followers to collect signatures for a clarification to the pending amendment which would deny the chancellorship to anyone under twenty-five—or over seventy-five.

"The court will find it a very difficult to rule out this clarification as *ultra vires* to the question being put before the public." Wintergrin almost laughed. His smile was broad.

"That will teach Der Alte. He is seventy-six."

"Assuming you get the clarification fused with the amendment, what do you think will happen?"

"If the Adenauer people lose in the courts, they'll drop their support of the amendment, and only Ollenhauer's people will pull for it. It has to get a plurality of sixty per cent to be enacted. That would never happen with Adenauer and me in opposition."

"I do not need to say"—Wintergrin sat up, taking out the sliver of blue glass and returning it neatly to its marked envelope—"that my analysis is confidential. I don't want to eliminate the surprise factor."

"Of course," Blackford said—as he reflected on which of the two standard means for communicating with his superior he should select to relay Wintergrin's confidence, and deciding there and then on the faster of the two. He thought as a precaution to say, "But surely somebody will figure out how you're going to maneuver?"

"In *fact*, no one has." Wintergrin leaned back in one of the two chairs in Blackford's office in the north transept. Blackford studied him as Wintergrin turned once again to the chapel. When would the sketches for the choir stalls be completed? Had a mosaicist been contracted for? Had Overstreet completed his examination of the timbers and cross-bearings? Would scaffolding be necessary at the spring lines to do the stonework on the vaults?

It was as though St. Anselm's was his vocation, and his political career his hobby. But both were compulsions, Blackford knew. The intensity of effort coiled from a single spring. The restoration of the chapel was one with the restoration of the republic. Wintergrin loved them equally, would devote himself no less passionately to either. Blackford could see him drawing strength from his discussions of the chapel, every detail of which Axel had apparently assimilated from childhood. He talked about the afternoon of his seventh birthday when he had taken refuge in the chapel during a flash storm rather than run the one hundred yards to the castle, and had seen, as if for the first time, the windows in the south aisle wall lit up like displays in a jewelry store, how he stood transfixed when the storm suddenly ended, the sun emerged, and they brightened as if they would burst under the golden pressure. His eyes shone as he recalled the moment.

"Wait until you see the light they shed on the columns, Oakes. It will be many months, I know, but I promise you will not find them wasted."

Blackford said impulsively, "Do you ever come in here to pray?"

Wintergrin looked at him, slowly straightening in his chair. "I believe in God," he said. "And for that reason, I do not pray to Him to grant me favors. That way I am never disillusioned. I express gratitude to Him when I feel His blessings. I feel Him in this building. I am, here, wired in to the will of God."

He rose, thanked Blackford formally (he always did, after every session, as though Blackford was a volunteer) and walked deliberately down the nave, past the narthex to the door, out through the porch to the courtyard, and to his castle.

The next morning at ten Adenauer was sitting in his office, tapping his fingers on his desk. He had himself taken the call from the high commissioner's office. Wintergrin would come out on Monday for a clarification to the amendment. The logic of the move, now that it was revealed, was instantly apparent. Wintergrin had outwitted them. Still . . . still, he thought, there might yet be ways to play it. Both he and Ollenhauer must now appeal jointly to the court. Perhaps that way they could keep the two constitutional proposals separate. He must persuade Ollenhauer that it would be dangerous to opportunize on Wintergrin's moves by backing the clarification maneuver. Adenauer was not comfortable dealing directly with the other camp, so he called in an aide and dispatched him to Berlin to concert with Ollenhauer on strategy.

Black added a sentence to the scramble he had read into the telephone from the public pay booth at the Westfalenkrug opposite the inn. It said: "I NEED TO TALK TO SOMEBODY. CAN YOU ARRANGE IT?"

That night, in bed, he stared out the window and rehearsed the reasons why, in betraying Wintergrin, he was serving his country's interests. How does it go? he thought. If A—whose intentions are to confound X, even as B intends to confound X—adopts different tactics from B, who is being backed by C, how actively should C get in the way of A? Sufficiently to line up with X for that purpose?

Screw the diagrammatic approach. The fact of the matter was he felt dirty. Was he in a dirty business? He wished his old friend Anthony Trust were here, and that they could go out and drink and talk together. It was one thing to bring a British traitor to heel, another to ingratiate himself with someone as high-minded as anyone he had ever known—for the purpose of putting that man's confidences on a conveyor belt to his enemies. If it had not been for St. Anselm's, he suddenly realized, he would go bonkers, as they used to say at Greyburn. As it stood, if tomorrow he was discharged by his employers, he would instantly seek out employment in the rebuilding of St. Anselm's. He had come to yearn now to see it recreated. (Which reminded him. By the book, his cover was near-perfect. He *was* doing what he would actually like to be doing, assuming there had been no . . . connection.) Reading in the journal of the architect, he came across a passage in antique German:

"It is regrettably not possible to position the church at this latitude in such a way as to lengthen its season. But from about 18 May until about 24 October, the confluence of light, as seen by parishioners who occupy the easternmost three-fifths of the nave—the rear section will be deprived of the perspective necessary to the blend—will provide during the daylight hours the desired balance of blues, yellows, and reds, and the pilgrims will follow the story, so well laid out on glass by Herr Tissault, of St. Anselm's philosophical journey to paradise." That, thought Oakes, was a medieval jam session. That was how they let themselves go. No ballistic-missile engineer cared more for the placement of his moving parts than Meister Gerard cared about the arrangement of the colors in St. Anselm's church. Blackford thought it truly miraculous that his involvement with the church had been entirely incidental to his reason for being in Germany. As finally he dropped off to sleep, he resolved he would join any movement primarily devoted to the reconstruction of St. Anselm's church. Come to think of it, he wondered: Was there an order of St. Anselm? He would be ready for it by the time he left Westphalia.

8

The German High Court agreed to hear arguments on the clarification proposal during the last week in September, so as to be able to rule in ample time to put the proposed amendment before the public, in final form, on election day, November 15. The pressures on the count were considerable, the comment indiscreet. One newspaper pointed out that if Adenauer at seventy-six was statutorily incompetent, why not also the members of the court appointed by him during his senility, which meant two-thirds. Opponents of clarification stressed the common-sense point that to argue that someone needed to be experienced in order to exercise the highest office in the land was not the equivalent of arguing that

too much experience—arbitrarily acquired at age
seventy-five—was *dis*qualifying. The young law
professor who pleaded Wintergrin's clarification
argument insisted that it was no more arbitrary to
presume senescence at seventy-five than to presume immaturity at thirty-four. Wintergrin's
strategy proved effective. By the time the judges
were finished with their questions, it was clear
that the pro-amendment forces desired the court
to give them an *ad hominem* ruling in respect of
Wintergrin, and an *ad rem* approach in respect of
Adenauer.

And so the ruling came as no surprise. The
clarification was ordered integrated into the
amendment and listed on the ballot for plebisci-
tary action at the general election. Although in
theory Wintergrin could be disqualified by rati-
fication of the amendment, that disqualification
would also extend to Adenauer. The day after the
court's ruling, the established German leaders,
meeting with their advisers, pronounced the Wintergrin strategy dead. More important, so did Joseph Stalin, who spoke of another strategy as now
necessary.

Returning to St. Anselm's from the week's
political activity, Wintergrin went straight to the
chapel, as was his custom, to see what progress
had been made. He found Oakes translating Overstreet's instructions to two German masons whose
assignment was to furrow onto the eight columns the stone traceries of the originals. They
were to use a paste that would pick up some of

the gold that came in through the windows as,
the history insisted—and one or two of the pictures demonstrated—the original pillars had done.
The question was to find the reflective element
and insinuate it into the stone in just the right
proportion. Too much would be, well, "too
much," said Blackford, happy to return to John-
Jane-Gyp German, after so ambitious a passage
in highly technical German. Wintergrin could
not refrain from firing off in his virtuosic German a fresh translation, the precision of which
Blackford admired, and said so, taking the opportunity to congratulate Wintergrin on his political victory, and despising himself on his hypoc-
risy: though he confessed he was not absolutely
sure which side of him was the dissimulator, the
one that congratulated Wintergrin, or the one
that consoled Washington. Wintergrin thanked
him matter-of-factly, looked expertly about the
church, and noted ruefully that there had been
little apparent progress over the preceding week.
Blackford said that was correct; most of the
week had been given over to experimentation and
research, and to problems in carpentry in antic-
ipation of a major effort to shore up the old
structure. Wintergrin said he would look it all
over in detail tomorrow as he planned to spend
the entire weekend at St. Anselm's, and would
Oakes by any chance be free to take dinner with
him tonight—he would have along only his
principal aide, Roland Himmelfarb, and his new
assistant, a most attractive woman who had just
joined his staff—Erika Chadinoff, the daughter of
the renowned novelist and scholar, Dimitri Cha-

dinoff. Oakes half-expected the invitation: Wintergrin had taken to asking Oakes to join him at the castle for dinner on the night of his weekly return to St. Anselm's, sometimes with one or more of his aides and friends, most of whom by now knew Oakes and spoke in his presence with candor; twice with Wintergrin alone, though on one of those occasions his mother had been present, and though Blackford had enjoyed the hour and a quarter devoted to the childhood triumphs of little Axel, grown-up Axel enjoyed it not at all, but was unable to restrain his premier fan. It was the only occasion on which Oakes had ever seen Wintergrin fail to assert his authority.

Oakes was late. The others were seated in a second living room, this one lined with panels describing a boar hunt in dark greens and blues and reds—the countess was having dinner with an old friend in her favorite room, leaving the dining hall to her son. The talk during a meal of trout, veal, fruit and cheese, as expected, was of the analysis being made throughout the country of the meaning of the court's decision. No analyst was quite yet attempting a projection of the number of voters who would be won over by the Reunification candidate in November, but everyone agreed that the maneuver to eliminate Wintergrin by constitutional amendment had backfired.

"Did you catch the piece by old Razzia?" Himmelfarb asked.

Wintergrin smiled. But Erika Chadinoff said in her deep, energetic voice that she had not seen the column, and asked what Razzia had said.

Himmelfarb drew himself up and delivered an imitation of the writer, whose mannerisms were widely known, and widely caricatured, because of his depressing ubiquity: he was a syndicated columnist, a television host, an author, editor of his own magazine, and had now announced he would also write novels!

"The court's decision in favor of Count Wintergrin," said Himmelfarb, imitating the tired, tiresome archness of Razzia and his euphuistic style, "is a tergiversation for the German people. We are afraid to learn from our own mistakes. Afraid to show the courage to amend our constitution in such a way as to save us from the possibility of such an embarrassment as history will deplore when it has examined all the evidence, notwithstanding the sophists who misconstrue it . . ."

But the room was already rocking with laughter—even Wintergrin laughed, a rare sight. Himmelfarb had perfectly captured the convolutions of the ubiquitous Razzia. Oakes had arrived and, still smiling, they rose and Wintergrin introduced him to Erika Chadinoff, who took his hand and smiled warmly at him. Wintergrin signaled the waiter for wine.

It was a pleasant evening, devoted to a progressively intense exploration, led by Wintergrin, of the problems that lay ahead. The following Monday he would formally launch his campaign at the party convention to be held in the famous Paulskirche in Frankfurt. On that occasion, he said, he would unveil more specifically than he had done heretofore the approaches his government would take in pursuit of East German liberation.

"Will it frighten us all, Count Wintergrin?" Erika Chadinoff asked.

"I cannot say whether it will frighten *you,* Erika," said Wintergrin. "It is certainly designed to frighten the Russians."

"How much of it will be bluster, Axel?" Only Roland Himmelfarb, who treated Wintergrin like a protective brother, would thus have addressed him or, for that matter, would have put such a question to him in the presence of others.

"That much of what I say that makes me sound like Gandhi will be bluster. Gandhi was right—like the Bhagavad-Gita—in saying that the whole of one's resources must be mobilized to consecrate a purpose. He was wrong in supposing that no human being is finally monstrous enough to run a locomotive over the incremental resister. The Communists are. That is why we shall have to be prepared to do more than Gandhi was ever prepared to do."

Oakes's heart began to pound.

"Who says A must say B," Wintergrin said, quoting Trotsky. And interrupted himself in midthought. "Have you read James Burnham's *Machiavellians*? Anybody? Spread it around." He pointed his finger at Himmelfarb, among whose responsibilities was the distribution to the inner guard of books and articles that attracted Wintergrin's attention.

"You were about to say, Count Wintergrin?" Erika Chadinoff said. She had violated Blackford's self-imposed protocol: never to push Wintergrin toward sensitive subjects, even by redirecting his own train of thought. Let him say things as he chose.

"Oh yes"—Wintergrin looked distracted—"it follows that we shall have to rearm."

There was silence. Wintergrin proffered nothing more. Himmelfarb smoked. Erika Chadinoff looked into the fireplace. Blackford noticed her hair as if coming to life, and the blue liquid eyes, and the inscrutable set of full red lips that pouted with curiosity and passion. Blackford leaned over and picked up the countess's cat, stroking her.

Wintergrin broke the silence. "I am glad, Erika, that you made your suggestions well before next Monday. Please thank your father for advancing so shrewd a point. It will prove very very helpful. I shall let you have the draft of my speech well ahead of anyone else." He rose and, as the others did, turned to Blackford, but his words were addressed equally to all.

"I regret to say that beginning tomorrow we shall be instituting a formal security system. I put it off as long as possible, but Jürgen Wagner is of course right. He is the chief security officer, and he is justified in saying that security officers should have something to say about security . . . so, it has to be done.

"Beginning at six A.M. tomorrow there will be guards at the entrance to the courtyard, in addition to guards here, outside the castle. The telephone people will be here tomorrow to install extra lines, including a line to the new guard-house. External security—outside St. Anselm's, on the road—will be supplied by the federal government. On top of everything else, Wagner has persuaded me to admit an amiable young gorilla into my entourage, a young man devoted to our cause who has taken a leave of absence from the police academy at Dortmund to serve as my bodyguard. His name is Wolfgang something-or-other—I have not met him, but Wagner promises me he is humorless, discreet, literal, and will not grow taller than his current height, which is six feet four. The type, I gather, who will not follow me into my own headquarters unless I prove I am myself. I mention this because he will arrive tomorrow, and I do not wish to frighten you if you should find him—a line from Milton, Oakes? Did you, at Greyburn, study with old Potpot? He read us all of *Paradise Lost.* I remember only a few lines:

> *Whence and what are thou, execrable shape,*
> *That dar'st, though grim and terrible, advance*
> *Thy miscreated Front athwart my way*
> *To yonder Gates?*

Wintergrin grinned with pleasure and, his friends now warned about the terrible Wolfgang, turned, businesslike once more, to Blackford:

"Would you, Oakes, drive Miss Chadinoff back to the inn? I must go with Roland to the study. I shall see you tomorrow at the chapel, two P.M. Goodnight." He bowed slightly to both of them and walked away, leaving Himmelfarb to show them to the door.

Would Erika care for a drink before retiring?

Of course.

They settled in the corner table in the near-empty *Bierstube* at the Westfalenkrug, forlorn, always, on Monday evenings. She wore a dark-blue skirt and a turquoise blouse and a commanding scent Blackford never knew before, which he reminded himself to ascertain the name of, to send his mother, whose only indulgence was exotic perfumes. She spoke to the waiter in pre-emptively fluent German. In the dim light they were silent for a moment.

"He is something, isn't he?" she began.

"He certainly is. I hope he doesn't turn out to be 'somebody' in the sense that Gavrilo Princip was 'somebody.' "

"Who?"

"The guy who started the First World War at Sarajevo by knocking off the Archduke."

"You don't really think that, do you, Mr. Oakes?"

"Call me Black. Do I really think so?" He thought it prudent to retreat. But cautiously . . .

"Of course I don't *think* so, in the sense that I predict Apocalypse. On the other hand, unless somebody does a lobotomy on Stalin he isn't going to hand over East Germany to our hero on account"—Blackford here imitated the well-known accents of Greta Garbo—"of his beautiful blue eyes."

"You sound like a cynic."

"I'm *not* a cynic! I profoundly *believe* in the sincerity of Stalin's evil intentions."

113

Erika paused, began a smile, then suppressed it. "How long have you known him?"

Black explained that he was by profession an engineer, commissioned by the Marshall Plan people to preside over the recreation of St. Anselm's chapel, and had met Wintergrin only a month or so earlier.

"Isn't it unusual, at your age, to be put in *charge* of something like this?"

Blackford wondered whether Erika's curiosity on this rather delicate point reflected something she had heard from Wintergrin or his associates. He decided on hyperbole, as against the alternative of a pompous recitation of his formal credentials.

"I'm older than Alexander was when he conquered Persia," Blackford said, in exaggerated dejection. "I'm embarrassed they gave me the chapel at St. Anselm's to rebuild instead of the cathedral at Cologne." She didn't answer, so he seized the initiative.

"What brought *you* to our leader's staff?"

"Blackford, in Germany we do not use that expression."

"Sorry. What brought you to our hero's staff?"

"It was my father's idea. You . . . know about my father?"

"At Yale, engineers are taught to recognize the names of Dante, Shakespeare, Milton, and Chadinoff."

She actually blushed, and added, "I didn't mean it that way."

"Oh, come on. I know you didn't. There are

114

plenty of people who don't know who your father is, but I'm not one of them. You see, I'm crazy-mad about bees. I hang on every word your father writes about them."

Erika was amused, and relaxed, and she smiled her pleasure at the conversation, and at the company. Her father would especially have enjoyed the exchange. Dimitri Chadinoff was famous as an apiarist, as one would say da Vinci was famous as a biologist. After leaving Russia in 1917, her father had come, if not to dominate, to figure hugely in the world of critical letters in three languages and in three countries. His works of imagination, evocation, and playfulness were grist for what sometimes seemed half the critics and graduate students of the world. From his eyrie in Switzerland—he despised the atmosphere at the level of the sea, and confessed, at a moment of singular candor with a visitor, that he thought the air pressure at sea level spiritually as well as metallurgically corrosive—he vouchsafed to the world one book per year, and always in its interstices one could experience the passion with which he scorned the political, social, and artistic work of the Communists in Russia.

Erika said, "In my father's other life—away from the bees—he has achieved a certain reputation as a verbal precisionist. He felt Wintergrin needed some help at this level."

"I don't understand you."

"You remember what *Pravda* did with his Heidelberg Manifesto in 1948? Wintergrin said, *'Germans must embrace their fellow Germans.' That* got translated into Russian as *'Germans*

115

must hang their fellow Germans.' And appeared under the headline: German Warmonger Demands Execution of Democratic Germans'—and story after story was broadcast in East Europe playing this line. My father's feeling is that although there is no way to prevent the Russians from distorting what Wintergrin says, we should at least try to make it *hard* for them. The idea is to send out exact translations from the German several hours before he delivers his speeches. Send out translations in Russian and Polish as well as in English, Italian, and French. In the Western languages there isn't as much to fear in the way of *intentional* distortion. But accuracy is terribly important . . ."

"So your job?"

"Is to supervise the translations. As a matter of fact"—her voice affected academic pomposity, effective except that laughter broke out—"my Polish is a little rusty."

Blackford whistled. "You mean, you can handle all the other languages with—precision?"

"Yes," she said. "You do know that I am a translator by profession?"

"Well, sure," Black said. "Rubinstein is a *musician* by profession. But he isn't expected to perform on the bass fiddle, *and* the piccolo, *and* the harp."

Erika nodded to the waiter, and pointed to her empty glass. Blackford, without looking away, raised his glass too, which the waiter removed, coming back in due course with replacements.

She said, "I shall retain one, perhaps two assistants to help. I gather from Himmelfarb that up to now Wintergrin has spoken mostly extemporaneously. If he continues to do so our job will be more difficult. We can rush out authorized translations, but the misconstructions get out ahead of them. He promises that beginning Monday at Frankfurt he'll try to get us his speech twenty-four hours ahead. That will mean round-the-clock work, getting that speech into seven languages."

"Let me know if you need any help with some of his tricky German words," Blackford said.

"I will." Erika's face lit up. "I'd offer to help *you* with the stained glass, but I know what an expert you are on it."

Blackford smiled at her suggestively and twirled his glass in his hand. What in the hell does she mean by that, he wondered. And repressed the thought. Hell, a few more years in this business and he would be suspicious of Shirley Temple. Come to think of it, how account for that sequence of miscegenative suggestiveness between Shirley Temple and Bill Robinson? Ah! Could that have been one of the scripts of the Hollywood Ten! To start all that commotion in the South! Senator Bilbo was right!

"What are you smiling about?" Erika asked him.

"Oh, just a little fantasy. I was entertaining myself . . . er, playing with myself." He looked up, and his smile was to the point.

"Tell me."

"Well," said Blackford, "I wondered whether maybe you were a spy from the camp of Kon-

rad Adenauer, and whether you would make it
your business in your translations to make our
leader—our hero—sound hungry for the roar of
tanks and the smell of death. But I put it out of
my mind, because I'm the trusting type."

She did not say anything, though her smile
was expressive, amused, coquettish, and Blackford's thought meandered during the silence on
how pleasurable it would be to take her to bed.
They would walk hand in hand across the street
to the inn, and in ten minutes he would scratch
lightly at her door, she would open it, and he
would sidle in through the opening. How *un-
thinking* all those writers who take it for granted
in their novels that men can slide into the bed-
chambers of their trysts past reluctant doors
opened only just wide enough to accommodate
the width of their lateral frame at rest: Erika
would open the door wide enough for him to
walk in frontally. He would speak to her only in
a child's German as he softly removed her night-
gown and, moving her into the moonlight, press
against her, and then tease her, using the German
words just slightly, pertly, provocatively wrong,
provoking her didactic instincts, and then inten-
tionally misunderstanding her instructions, as he
laid her down and—he bit his lip, feeling sweat
on his brow, and dryness in his mouth. He caught
her eye, she returned his glance fully and, with
her eyes, said No. In seven languages.

9

The Frankfurt Convention, as the occasion was ever after referred to, dispelled any lingering complacency in Moscow, in Washington, and in Bonn. The meeting was held on October 15 in the old homesite of the Frankfurt National Assembly, the imposing Paulskirche. Reporters, television and movie cameramen trained their attention on the assembly, endeavoring to discern any special characteristics. There were none. There were burghers and farmers and merchants. There were at least five hundred student-aged men and women. Here and there those who knew the academic elite spotted a distinguished professor. Moreover, the assembly was composed not merely of the curious. This was a formal political convention fashioned after the American model, brought together for the purpose of nominating the leader of the Reunification Party. Everyone there, except the press and a few hundred friends and family, was a delegate or an alternate delegate—almost three thousand in all. They were accredited members of the movement, committed to its cause, and they came from every part of Germany.

There was music from a considerable orchestra—conveniently situated in the choir—as expected; but no hilarity. Germans had gone a long time since experiencing a political convention, and most did not even know what traditional behavior at a German political convention was. But the mood was set by the clear historical mandate of the meeting: to validate the claim to leadership of a young man who had risked his life to free Germany from domestic tyrants, and was prepared to risk it again to free Germany from foreign tyrants. To this awesome end this party was convened, formally consecrating itself; and from that exhilarating purpose it drew its strength. During the day the delegates heard a number of speeches from regional representatives of the party. The platform committee cautiously refrained from specifying the means by which the goal the party sought would be achieved: that exegetical responsibility would be for the party leader, in his own time, to discharge. So the platform was merely a paraphrasing of the speeches of Axel Wintergrin.

At six there was a break for dinner. The balloting was at eight. With no competing candidate, the balloting and the formal designation were a formality. At three minutes after nine the chairman of the convention rang down the gavel and announced that the leader and candidate of the Renuification Party was—Axel Wintergrin. The crowd rose, cheering from the heart, as the slim young man, dressed in his familiar tweed suit, walked out to the podium. The cheering would not stop, even though Wintergrin raised his right hand imploring the audience to be still as, with his left, he buttoned and unbuttoned his jacket. The restoring of order would take another fifteen minutes and, of course, comparisons were extruded in much of the press with the hypnotic ovations given to Adolf Hitler. But there were men and women there who had been at Hitler's rallies and they knew the difference: Hitler was preaching the necessity of asserting the national will for the purpose of aggrandizing the State and hating The Enemy. Wintergrin also preached the necessity of mobilizing the national will—but in order to undo a legacy of Hitler: the loss of one half the nation. Wintergrin's objectives were unassailable: No one, save a few German Communists who counted it more important that East Germans should live under Communism than that they should live as free men in a single German republic, could doubt the desirability of the goal. The quarrel, and the indecision, were over the question of means.

Axel Wintergrin could no longer put off specific statements of his intentions if elected, so he arrived quickly at the eagerly anticipated "platform of policies."

—The Soviet Union would be given an ultimatum: To conduct free elections in East Germany under United Nations supervision by February 1.

—If the people of East Germany opted for reunification, that must be effected by April 1. (At the press table there was commotion. No one had suspected a timetable so wildly audacious.) Wintergrin did not bother even to allude to the hypothetical possibility that the East Germans would vote against reunification. To have done so, he implied, would have been to dishonor rational processes.

—If the Russians declined to hold the elections, the Government of West Germany would declare war against—and here Wintergrin said it carefully, twice, exactly—*not against the Soviet Union, but against any Soviet agent, irrespective of his nationality, who continued illegally to reside in East Germany.*

—To achieve the strength to carry out that war against foreign invaders, the West German Government would rearm. Such provisions in peace treaties, finalized or prospective, as forbade such rearmament would be considered null and void inasmuch as they were imposed on a people at the expense of that people's freedom, in violation of the United Nations covenant on human rights and of the axiomatic rights of nations, to rule themselves. No German weapons, said Count Wintergrin, would be aimed at anyone outside the boundaries of Germany.

—But this pledge, Count Wintergrin said, was contingent on no foreign troops being sent into

Germany. If such troops were sent in, Germany would retaliate against the aggressor as necessary.

—Finally he came to the means. "I am in touch," said Count Wintergrin, "with German scientists who are agreed that rather than risk the annihilation of the German people, whether resident in East or in West Germany, they will make available to our own army the definitive weapon of defense."

He could not deliver his carefully prepared peroration. The crowd would not permit him to go on. The press was stampeding out to their typewriters, telephones, cable offices. The cameramen pulled out reels of film to be whisked off to the developers, and with fresh reels photographed the hysteria of the crowd. It was the hysteria of a people who only a few years earlier had been summoned to sacrifice everything for a cause that proved ignoble—and now were being asked to be prepared to sacrifice everything for a cause indisputably fine. It was the full cry of gratitude for a formula to erase, insofar as it was possible to do so, the awful consequences of the things done in the name of the German people. It was the road to self-esteem.

When the meeting in the White House adjourned it was after eleven. It had begun at two in the afternoon. At various stages it was a session on military strategy, a seminar on ethics, a debate on psychology, a hypothetical discussion of pre-emptive war, a history of assassinations, reflections on the Constitutional Convention, and

a dispute on the rule of civil behavior at such
meetings as this. The President sent word he
would not attend the meeting and, moreover,
that he would leave it to the Secretary of State to
decide whether the President should be informed
of the meeting's outcome. At one point, three
hours after the sandwiches were eaten, and after
the twelvth pitcher of coffee had been brought in,
the Secretary of Defense, pointing his hand upstairs in the general direction of the Oval Office,
made a heated reference to "old Pontius Pilate up
there." Presiding, the Secretary of State said
that as the son of a Christian clergyman, he
could not make out a case for Pontius Pilate, but
as a former partner of Sullivan and Cromwell,
he'd have advised Pilate to do exactly what he
did. Over and over the variables were considered. Three times conversation stopped entirely
until a specific piece of information was elicited
—from Defense, from the CIA research division,
from a nineteenth-century diplomatic protocol.
At eight P.M., the chair ruled that no further
legal discussion would be permitted. By nine, anybody who mentioned the Constitution of the
United States one more time would have run the
risk of being dragged out from the Situation
Room, turned over to the marine guard, and
shot. By eleven it had become clear to the exhausted assembly of five persons that whatever
course of action the Secretary of State recommended was the course of action that would be
taken. There was no other way to interpret his
mandate from the President. And so it was left:
He would make a decision. He would then re-

port back to the executive committee of the National Security Council on the probable effects of that decision. Then the agencies of the government would deploy. The dapper Secretary motioned to the Director as, with some physical effort after so many sedentary hours, he pried himself up from the chair. "Let's go to my place, Allen."

They did, settling gratefully for a scotch and soda, sitting deep in the Georgtown chintz, the windows tightly shut, the secret service guard discreetly at his station near the kitchen; the house otherwise empty, except for the cook and the maid, asleep on the third floor.

The Director spoke first. "Some of the points made tonight stick in my mind. Maybe it's true. Maybe Stalin *wants* Wintergrin to win the election and hand him that ultimatum."

"Stalin certainly would want that if he had heard the nine-hour conversation in that room tonight. That festival of indecision. Dear Allen, reassure me on at least that much. Was anyone in that room a Soviet agent? You're not by any chance a Soviet agent, are you, Allen?" The Director managed a weak smile.

"You wouldn't think, would you, that *we* were the world power with three hundred and sixty nuclear warheads, and the Soviet Union the power with nine paleolithic atomic bombs? That *we* have the air force to deliver those bombs, whereas they don't? That, after all, Wintergrin is asserting rights guaranteed under the UN Charter to which the Soviets are signatories? No, you would think that *we* were the aggressor, the threat

125

to world peace, the weak sister, and Wintergrin the imperialist. It is inexplicable how these inversions come about."

"It isn't really so inexplicable, Dean. We have a conscience. Isn't it *that* easy? And that difficult? We are required to think in terms from which Stalin is totally liberated. Even if we reject—or 'transcend'—the norms, we are aware of them. And we are fatigued by the experience. We are . . . ambiguists."

"Stalin himself has plenty to weigh. Well, not *plenty*, exactly. He has to weigh *our* reaction. He has never really cared about world opinion, and here Wintergrin has played into his hands. Have you noticed the cables? Wonderful! The line is exactly what any Soviet-watcher would have supposed: WINTERGRIN THREATENS ATOMIC WAR AGAINST SOVIET PEOPLE: WORLD HOLOCAUST POSSIBLE. That line, played over and over again during the next two months, would provide the Communists with cover for the resurrection of extermination camps for the purpose of providing a final solution to anyone in Germany who by his vote in the November elections signified a desire to live in freedom."

"You're right, you're right. The only thing that's going to stop them is if we tell 'em, and if we tell 'em in a way that leaves them in no doubt that if they march into Germany, we'll dump on Moscow: right down in the Kremlin courtyard—"

"And send John Hersey over a month later in a gas mask to lucubrate on it all—" the Secretary interrupted.

"But who's going to tell them that?"

The Secretary sipped at his drink. "Let me see now. The Voice of America. Or shall we send a delegation to Moscow? Ah, yes. A bipartisan commission headed by Adlai Stevenson—he could take a couple of weeks off from the campaign: nobody would notice. And as delegates, let's see: Norman Cousins? Of course. Archibald MacLeish? He *terrified* Hitler. What's the name of that tiger in Greenwich Village? The woman. Yes. Mary McCarthy. 'We are here, Comrade Stalin, to have one last look at the Kremlin because, you see, the day after tomorrow it will cease to exist. That is the message from our government. Bipartisan message. That's why Adlai Stevenson is the head of the delegation.' Allen, am I going nuts?"

"From all appearances, I would say yes, Dean."

"That will prove a terrible loss to mankind."

"You forget, there won't be any mankind left."

"I forgot."

"It does seem late in the evening to worry about mankind."

They went back to their scotches and said nothing for a few minutes. The Secretary looked at his watch. It was after midnight.

"Let's meet here for breakfast at six A.M., Allen."

"I'll be here," the Director said, rising. He took his overcoat from the rack, but didn't put it on. "I'll manage, thanks." He opened the door, and slid into the waiting limousine.

The next morning when he returned, he found the Secretary in the kitchen, making the toast. Without looking up, he began right away. "We shall have to go along with them, Allen. As you turn it over in your mind, there is, really, no alternative."

"I've reached the same conclusion."

"But here is where I think we can make a point with old hatchet face." They were seated now at the kitchen table, the juice was already served, and the Secretary poured the coffee as he sat down. "Why shouldn't *they* do it?"

"Well, there's no reason why they shouldn't. But remember, Wintergrin's alleged to be *our* operation. I don't think even Stalin really believes that. But it's convenient clothes horse for all their complaints.

"But listen. Even if it were so. Even if Wintergrin *were* our man. So, we take the position: 'Okay, go ahead and get rid of him, even though he *is* our man.' What better evidence that he *isn't* our man than that we're willing to see him disappear from the scene?"

"It's worth trying."

"I'm going to do more than that. I'm going to say, Either they do it or it won't be done."

"Do you have a fallback position?"

"Yes. If they insist, I'll shoot Wintergrin myself."

The Director smiled. And was silent.

The Secretary spoke again, stirring his coffee for no apparent reason, since he had put neither sugar nor cream in it. "What is his security like?"

"Up until Frankfurt, Laurel and Hardy

could have bumped him off. It was loose, loose as hell. Now it's pretty tight. Oakes reports that a real pro has taken on the responsibility of keeping the candidate alive. You can't get near St. Anselm's any more. Even the press are frisked when they go see him."

"What a wonderful opportunity."

"To do what?"

"To emasculate the press, dear Allen."

"And he travels behind an armed car, with radio. He's been protesting the appearance of all this, because Adenauer and Ollenhauer are moving about conspicuously unescorted. But there doesn't seem to be any negative public reaction. Incidentally, don't eliminate the possibility that somebody else will try to bump him off. The opposition isn't all from the left. *Der Spielgel* is off-its-rocker-mad at him, says he's going to cause the destruction not only of East Germany but of West Germany. Oakes says there's a lot of randomly motivated hate mail."

"Any of it signed 'Harry Truman'?"

"And the police, a few days ago, arrested a young guy at a rally with a loaded pistol in his pocket. He's being interrogated. They've established he is a member of the United World Federalists."

"Allen, did you ever read *Murder on the Orient Express*?"

"No, but I could use Hercule Poriot right now."

"Well, the murdered man has thirteen knife wounds. And there are thirteen passengers on the train. And M. Poirot establishes that every one of

129

them had a motive to kill him. And the denouement is: They all did—took turns with the knife . . . . That would be a *hell* of a coincidence if, a few days before the election, Count Wintergrin was simultaneously shot, stabbed, asphyxiated, poisoned and drowned."

"Some people would know it was a CIA job then."

"Well," said the Secretary, leading the way into the living room, coffee cup in hand, "now let's go and get grim together. You go and see your man Rufus, and get him into the act. I'll bring in hatchet face. My office will tell him ten A.M."

"We're both lawyers, Dean. You're a constitutionalist, or anyway you pose as one. The mandate here is a little irregular. What, in your opinion, are my direct responsibilities to the President?"

"In my opinion, your responsibilities to the President are never to mention the name of Wintergrin in his presence. His responsibility to you is identical."

10

When Blackford called the number in Bonn, he was told to ring a second number and to ask for "Bob." He rang it, giving—when asked by the voice at the other end of the telephone, "Who is calling?"—his agency name. On hearing "This is Singer!" Blackford felt, for the first time since arriving at St. Anselm's, that he was back in touch with his own country. For eight weeks he had been reporting only to a disembodied voice at the other number, and nothing had come of his request to go to Bonn and speak directly with his superior. He would receive his instructions over the telephone, file his reports either over the telephone, or by mail to Bonn, depending on their character. He had no knowledge of the uses to which his information was being put, or any acknowledgment of the work he was doing.

"God, am I glad to talk to you!"

"Me too, buddy. I want you to come around and see me."

"When?"

"Tomorrow."

"Where?"

"Call the other number at noon, and they'll tell you. Got to go. See you tomorrow."

Blackford could easily account to his associates for any trip to Bonn. Bonn, after all, was where Washington sent the money. It was the administrative center of all German reconstruction projects financed or partly financed by Marshall Aid. And, of course, Blackford would take the precaution of checking in with the foreign aid mission office to report on progress.

He was at the chapel at eight, to go over the day's work with Overstreet and Conditti. At nine he was to see Wintergrin, who had asked him to stop by. Getting in and out of the courtyard had become something of an operation. The additional sentry was posted at the top of the hill at the entrance to the courtyard. There were guards outside the castle. The inner sanctum was defended by three men casually distributed in the corridor with automatic weapons. They all knew Oakes by sight, and several times saw him stroll in and out of the church and the castle in the relaxed company of Count Wintergrin; still, with Teutonic thoroughness, they went through the motions of inspecting his credentials as if for the first time, until Count Wintergrin caught them doing it. At the stormy ensuing session with Wagner, Wolfgang was called in and specifically reprimanded, and now Blackford could circulate without interruption.

He found Wintergrin alone in his study. The adjacent room, once a refectory for hunting parties, was now a press office of sorts. It was there, surrounded by antlers, boars' heads, strutting stanchions with jaded banners of war, that Erika worked, sharing the huge room with half the staff of twenty involved in scheduling, policy, and organization. Roland Himmelfarb occupied a small office between the refectory and the dark, book-filled office of the count, into which Blackford was escorted by an appointments secretary.

Wintergrin never appeared to feel harassed, but with Oakes he had become unusually relaxed, carefree. "I sneaked past the gorillas last night at six and took a look. It really is very exciting. The joinerwork up from the panels to the rood screen is first-rate work, first-rate. And the traceried panels themselves, as I've told you, are indistinguishable from the originals. The wood will have to age, but that will happen . . ." He rippled on about the details of the woodwork in the choir and returned to his continuing preoccupation: the blue glass. Blackford wished he could divert him to the subject of his political campaign, but the occasion was too formal. Count Wintergrin had summoned his architect to discuss the business at hand, and so Blackford was resigned to a week with nothing to report to his employers when Wintergrin, almost without pausing, said:

"I would like to get away for an evening. I have not been free from my staff since Frankfurt. I know a good restaurant, with private dining rooms. It is located, improbably enough, at Gummersbach, a dull little town, in case you don't know it, between Düsseldorf and Bonn, but much closer. The maître d'hôtel there is called Walter (he pronounced it Valter). There are also discreet opportunities for postprandial relaxation, if that is the mood of the patron. I have two questions: Would you be disposed to accompany me? Second, if so, would you kindly make the reservations in your name only?"

All this, thought Blackford, and Singer Callaway too, in a single day.

"I should be delighted, Count Wintergrin."

"Axel," he said, scratching the name of the restaurant on a notepad and handing it to Oakes. "I told you once, I shan't tell you again. You may call me, in due course, 'Chancellor.' But that will have to wait."

"Do you get to be called anything special after you unify Germany?"

"I should think 'Liberator' would do."

"And if you fail—'Liberator Manqué'?"

"If I fail, you will probably be referring to me as 'The Late Count Wintergrin.' "

"Who would be the successor to . . . all this . . . if that . . . happened?"

Wintergrin took the narrow road in his answer, as if Oakes's question were of purely biological concern.

"I have a natural son in England. My lawyers have the documents. If all goes well I shall adopt him legally. If not, he will be acknowledged by my estate as the rightful heir ... But go away, Blackford, I am busy, and I shall look forward to your impertinent questions tonight." He smiled, more warmly than ever.

"Fine. I have to go to Bonn anyway."

"Oh?"

"Don't worry. They're not running out of money. Routine stuff."

"You know to take the road north to Schmallenberg?"

"I know to take the road north to Schmallenberg."

Count Wintergrin smiled, a little shyly. He reached out his hand. Blackford rose and started to extend his own but saw that the impatient count was pointing now at the door.

"Don't get corrupted in Bonn. And don't forget to make the reservations. For eight P.M. At exactly seven-thirty I'll walk out of my car, parked opposite the library at St. Anselm's, wearing a raincoat, a fedora, and glasses."

"I'll be there. Wearing a suit, over a shirt, tie, and underwear."

At Bonn, Blackford was directed to an apartment on Remagenerstrasse, within a block of the building where Beethoven was born. The door of the ground-floor apartment was opened by Singer Callaway himself, and he looked exactly as he had on that morning he had opened the door at Park Street in London to introduce Blackford to his mission there, almost exactly a year ago. Callaway was buoyant as ever, orotund in speech, conspiratorial in tone: and Blackford knew in his bones that the Wintergrin matter was coming to a head. All they needed now was someone like Rufus, and he would know that he was stationed on the forwardmost line. Callaway smiled broadly, led him silently through a moderate-sized, overstuffed living room into an adjacent study where, sitting at the desk, was: Rufus.

"Oh, my God!"

Rufus rose, smiled as warmly as he ever did, and quickly sat his thin frame (hung in clerical dress, including the Phi Beta Kappa key) down again, his eyes somber-brown behind the thick glasses, his hair neatly plastered on his balding dome.

"I thought you had retired, Rufus."

"I thought I had too."

"What brought you back?" Blackford took the chair toward which Rufus waved him. Singer Callaway sat at the end of the desk, his elbows on it, his chin in his hands, prepared to concentrate.

"What brought me back is the threat of a world war."

"Is it really that bad?"

"It is really that bad."

"Intending no offense, Rufus, what do you know about it that I don't know? I mean, that anybody following the news closely, and listening to the shouting and yelling couldn't deduce?"

"We now know the nature of the ultimatum of the Soviet Union."

136

Blackford waited to be told what it was. Rufus did not divulge it.

He continued. "What we cannot know is exactly when or how the Soviets would move. We know what they are in a position to do on the ground. We're fighting a war in Korea, where we've concentrated practically everything we have. We all but demobilized the army during the panic to get home after the war. We wrote a treaty that forbade West German participation in a joint military command. The French economy is on the floor, and the French military is completely absorbed all to hell and gone, off in Indochina. The British are exhausted, and engaged in full-time decolonization. We put up a good front about NATO, and Ike made some nice speeches over here, but here are the facts. The Russians have three million men on their western border, comprising one hundred and seventy-five divisions. Twenty-two of these divisions are in East Germany and are mostly motorized, backed by sixty divisions facing west; East Europe has sixty to seventy divisions under arms. We have ten divisions in West Germany—most of them under strength, backed by commitments for twenty divisions. The Russian presence in Korea is negligible. So they have available to fight in Europe the whole of their military machine. We figure they'd mass on the West German border, and twenty-four hours after they move, they'd reach the Rhine. Three days later, Paris. Either there would be no resistance at all—which is a strong possibility if NATO collapsed right away; or there'd be a fierce resistance of a partisan nature, and bloodletting on the scale of what went on in western Russia in the early days of the war. It is"—Rufus looked up at Blackford—"the worst potential situation I have seen since the Battle of Britain."

"Hell, Rufus, what about our bomb?"

"There's something we *don't* know. We don't know whether the President of the United States would order the use of atomic weapons to stop the Russians if they did move."

"But you do know—I assume—what can be done to keep the Russians from moving?"

"I think so. But first, consider three alternative constructions.

"Alternative One: Stalin is anxious to strike, desires Wintergrin to win the election, challenge it, and so give him an excuse to go ahead and gobble up the rest of Europe.

"Alternative Two: The Soviet Union is *not* anxious to take on the West but is prepared to do it—if Wintergrin is elected and issues his ultimatum."

"Alternative Three: The Soviet Union isn't anxious to take on the West—and won't take us on *even if Wintergrin is elected and presents his ultimatum.*"

"Surely the third alternative is too remote even to think about?" Blackford ventured. He had by now ten weeks' intensive familiarity with the German press, on both sides of the Iron Curtain, and his observations of the working of Stalin's iron will were well integrated. Stalin yield to Wintergrin?

"I list it out of a sense of obligation to list all the alternatives. Now, as for Alternative One, which early on was popular at Defense, I was always skeptical. The weakness of NATO apart, the American atomic deterrent apart, to take on all of Europe is something very few military men would counsel Stalin to do at this moment. If he *has* to do it in order to keep East Germany, that's one thing. Otherwise—later, maybe. It would mean occupying Italy, the parts of Austria they don't already occupy, West Germany, France, the Low Countries, Scandinavia; then war, along whatever ground rules, with England and the United States. No, they can't be *anxious* for that."

"So it comes down to Alternative Two?"

"In my opinion it comes down to Alternative Two."

"What are they saying in Washington about the chance of Wintergrin's winning?"

"We have been running polls every week. The week before Frankfurt, it was Wintergrin twenty per cent. The week after, it was Wintergrin twenty-eight per cent. A week ago he slipped— some of the criticism is beginning to tell—down to twenty-four per cent. But now listen to this: the poll four days ago, after his television press conference in Berlin, put him at thirty-four per cent—only four per cent behind Adenauer, and ten per cent ahead of Ollenhauer.

"There are three weeks before the election. Wintergrin's tide is rising. We are directed to proceed on the assumption that he will be elected the next Chancellor of West Germany unless he

139

sinks to below thirty per cent, or unless Adenauer's lead should rise to eight points. As a result of this week's upset, we are now polling continuously, making collations twice a week, Tuesdays and Fridays. The election is on November fifteenth. If on November eleventh the polls still show him at thirty-plus and Adenauer less than thirty-eight, we must, to be safe, assume that he would be elected."

"Well, what are we supposed to do about it? To be 'safe.' "

"We're supposed to do what we can to lower his standing in the polls."

"That will be an interesting job. Shall we begin by coming up with documents showing that he was really working for the Nazis in Norway?"

"That possibility is being studied."

"Shit," Blackford said, and instantly regretted it. One didn't say that kind of thing in Rufus's presence. Not because Rufus was a prude. But because it was an affront to his professionalism. Rather like a doctor swearing at an inflamed appendix. Rufus, of course, overlooked it. He said only, "There are a good many other possibilities, of course."

Blackford started to say, "All of them equally distasteful?" but checked himself. The questions being pondered by Rufus had nothing to do with good taste or bad, delicacy or indelicacy. He said instead: "I suppose we could fan the Wintergrin-will-lead-us-to-a-third-world-war movement."

"There is always that."

"Well, what happens if on the eleventh of

November he's still got more than thirty per cent of the vote?"

"He will have to be killed."

Blackford stood up, his pale face suddenly burning, his lithe body stiff, tilting forward. He could only think to say softly, reproachfully, "Rufus!"

"Moreover, there is only one person who could do it, expeditiously, who could get inside security, arrange for it to happen without suspicion. Who is, in fact, inside."

Blackford sat down. The pause was long. "Rufus. *I* couldn't. I *couldn't*. *You* couldn't, if you knew him . . ."

Rufus snapped: "The matter does not hang on Wintergrin's amiability." And, in a different tone of voice: "Nobody can *make* you do it, Blackford. And it may not prove necessary to try. It is necessary to guard against the high possibility of a world war and the loss of Europe. We must get on with these preparations irrespective of whether we ever trip the wire. To do that we need at least your cooperation, deferring until another time the question whether you would . . . act as executioner. I must ask you to cooperate at this critical stage." Rufus rose solemnly, and Blackford was reminded that he was facing the man Churchill had acknowledged as the single principal asset of the Allies during the Second World War.

Blackford didn't have the stomach to discuss the matter at any greater length with Rufus. He needed someone human to argue with. "Let me talk with Singer, please."

"Of course. Lunch is waiting for you in the dining room upstairs."

He was there at exactly seven-thirty. Blackford, true to his training, pulled up across the street exactly on time, so that there was no moment during which Wintergrin was waiting for an automobile, or an automobile was waiting for Wintergrin. On reflection, Blackford thought as Wintergrin opened the door and moved in next to him, the clockwork rendezvous—assuming anyone observed it—looked more suspicious than if one party had had to wait a moment or two for the other. The fine synchronization made it look like a getaway car.

Blackford had had a stiff drink of scotch in his room at the inn, seeking to tranquilize the day's events, and was struggling now to act natural. Wintergrin helped; he was in high spirits as they went down Goethestrasse, toward the highway west. Stopping at a light, Blackford looked across and noticed for the first time that in addition to the unaccustomed fedora, Count Wintergrin had a mustache.

"Not bad. I wonder what Hitler did when he wanted to go out incognito? Wear a yarmulke? How long have you had that?"

"Since becoming a fixture on television. I have used it perhaps five times, and it is quite wonderful. I have never been recognized with it on. I wish I could fool Wolfgang with it—but I can't; I have to get his permission to use it. The authenticity I owe to my sainted mother. When,

after three months' progressive disgust, I decided
to shave off the mustache I grew at college, mother persuaded me to let her clip off the ends, which
I now use. I am surprised dear mother does not
ask me to save my fingernails. Sometimes, after
hearing Roland Himmelfarb's dire reports on our
financial problems, I am tempted to auction off
my fingernails. Do you suppose you could persuade your Marshall Plan people to buy some at
a price consistent with German dignity and American resources?"

"I'll try . . . Axel"—that was the first time,
and the scotch helped to make it possible; besides,
Blackford thought wildly, what *is* the proper
mode of address between executioner and execu-
tionee? He would have to research this. He could
not think, offhand, of a course at Yale that covered the subject adequately, though no doubt
Professor Lewis Curtis, professor among other
things of European arcana, could at a moment's
prodding deliver a lecture on the subject. Surely,
in a democratic age, matters had advanced from
such stiffness as the axeman's who asked Mary,
Queen of Scot's: "Your Majesty, would you bend
your head down a little lower, please, ma'am?"

Blackford said: "Bonn has been pretty good
about expenses. Needless to say, we're over the
budget—that's always expected. But I'll tell you
what: If you would agree to get yourself mar-
tyred, I'm sure I could persuade Washington to
requisition—that is the word, Axel: never just
plain *'acquire'*—your fingernails as relics for the
altar at St. Anselm's."

"Thank you, Blackford. I shall take up your

proposal with my staff at our meeting at ten tomorrow. I am quite certain that Weil, my finance chairman, will give it every consideration."

They reached the Gummersbacher Hof, and Blackford went in ahead and asked for Walter, informing him that Blackford's guest was parking the car. Was everything in order?

Perfectly. They would have *Chambre séparée 3*, entirely private, and Walter's first waiter, Karl, would take care of the dinner order, and there would be a bottle of champagne in gratitude to the Americans who were rebuilding the beautiful chapel of St. Anselm's. Blackford, desiring leverage for his request for privacy, had let drop his mission in making the reservation. Walter led him through the dimly lit *fin-de-siècle* dining room, past crystal and candles and roast goose and crepes suzettes and animated Germans, a few with wives, others with women as conspicuously nubile as they were unattached; and finally to the little room sheltered, like one or two others, by a curtain. A single candleflame held the darkness at bay. At the sides of the table were upholstered chairs. Walter showed Blackford where the bell button was located (on the wall, by the head of the table), and reiterated that Herr Oakes had only to *mention* Walter's name to Karl and, without a moment's hesitation, Walter would materialize. Blackford went out to the parking lot and brought in the Liberator, who slithered by the twenty couples without problem—twenty couples whose thought, in any event, was not, at that particular time and place, easily arrested by politics.

Wintergrin seated, the curtain drawn, was expansive. He drank quickly from the champagne at the table, in sharp contrast with his habit of ordering a single glass of white wine and leaving it virtually untouched. Blackford too drank copiously as they looked unhurriedly at the menu. Wintergrin's paternalistic inclinations were not, however, adjourned, and Blackford was amused to hear his host say, as if in a soliloquy: "Let me see . . . they have fresh crayfish tonight. But also trout. I think we'll have the crayfish. Yes, don't you agree, Blackford?"—without looking up, and without anticipating any verbal reaction. "To begin. Yes, to begin. If my mother didn't always serve trout, I would order it here, since they are superbly done. But under the circumstances, we must have something else. Yes. Something else. Of *course*." This time he did not bother even to say what his selection was. He pushed the button, and in seconds Karl arrived with his notepad.

"The wine list." Karl had it in hand. Count Wintergrin drank infrequently, so his attention tended to focus on the familiar wines, and he picked out a Schorlemmer Mosel, then a Lafitte, and gave the order for the meal. Karl walked out. For the first time Wintergrin looked up.

"Will the United States work very hard against us?"

Blackford's mind ran to the joke passed around at school about the Prussian disporting himself with the whore who, it transpired, was palpably enjoying herself, causing the Prussian to pause in mid-enterprise and say: "Now vait a minute, Frieda. Just *who* is fucking whom?" So

145

now *Blackford Oakes,* a.k.a. Geoffrey Truax, was invited to inform Count Wintergrin of United States policy toward the reunification movement! Blackford was confident of his instincts about Wintergrin's preternatural innocence respecting Oakes's role at St. Anselm's. What, then, was Wintergrin after, asking him such a question? Did he mean to probe Blackford's knowledge of what U.S. officials were saying in Bonn, the principal Western listening post for American diplomacy? If that was Wintergrin's intention, surely he'd have approached the question more obliquely? If the idea was to suborn Blackford's good nature by teasing him into indiscretion, Wintergrin would surely have waited—a long evening lay ahead of them—until the wine had done its notoriously good work in softening preprandial resolution. No, Wintergrin was being characteristically frank, surely—ingenuous.

He took a long, slow drink of champagne. "Well, as you know, the Administration is backing Adenauer."

"Of course I know. That much is obvious. They've backed him from the beginning. And I am not unsympathetic with their motives for doing so. They didn't anticipate a reunification movement. Now they have one. The Soviet press and the left press throughout Europe have responded to our challenge exactly as one might suppose they would. But is it inconceivable that the U.S. Government—are you aware, Blackford, that not *one* American official has interrogated me, however indirectly?—might change its mind? Or even that it would remain neutral? What puzzles me, now that there are only three weeks to go, is: What will they do to reinforce Adenauer's position? And what will they do if they conclude that Adenauer is going to lose—that I am going to win? I'll tell you something confidential." He drank his champagne. Blackford followed suit. Wintergrin leaned toward him. "The Americans are conducting polls. You know, we are not yet officially permitted to do so. But even if *Der Spiegel* goes ahead, as it threatens to do, American polling techniques are far advanced, thanks to your Truman-Dewey experience. Now, I happen to know—one of our people is, well, nicely situated in there—what the most recent poll says. Do you know?"

"No," Blackford lied, tilting his glass to hide his face.

"I am at *thirty-four per cent*. Adenauer is only four points ahead of me. I began at twenty per cent. There have been ups and downs. But the upward graph is steady. And"—he drank slowly now from what was left in his glass, and looked directly at Blackford, his face calm, resolute, solemn, his eyes slightly raised as if the subject were, somehow, slightly indiscreet—"I am going to win. Assuming an exact three-way split, I would need only thirty-four per cent. But I am every day taking votes from Adenauer. And why not? Adenauer's position is no longer interesting. It is the position of . . . an . . . *inchoate* reunifier. He is progressively seen as the impotent candidate. I make this prediction: When the votes are counted, *Ollenhauer* will be ahead of Adenauer. The publicity against me is—if only my enemies knew it"—he chuckled, a little nervously—"if only you people realized it—at the strategic expense of Adenauer. Everyone who is persuaded by what they say about me—that I'll bring on a war—will be frightened into *Ollenhauer's* camp, don't you see? If they are scared to death of any confrontation with the Soviet Union, won't they go, after the battering they are taking, as far away from confrontation as possible? Ollenhauer is a good German, but his idea of reunification is something that will happen when Stalin's grandson gives away East Germany as a wedding present to his German bride."

Blackford tasted the first course before answering, waited for Karl to leave, and said, cautiously: "Well, I don't know what they're saying in Washington But I can guess. They're probably saying: What in the hell are *we* supposed to do if Wintergrin's elected, gives Stalin his Frankfurt ultimatum. Stalin says screw you, and oils up his legions to overrun West Germany? Washington is not prepared for that, I'd guess. What *could* it do? NATO isn't strong enough. The Bomb means a third world war, and that probably means the last war. I assume the Russians wouldn't give you time to develop your own strength to resist the Russian Army . . ."

"The Russians"—Wintergrin edged his chair closer to the table, and gripped his glass of wine —"the Russians," he said in a strident whisper, *"are scared to death.* Don't ask me how I know. But I do. They are *counting on* threats and bluff to dispose of the Wintergrin problem." He took from his pocket an envelope on which he had made notes. "This is very confidential. We have someone in Ulbricht's entourage. He reports that Ulbricht sent on dutifully to Moscow an intelligence report taken by his own people predicting that any move by the Russian military across East Germany would mobilize the whole country in opposition, which would rip right across Eastern Europe, endangering the whole Soviet postwar position. I wonder if the CIA knows, or guesses, this? With these problems in the countries they presently occupy, can you *imagine* the Russian situation if they moved and tried to take over *West* Germany? Let alone our NATO neighbors?"

"Well, yes. I imagine that, among other things, previously ill-fed Russian military officials would be eating the crayfish here tonight."

"Blackford, there is a limit even to what the Russians can ingest. The prime minister Count Witte warned Nicholas II on the eve of the First World War on that point, trying to dissuade him from declaring war against the Germans. Stalin is everything evil and avaricious you want to say about him. But he has practically *never*—in his career—shown a disregard for strategic prudence. His only lapse caused him to be taken by surprise by the Nazis. He very nearly lost Russia, never mind the world revolution. Do you want to know what *I* think would happen—what I think *will* happen? The Russians will reply to my ultimatum with a series of face-saving qualifications. I am telling *you*, swearing you to silence, that *I will let them get away with it*. I would even extend the deadline. I would sign a nonaggression treaty. I

149

would go to Moscow. *I would even push NATO out of Germany* . . . But when the final moment comes, they will give us back Germany. I'm telling you, Blackford, they will give us back Germany without war. Of this I am confident. More confident than I am that the West—that *you*"—he looked up directly at Blackford, as though Axel were addressing the President of the United States—"will take the historical opportunity my movement presents you. The temptation to prudence is *so* great. And the means of effecting prudence can be ugly—I know; I was involved, once, in effecting prudence (we were right, in the circumstances) in Norway, in 1944, there was a dead Norwegian left over. He might—conceivably—have escaped us, with tighter security. I could never escape the West, if the fatal decision were made. I can only hope that the West will see: through my eyes if necessary; through their own eyes, if only they will widen them. Don't you see, Blackford, I have got hold of the key to the eventual liberation of Eastern Europe?"

Blackford studied his face. In Axel's words there was assurance, but not a trace of that triumphalism that marks the fanatic, or the politician-on-the-stump. He was struck by Wintergrin's conviction, and its gnawing plausibility. Question: Was there more that Blackford should pursue? Out of professional concern? Or should he feign now only the dilettante's interest in the subject? What, he thought bitterly, would Rufus want him to say? He sensed he knew the answer to that question, and out of a sense of professional obligation he pursued the point.

"Surely those scientists you spoke about at Frankfurt must be known to the Russians? I can't see any *way* the Soviets would sit around and let you develop an atom bomb."

Wintergrin looked at him, and hesitated. He replied with manifest caution. "The scientists have already done their work."

Blackford chose to sacrifice his vanity and appear obtuse: "Done their work? What do you mean?"

Again, Wintergrin paused. And then said, "The defense we would under extraordinary circumstances deploy against the Soviet Union is ours to deploy."

Again Blackford affected to misunderstand the electric reply, taking cover behind a handy cliché: "Of course, of course. Scientific knowledge is universal. You can't take $E=mc^2$ and send it to Siberia. Good point, Axel."

Wintergrin accepted the evasion and changed the subject. Over the next course he recounted to Blackford the special problems involved in producing the crayfish. Blackford, tasting it, pronounced the problems well solved. Wintergrin said—the Cold War was well behind them —"This doesn't quite remind one of our old school, Greyburn, does it?"

Blackford said, "I haven't been reminded of Greyburn since visiting Sing Sing."

Wintergrin laughed. "Come now, it wasn't that bad, though your hyperbole is in the Greyburn tradition."

Blackford said, in diligent pursuit of irrelevance, "I doubt the poor English can find food

151

like this *anywhere*. And to think, *they* won the war!"

Wintergrin agreed. "Not even at Buckingham Palace"—and stopped, as if to undo the clear suggestion that he was familiar with the fare at Buckingham Palace. Blackford, who had drunk more than usual and more then he should have, began to feel giddy. "Ah, yes. But of course, Axel, you are a second cousin of the Queen, a relationship frequently remarked in the press. Now let me tell you something *you* don't know: I have tasted the food both at Buckingham Palace *and* at Windsor Castle."

"Oh?" said Wintergrin, taking the last of the red wine.

"Oh, yes. I said to the Queen, I said, 'Ma'am The grub here is okay, but I can tell you where in Atlantic City you can get better.' "

Wintergrin smiled. Blackford hated himself, but could not stop. He hoped, hoped, he could stop in time, but meanwhile, under the impulse of champagne, Mosel, claret, and Rufus, he barreled on. "Oh, yes, Axel, that's what I, er, said to the Queen. Then I went to Windsor Castle. Spent a couple of days there. Went riding with her, right around Windsor Park. Then we went back to the castle and had dinner, just the two of us. Then" —Blackford felt like weeping, for the first time since, at fifteen, he learned at summer camp about his parents' divorce. Was it seriously proposed— surely the most macabre coincidence in history— that he execute *another* second cousin of the Queen? And this one, moreover—unlike the other

—the most convincing relic, in the world of jaded human resolution, of a will to resist the bad guys? The liars, cheats, murderers, torturers, slavemasters? Was he—Blackford Oakes—conscripted to serve the West to *that* end? He sensed the nervous immobility at the other end of the table, the awful fear of hearing an indiscretion . . . "And after dinner, I said to her: 'Ma'am, it's been a wonderful day.'" Blackford had pulled out of his nose dive seconds before hitting the treetops. "You see, I was there to look over the archives, to file an engineering report—and she was swell; she invited me, as a favor to the ambassador; talked about everything, including your common cousin Peregrin Kirk, who had taught her to ride horseback. When I went down to my room, I have to confess, Axel, I used some Windsor Castle stationery to write a letter to my girl in Washington."

Wintergrin was relaxed again. "Here is the money to pay the bill"—he slipped one hundred marks to Blackford. "Remember, it's my party, though you're the host as far as Walter is concerned. Give him ten marks. Now, if you want to go upstairs, talk to Karl. He will make the whole thing very easy for you, no fuss. I shall be gone until"—he looked at his watch—"it is now ten-thirty. At twelve-thirty I'll be here, with a glass of brandy for you. We will now go our separate ways. Tell Washington that." Blackford looked up, though the focus was a little unclear, rather like the night he ended his three-year ordeal of abstinence for the greater good of the swimming team at Yale.

Blackford said: "No, Axel, thanks. I'm not in the mood. Let's go home, unless you want me to sit here and wait for you."

Axel rose silently. Blackford rang for Karl, settled the account, and walked out. Axel was sitting in the car, and they drove home. Axel talked about the days at Greyburn. They had been happy days, even though he was the resident Hun, and the martial winds were blowing. Blackford asked whether these were also happy days, even though the martial winds were blowing yet again, and Axel said he was happy for many blessings, among them that he had such a friend as Blackford; that the future was for Providence to worry about, and that Providence, with so much weight on its shoulders, cannot be supposed to be happy except in the special sense that Sisyphus, rolling the stone up the mountainside again and again, could be thought to be happy. Both men had read Camus.

11

On the following day Blackford informed Overstreet he would be bringing in two electricians to
lay out the wiring. This was two months ahead of
schedule; but, he said, he had been told while in
Bonn that two expert electricians had finished
their work on the reconstruction of Monte Cassi-
no in Italy, and Washington had decided to send
them directly to St. Anselm's rather than back to
the States, and back again to Europe in February,
as the St. Anselm's reconstruction schedule called
for. Overstreet grumbled that the chapel was
hardly ready to rewire, and Blackford consoled
him by saying he had said exactly that at Bonn,
but that Colonel Morley had replied: "What the
hell, you want me to argue with Washington? Let

'em go to St. Anselm's. If there's nothing for 'em to do, ship their asses back to Washington." Blackford's imitation of the cigar-chomping colonel pacified Overstreet, who shrugged his shoulders and said, Well, he supposed they could work on the schematics even if they couldn't do any installations, and Blacky said sure, they could work on the schematics, and the next morning, having got two passes for them from Jürgen Wagner, he introduced Overstreet and Conditti to Hallam Spring and Bruce Pulling. Spring, in his early forties, was the senior. He was paunchy, direct in manner, had worked as an electrical engineer during the war, never married, and moved around the world now doing special jobs for the government. Usually—it depended on the assignment—he traveled with Bruce Pulling, a diminutive man in his thirties who wore thick glasses and seemed forever to be making squiggly notes on a pad, bending over, which in his case was never very far, to look at something—a circuit plug, a light socket; but, sometimes, seemingly at nothing at all—a bit of wall, a piece of carpet. He spoke hardly a word. Hallam Spring, a Californian who wore Levi's, an open shirt and, on formal occasions, a string tie, didn't say much either, though he was pleasant enough. He maneuvered with Blackford around the chapel, Bruce Pulling made a few notes, and Spring said they'd be back in the morning after settling down at the inn and resting from the long drive. Blackford led them around the courtyard to give them a tourist's-eye view of St. Anselm's before escorting them back to his car and driving them to the gasthof. In the car, past the sentry, Blackford said: "Did you come with any ideas, or are you going to work out some ideas here?"

Spring exhaled his cigarette smoke. "Don't know what Singer has in mind for us yet. He'll be letting us know in a few days. Meanwhile, we can keep busy, don't worry. There's a lot in and around that chapel we can be doing. We've got a little sweeping to do." Hallam Spring was one of the Agency's finest communications technicians and electrical experts. Bruce Pulling, early in the war, had been assigned as a demolitions instructor but he proved impossible as a teacher, so was sent to the field. Soon he was given the assignment of passing on unusual and complicated demolition problems. Occasionally he would venture out himself and take on an assignment: always when Rufus asked him to. Singer had said of him to Blackford: "Pulling plays explosives like Pablo Casals plays the cello."

Blackford was correct with his new associates, but not quite his old-boy self. Face it, he told himself ruefully: It wasn't all high principle that was churning him up. It was also the debauch of the night before. What *would* he have done without that last bottle of champagne at three in the morning? he wondered. Died of thirst maybe? He lunched briefly with his electricians, answered their questions, and returned to the chapel to work during the afternoon, and to think.

As he drove into the courtyard, Count Wintergrin's caravan was preparing to move out. That night the speech would be at Bremen. In front there was a police motorcycle, courtesy of the federal government. Then a passenger car, a middle-sized Mercedes, with two men in front, one in the rear—members of the Freiwillige Schutzwehr, the voluntary security corps organized by Jürgen Wagner to protect Wintergrin during the campaign. Then the candidate's own car, a 1941 Opel Admiral belonging to the countess. The windows had been bulletproofed; the bullet-resistant tires were reputed to weigh 175 pounds apiece. The chauffeur was a trained bodyguard like the grim Wolfgang who sat next to him. Behind, but not easily visible—though he could open the car's roof and stand up through the opening—was Count Wintergrin, and the ever-present Roland Himmelfarb. Following the car, a bus—a traveling office, really, with three well-appointed desks, two mimeograph machines, six typewriters, two radio-telephones, and another half-dozen phones that could be quickly connected to a circuit when the bus drove up alongside either a hotel where the candidate was staying, or a theater or gymnasium where he would speak. In the bus were Wintergrin's communications chief Heinrich Stiller, his press chief Kurt Grossmann, his chief translator Erika Chadinoff, and their staffs, plus two security men, heavily armed. Behind that the press bus would attach itself, completing the caravan. Wintergrin, talking with an aide, a leather portfolio in the crook of his arm, approached his car and waved a greeting to Blackford, who waved back but did not approach him. Instead he walked toward Erika, who was looking over a clipboard held up to her by an elderly woman. In a language Blackford was unfamiliar with, they were obviously wrangling, presumably about the proper translation of a passage from the evening's text. Erika smiled at Blackford. "Why don't you come along? We should all be back by one or two at the latest."

"Is he going to say anything interesting?"

"Very interesting. He's going to declare war on the Poles."

"Oh? What've *they* done?"

"They've refused to declare war against Russia."

"Well," said Blackford cheerily. "Serves them right. Be sure you get the translation right. We wouldn't want Count Wintergrin to be misunderstood."

She laughed. Blackford asked her to dine with him tomorrow, and she said yes, but it might have to be late, was eight-thirty all right? He waved his assent. Heinrich Stiller was talking into his radio. The press bus waited at the junction in St. Anselm's to join the caravan. A whistle sounded. Wintergrin walked toward the door of his car, and on reaching it stopped. There was no accounting for the silence, but for a few seconds, as Wintergrin gazed out toward the chapel and the castle, lit yellow by a brilliant October sun, the courtyard was motionless. The whistle stopped blowing, the passengers were all in their cars, the coordinators stopped speaking into their squawk boxes. The scene froze in Blackford's mind: motorcade, entourage, the tall slim aristocrat setting out on a crusade. Perhaps almost a thousand years earlier from this courtyard, with a gaudier entourage, horses and infantrymen and archers had surrounded Ritter Erik von Winter-grin setting out on the first crusade while St. Anselm was still alive, coping with the heathen kings of England. Had anything changed?

The policeman fired his motorcycle, the other drivers followed suit, the count stepped into his car, closing the door, engines raced, the sentry opened the gate, and the procession moved fitfully out, to reach cruising speed only after descending the hill and picking up the press bus at St. Anselm's. Blackford watched them go, and as he turned was startled at seeing Countess Wintergrin standing directly behind him. She was dressed in a tweed suit, wearing a floppy felt hat, and carrying a basket of oils and brushes and sketching materials. She spoke slowly:

"They will never allow him to succeed, will they, Mr. Oakes?"

Blackford answered evasively. "Of course, Countess, he has a great many enemies. I don't think Count Wintergrin underestimates that."

"But does he know who all his enemies are?" she asked.

Blackford struggled to escape her intense eyes. Again he tried evasion:

"Perhaps you are saying that we are our own worst enemies? I suppose that is true. Your son, though, has never shrunk from risks."

The countess smiled, nodded her head, and moved on with her basket toward the west garden. Shaken, Blackford walked into the chapel where, after a time, he felt, for the first moment since noon the day before, a certain composure. He worked for five hours gratefully with Overstreet and Conditti. He wished he could work there without end, wished he could exchange roles with Overstreet.

They walked silently to the Westfalenkrug, advertised by an old sign depicting crossed swords, the shield of Wintergrin, and the legend, *Nobly live, nobly dine.* Blackford led the way. He knew the waitress, who conducted him routinely to the usual table in the corner, removed from the jukebox which played, endlessly, bouncy German Volkslieder and lush American Volkslieder, of the Glenn Miller age. Weeks before, Blackford had made a mental note to requisition twenty new phonograph records from Bonn, intending to make a gift of them to Herr Musiktorturer. Three men and two couples were at the bar, one pair fiercely debating the political campaign, the man gesticulating to his wife and pointing to an iron cross he wore conspicuously on his corduroy jacket. She was pointing to a picture of Wintergrin and saying, repeatedly, *Er hat recht! Er hat recht! Er hat recht!* (He is right! He is right! He is right!) Blackford sat down wearily, told the waitress he would have a beer, and asked his two companions what they wanted. Spring wanted bourbon, but they didn't have it, so he said, "gin mit anything." Pulling bent over the list of beverages for a full two minutes, cleared his throat, and asked for water. They glanced over the menu.

"The sausage is good, so is the sauerkraut. If you're feeling flush, the *entrecôte*—steak—is okay. So is the veal." They ordered, and Hallam Spring began.

"We swept your room at the inn."

"And?"

"Bingo."

"Come on."

"Yup."

"Wintergrin's people?"

"Maybe. If so, they've got an expert on the team. Well, why not? He's surrounded by people who just finished waging a pretty sophisticated world war."

"Straight bug?"

"Straight bug."

"Where?"

"In the light socket on the floor lamp by your desk."

Quickly Blackford thought back. Had he ever said anything indiscreet over the telephone? He was satisfied he hadn't. He tended not to deviate from his training. All his calls to Bonn from that telephone had been to Colonel Morley, on straight chapel business. He had telephoned his mother in England, Sally in Washington. He had called Anthony Trust on his birthday. What had he said? He struggled to remember exactly. But he was certain he had been cautious.

"Did you track it?"

"Yup."

"All right, to where?"

"Not very far. To the translator's room. Chadinoff."

"Erika Chadinoff? I'll be *damned."* He decided to approach the news professionally, ana-

lytically. "Well, that's interesting. So Miss Chad-inoff is either—let's look at the possibilities: One, she is doing extracurricular duty for Wintergrin. Or two, she is an agent of Adenauer. Or three, she is an agent of Ollenhauer. Or four, she is an agent of the Commies. Or five, she's a free-lancer of some sort."

"Well, that's for you people to figure out."

Spring, his mind on the artistic possibilities of explosives, began asking about the configuration of Wintergrin's caravan.

"Look, please. Not tonight. I know you're on assignment, and I'll give you what I got. But not tonight, okay?"

"Okay," said Spring. "What do you want to talk about? The Yale-Harvard game?"

Blackford was in just the mood to get up and poke him and, while he was at it, take the little shrimp by the neck, bury his nose in the soup and tell him if there was anything suspicious in it to write it in his notebook. He felt color rising in his cheeks. He got up. "Take care of my bill. I'll see you tomorrow." He felt sick, but managed to walk to the pay telephone in the rear and ring Singer. He was at yesterday's number.

Singer listened while Blackford spoke. Blackford strained to recall the code name for Erika Chadinoff—there was one for each of a half-dozen St. Anselm-based members of Wintergrin's staff. "Have you thought of inviting Eleina to the party? It's not that far from Cologne. She'd probably like to come, get a little relief from the routine. Nice girl, really inquisitive."

"Sure," Callaway said. "I'll send her a card.

I have her address. When are you coming up to Bonn? I've got some material here might be useful to you."

The interrogatory had a special meaning: It was a summons. "I thought I'd go up tomorrow morning. I've got several things to do. I'll give you a ring."

Back in his room, he looked carefully at the light socket. With his lips, he formed the words, *Up-yours-Erika.*

Then he sat down and wrote to Sally the most ardent note since arriving in Germany. ("Do you know this is my seventy-first night in this dreary inn without you? Why are you so faithless? What does Chaucer have that I don't have? You probably think we engineers know nothing about Chaucer. Well, you're wrong, my favorite of his is *Romeo and Juliet.* How are you, Juliet? Do you find me like the moon? Do you look out your window in New Haven, see the moon, and tell that impostor in your room, whoever he is, that the moon reminds you of Blacky, your beautiful Blacky who is going crazy without his Juliet? That last line should convince you I'm sick. Come, give me an aspirin. When I finish, I'm going to handcuff myself to the bedpost and enclose the key with this letter. I can go without food or water for four days. . . .") Then he tried to read his Goethe, but his mind would not focus on the German. He picked up Whittaker Chambers' book on the Hiss case, and for a while was absorbed by the account of the net the interrogator drew so artfully, and was struck by the historical irony, as given by Chambers. What he said about

himself, Blackford thought, he—Blackford—
might as well apply to his own circumstances. . . .

"And as, hour by hour, the agony mounted,
died away and mounted again, point by damning
point, I was more and more bowed under the
sense of how much each of us was the prey,
rather than an actor, in this historic experience to
which what had been best in us had led us, from
motives incomprehensible to most of those who
watched or heard us, to this end.

"The exchange with Nixon began almost off-
handedly.

> MR. NIXON: Mr. Hiss was your closest
> friend?
> MR. CHAMBERS: Mr. Hiss was certainly
> the closest friend I ever had in the
> Communist Party.

"Alger Hiss was now sitting behind me
among the spectators, surrounded by a little group
of friends. As I testified, I could hear Hiss making
sotto-voce sallies, and the titters of the others.

> MR. NIXON: Mr. Chambers, can you
> search your memory now to see what
> motive you can have for accusing
> Mr. Hiss of being a Communist at
> the present time?
> MR. CHAMBERS: What motive I can have?
> MR. NIXON: Yes. I mean, do you—is there
> any grudge that you have against
> Mr. Hiss over anything that he has
> done to you?

"That single question slipped the cord on all the pent emotion that had been built up through the day. Until that moment, I had been testifying as a public witness, trying to answer questions carefully and briefly. Now I ceased to answer in that way. As I struggled to control my feelings, slowly and deliberately, I heard myself saying, rather than said: 'The story has spread that in testifying against Mr. Hiss I am working out some old grudge, or motives of revenge or hatred. I do not hate Mr. Hiss. We were close friends, but we are caught in a tragedy of history. Mr. Hiss represents the concealed enemy against which we are all fighting, and I am fighting. I have testified against him with remorse and pity, but in a moment of history in which this Nation now stands, so help me God, I could not do otherwise.' "

He put the Chambers' book down and picked up *Time* magazine, flipped to the foreign news section, and read there the account of the growing apprehension in the capitals of Europe over the enthusiastic public response to Wintergrin's speeches and press conferences. *"Leaving the amphitheater, the roaring of the crowd still audible, a young man dressed in an old army trenchcoat walked slowly out, dragging his wooden leg like a ball and chain. 'Don't they understand? Do they really want another war?' That was the question all thoughtful men in Europe were asking themselves last week as the dashing young count went from rally to rally preaching his simplistic solution to the problem of a divided Germany. Everywhere the scientists were asking themselves the same questions: Is it possible that*

166

*young Wintergrin actually has access to a nuclear
bomb? Everywhere the answer was: 'Impossible.'
But what is going on in Germany at the moment
would have been thought impossible only a few
months ago."*

Blackford threw the magazine on the floor
and looked at his watch. It was after midnight. He
was tempted to approach the floor lamp and coo,
"Goodnight, dear Erika." Instead he went to the
cupboard and poured four ounces of gin into his
toothbrush glass, stared at it, walked to the bathroom, and splashed the contents into the toilet.
Back in bed he reached impulsively to open the
drawer at the bedside, taking out the German
hotel Bible. He flipped the pages to the psalms. He
read ten of them and then reached for a pencil and
his clipboard, and set out to translate the final
one. He surveyed the result, and concluded he
would not have qualified to serve on King James's
commission. Now, finally, he felt he could sleep.
The psalmist had revived his spirits, and as he began to doze off he thought, Really, I must join a
religious order, and let other people worry about
rights and wrongs. It is only vital, he reminded
himself as he dropped off to sleep, to remember
that there is a difference between the two.

12

The parents of her friends in America would make references to her "privileged" upbringing and now and then would imply, not without admiration, and not without envy, that she had been spoiled. Sometimes over a weekend visit or vacation, Erika's hosts, in the effusive style of the forties, would push Erika forward to exhibit one of her accomplishments, even as they might ask an older brother to show off a card trick. Erika went through the usual stages: she would be shy, she would be recalcitrant, she would use evasive tactics, but after her third year at the Ethel Walker School in Simsbury, Connecticut, she surprised everybody who knew her. Her fat friend Alice begged her after dinner one night to play on the piano excerpts from the first movement of the Grieg A-Minor Concerto, which Erika had played before the entire school at the annual concert only the week before—accompanied by the school piano teacher, who knew very little about music, but that didn't matter because it was recorded and rerecorded that in her youth she had actually studied under Clara Schumann. Erika surprised Alice, and rather dismayed Alice's parents, who went once every summer to the Lewisohn Stadium when Alexander Smallens did *Porgy and Bess* and thought themselves thereby to have acquitted a full year's responsibility to music, by getting up without demurral and proceeding through twenty-two minutes of music, stopping only to sing at the top of her husky voice the parts written by Grieg for the missing orchestra.

"You certainly are a privileged young girl," Alice's mother said admiringly while the father, fearful that his daughter would suggest that Erika play an encore—had Grieg written another concerto? he worried . . . everyone knew that Mozart had written over, was it 400 concertos?—clapped loudly, looked at his watch, and said as a treat he would drive them all to the late movie with Bob Hope and Bing Crosby off on the Road to Morocco. The girls went happily to get their coats and Erika had time in the car to muse over her privileged unbringing, in Germany and England, before coming to the United States three years ago at age thirteen.

Of course, being the daughter of Dimitri and Anna Chadinoff *was* a privilege, this she did not deny, though she wondered—she truly wondered

—what her parents would have done about her if she had not been . . . clever. She had picked up that word in England and thereafter used it—there being no satisfactory American substitute, as she told Alice. Her friends supposed that her early memories of Germany were of intellectuals and artists coming to her parents' elegant apartment to eat stuffed goose and read aloud each other's poems and short stories and argue long into the night the meaning of a fable by Pushkin. What Erika in fact remembered was the awful physical discomforts and the utter indifference of her father to them. She was very young when she learned that something called "money" was terribly important. When her mother looked into her handbag, either there was money in it or there was not money in it. In the former event Erika would eat dinner, in the latter event she would not. Beginning in midafternoon, Erika would find that her attention was substantially given over to the question, Would there be money that night when her mother opened her handbag? Her mother, though not as stoical as her father, was twice as vague. If, on opening her handbag, she had pulled out a diamond necklace, she'd have said, "Dimitri, dear, I apparently have a diamond necklace here I hadn't reckoned on." Dimitri would have said, "That's fine, my dear," which he would also have said if his wife had announced that she had found an armadillo in her handbag. Her mother did concern herself for Erika, and in the especially cold winter of 1936, washed dishes at the corner restaurant in return for bread and potatoes left over at the end of the evening's meal. Sometimes

Erika had her dinner at one in the morning on her mother's return. Sometimes there was food left over from the night before. But sometimes there was no food at all. During these daily struggles her father was always reading or writing. He had access to the public library and spent much of his time there, often taking Erika because that way she could be warm. It was troublesome to do this at first because the guard at the door announced that the library was not a nursery in which to keep little girls. Dimitri Chadinoff asked just when could children be brought into the library, and the answer was: When they are old enough to read. Dimitri turned around, took Erika home, and was with her for three days, interrupted only when Erika could no longer stay awake. On the fourth day, triumphantly, he led her back and was stopped at the same entrance by the same guard. Calmly, Dimitri made his announcement. The guard leaned over from his high desk, put a newspaper into the girl's hands and, pointing to the headline, said: "Read this, little girl." Her face solemn, Erika read, haltingly, but without error: "Roosevelt Sweeps Country/Dems Control Both Houses." She was three years old. Her father showed no particular pride in his daughter, then or later when, at age seven, she earned a few pennies by drilling two dull teen-age boys, sons of a noble family, in English; or when Anna's friend Valerian Bibikoff, a fellow expatriate from Russia who taught piano and gave lessons to Erika, reported that the girl was singularly talented. Her father was as surprised as if he had been informed that his daughter was remarkable because she had

172

ten fingers. He showed displeasure as rarely as he showed pleasure. When, freshly arrived in England, Erika returned to their flat to say she had made friends at school with the daughter of the Soviet military attaché, Dimitri looked down at her from his desk and told her that he would just as soon she did not associate with the children of barbarians. "Why are they barbarians?" Erika asked in French, that being the only language spoken at the Chadinoff household on Thursdays (Monday, German; Tuesday, English; Wednesday, Italian; Thursday, French; Friday, Saturday, and Sunday any language save the language spoken in the country being inhabited). "They are barbarians," said Dimitri Chadinoff, "because they wish to obliterate everything important that human beings have learned about how to treat each other in three thousand years." "Why do they want to obliterate it?"—Erika had no difficulty with unusual words. Her problem, at school, was in learning that some words *were* unusual: she had to study them attentively and learn to use them with great discretion, or preferably not at all, since at home they were used as nonchalantly as kitchen utensils. She got off to a bad start her first day at Blessed Sir Thomas More's School in Cadogan Square by asking a girl whether the policies of the school were "latitudinarian." It was years before she could explain to anyone—the solemn Paul, at the Sorbonne—that she had been guilty of affectation throughout much of her youth only by searching out simple substitute words for those that occurred to her naturally.

"They want to obliterate it," said her father,

173

"because they are bewitched by the secular superstition of Communism, which is a huge enterprise that will settle for nothing less than bringing misery to all the people of the world."

"Why should they want to bring misery to all the people of the world?" Erika repeated her father's formulation piously.

"It isn't that they want to bring misery, though some do. They strut up and down in their baggy clothes swinging golden chains from their vests as if the keys to happiness were attached. All they have succeeded in doing is killing and torturing people and promising to do as much to people fortunate enough not to live in Russia during this period. To think that they have done it to Russia, the most beautiful land in the world," said Dimitri Chadinoff, and Anna agreed, recalling how the weather would be now in their native hills outside St. Petersburg.

"Did they take away all your money?" Erika wanted to know.

"Yes, they took away all our money."

Such an indifference as Dimitri Chadinoff's to money had not been seen since the natives begged St. Francis to accept a copper if only to have the pleasure of giving it away. But he did not deign to express where, in the hierarchy of Soviet offenses, the loss of the family money had come. *Infra dignitate.* Erika, a thoughtful girl, assumed that her father was correct but promised herself one day to think the matter over more exhaustively, and turned to her homework in mathematics, which she was always pleased to express her concern with because she knew it was the

174

single subject in which neither her father nor her mother could help her.

"What exactly is an integer? I don't understand."

"Ask your teacher. He's getting well paid," said her father.

Well, not so well paid by modern standards, but the school was well staffed and now Dimitri was making five pounds per week translating for a London publisher on a piecemeal basis, and that same publisher had sent out Chadinoff's fresh translation of Pushkin to be assessed by scholars at Oxford and Cambridge. "I could advise you," Chadinoff wrote to his editor, "which of the scholars at Cambridge and Oxford are competent to evaluate my work, but I suppose that if you agreed to accept my judgment in the matter the entire enterprise would be circular. Anyway, for the record the only man at either university who has the necessary background is Adam Sokolin at Cambridge. He studied under my old tutor, who beat some sense into him thirty years ago. Sokolin has done good work on Pushkin, from which we may safely conclude that he will not get very far in Cambridge." The editor took the letter by the corner, his fingers raised as if carrying a dead rat by the tail, walked into the office of his superior, dropped it on his desk and asked: "Have I your permission to tell this egomaniac to go and peddle his Pushkin elsewhere?"

The next day, manuscript back in hand, Chadinoff sent it to the Harvard University Press. The following day, the London publisher dropped him as a part-time editor and then, after Erika had gone to sleep, Anna took Dimitri aside and, even though it was Tuesday, spoke to him in Russian and said that they had to do something to bring in some money, that all their friends and relatives were equally impoverished, that there was no money for the next week's rent, nor for the next month's school bills for Erika. Well, said Dimitri—ever so slightly disposed to point out, by twiddling his fingers on the open page of his book, that Anna had interrupted his reading— did she have any suggestions? Yes, she said, she had recently been talking to her friend Selnikov (former colonel in the Czar's prime equestrian unit). Poor Sergei Babevich had not only himself and his wife to look after but three daughters and a son. He had taken a position as a maître d'hôtel at a medium-priced restaurant where a knowledge of several languages was useful. "The trouble with you, dear Dimitri, is that your knowledge of food is really not very refined. You could write a scholarly book about the feasts of Lucullus, but you would not be able to distinguish the actual food from fish and chips at Lyons. So I have another idea."

Dimitri had sat without any show of emotion thus far. "Well?"

Anna couldn't, at first, remember what her other idea was, and Dimitri waited. Finally the newspaper caught her eye.

"Ah yes. There is an advertisement in the paper for a concierge. He must be presentable— here." She reached for the paper, shuffling through to the marked section. "Presentable, must

176

be fluent in French and German. Some Italian and Spanish desirable. References."

Dimitri took the job. His hours were from one until midnight. He would sleep until six and then resume his own work. Erika was not permitted to see her father at the hotel during working hours. Once she decided mischievously to do so. She was small for twelve years, so that her head only just reached the counter. She had on a friend's hat, and her light-brown hair was knotted under it. She put on spectacles and, carrying a handbag, she said in a little girl's voice, imitating her father's own imperious accent and speaking in German: "Concierge, please get me a sleeper to the Finland Station!" Dimitri permitted himself a smile, and then in Russian said to her: "Get yourself out of here, Rikushka, before I invite the manager to paddle your behind." She went out roaring, and told her mother, who laughed, and then said not, ever, to do such a thing again. The following morning, when she went off to school, she found tucked into her notebook, in her father's unmistakable hand, a fable dedicated to her. It was called "The Little Girl Who Took the Train to the Finland Station, and Woke Up Lenin." That day, she thought, she was closer to her father than she had ever been before.

When the letter came from the Harvard University Press, Chadinoff was pleased, but not particularly surprised. He knew his Pushkin was superior. But he was surprised a month later to be invited by the Department of Slavic and Romance Languages to go to Harvard to lecture during the spring term. Chadinoff replied that, thanks very much, he would be happy to do so, and able to do so inasmuch as his job as concierge at the Basil Street Hotel required him to give only three weeks' notice, and February was still three months away.

They made reservations for the tenth of December on the S. S. *Mount Vernon,* and it was well that they did, because after the seventh of December, which was the day of Pearl Harbor, no reservations were accepted save for returning residents of the United States. Chadinoff and his family carried Nansen passports, and his excited wife and daughter were apprehensive, up until the moment the gangplank was lifted, about having to yield their room to returning U.S. residents.

During the commotion Erika, snugly dressed in a white skirt, peasant blouse, and tweed jacket, excitedly accosted a tall, handsome blond boy—at least two years older, she judged—wearing an English public-school blazer, chewing an apple, and affecting the ways of the cosmopolitan traveler.

"Do you think we will pull out on time?" she began the conversation.

"Oh, sure," he said. She was surprised his accent was American. "They always pull out on time. Especially when there are submarines."

"Why should a ship be punctual for the sake of the submarines?"

Blackford Oakes looked at her pert face, and frank, inquisitive eyes accented by her austerely coiled braids. "Because"—he spoke just a little less casually than before—"there are escort vessels, and it is quite a muddle if every boat decides for itself when to start out."

She did not answer, but looked at her lumpy watch. She would wait—for what, later at Smith College, the philosophy professor would tell her is called "empirical verification." And, in fact, at exactly one forty-five in the afternoon the gangplank was pulled, the whistles and horns blew, the crowd at the pier interrupted its waving and yelling, and her parents rejoined her. Before skipping off she turned to the boy, munching a fresh apple and looking very self-satisfied.

"You were right."

He smiled—it was a splendid smile, warm, animated. He reached into the brown paper bag and said, "Here, have an apple." She looked up at her mother, who nodded her head, so she took it and said, "Thank you," and then with her free hand grabbed her straw hat, which almost blew away as the great steamship slid out of the lee of the quay.

By the time Erika was sixteen her father was well known in the academic world and now held down a chair at Brown University, delivering learned, acidulous, witty lectures that would become famous. There was now money enough to pay the tuitions at the Ethel Walker School and, later, Smith College, and in her senior year her father gave her a secondhand car which Erika rejoiced in, traveling about New England tirelessly, to celebrate the end of gas rationing. She took on every challenge, competing for the classics prize, the philosophy prize, winning one, placing second in the other. In her junior year the dean had called her in to ask whether she would consider *not* competing for the Russian, German, French, and Italian prizes. She had won them all in her freshman and sophomore years, and now the teachers were finding it hard to persuade anyone to compete against so certain a winner. Erika said she would have to consult with her father, whose instructions to her had been to enter every competition. He wrote back and told his daughter that, noblesse oblige, she should allow other girls a chance at the prizes, but if she wanted to compete for the big Prix Giscard she might focus her energies on winning it. This prize went annually to four girls selected from applicants throughout the country to study in Paris, all expenses paid, and its renewal, now that the war was over, had recently been advertised.

Erika competed and won without much difficulty, and without causing resentment. Though serious by nature, she could participate in gaiety and do so convincingly. Her friends now accepted matter-of-factly her prolix virtuosity and had long since ceased to think anything about it. She was like the boy or girl at graduation whose name recurs and recurs and who has to walk up to the headmaster fifteen times before he is done collecting the silver: Best Athlete, Best Student Leader, Best Scholar—Best Prig, often as not. But Erika got on well with her friends, all of whom assumed that she would either go on to become a professor of almost anything, or else that a very gallant and very rich man, desiring a beautiful girl of exotic

180

manner and prodigious attainments, would take her off and make her duchess of something where she would preside over salons for a couple of generations of Princes of Wales. At home the night before leaving, in the comfortable house in Providence exploding with books and order, she actually managed to catch her mother's and father's attention at dinner by saying, "Are you glad we won the war, Father?"

Chandinoff, dressed in his velvet smoking jacket, finished chewing what he had in his mouth.

"I am glad we won. I am sorry *they* won. I am sorry that they now occupy Eastern Europe. I predict they will still occupy East Europe one, maybe two years from now."

Erika remembered the night her father so greatly embarassed her during her last year at Ethel Walker, before two friends spending the weekend in Province. It was the critical weekend when at first Stalingrad was reported captured by the Germans, then the Russians were reported holding out. As the radio reports came in the girls cheered on all the news of Russian advances, and hissed all the news of German advances. It soon became uncomfortably clear that their host, Professor Dimitri Chadinoff, was unmistakably cheering the other side. Alice, who was well known for her ingenuous candor, looked up during the late morning and said, "Professor Chadinoff, are you pro-Nazi?"

"No, Alice," said Chadinoff. "Permit me, are you pro-Communist?"

"Why, no," said Alice.

"Very well, then?" Chadinoff's eyebrows

lifted, and he was evidently prepared to change the subject.

"But we are at war with the Nazis."

"Who is 'We?" Chadinoff replied.

"Well, Americans . . ." Then she gasped. She hadn't thought about it before. She turned to Erika, hoping for help. But Erika's father was in charge.

"We carry Nansen passports, Alice. They are a kind of diplomatic Man-Without-a-Country passports. We are grateful to the United States for its hospitality and express our gratitude by paying exactly the same taxes we would be paying if we had been born and raised in Topeka, Kansas. We have not taken any oath to support America's foreign policy and, my dear Alice, if truth were told, no one's reputation for intelligence could survive the taking of such an oath."

Alice was a fair student of biology, a little backward in languages, including English, so she thought at least she could charm the famous linguist by trotting up a phrase from her Ethel Walker School French: "Well, Professor, *chacun à son goût.*"

"Chacun à sa bêtise," Professor Chadinoff retorted and returned to his reading.

That afternoon, when her guests were dressing for the Brown-Yale football game, Erika pleaded illness, sending her date off alone to the game. She then turned to her father as she had never done before and, fire in her eyes and a great ball of resentment in her stomach, she blurted out: "I think what you did to Alice was disgust-

ing! Doesn't it matter to you that one million—
one million—Russians have died in the last two
months defending Stalingrad? They can't be as
mad as you are at Communism for having taken
away *their* landed estates!" She flung the door
shut, went up to her room, locked the door, and
wept. She wept fitfully through the afternoon and
her intelligence alerted her, after a while, that her
discomposure was deeply rooted. She did not
know exactly what was the cause or causes of it,
and now, three years later, she still did not know.
Characteristically, neither her father nor her
mother had ever again alluded to the incident.

This time she said, "Father, do you believe
in God?"

"No. But I believe in some of the things
attributed to God."

"Like what?"

"Like the Ten Commandments. Most of the
Ten Commandments. One or two are arguable,
explained by Jewish cultural idiosyncrasies."

"What do you believe in?"

"I believe in the life of the mind, and in human fancy, and in the everlasting struggle against
vulgarity."

"What do you mean, you believe in *the struggle against vulgarity*? Does that mean you believe
that that struggle is going to happen, or does that
mean that you believe that that struggle is worth
winning?"

"It is obviously worth winning. But it will
never be won. That is why I qualify it by calling it
an everlasting struggle."

"The Communists believe more than you do."

"That is certainly correct. So do African witch doctors."

Her mother was following the argument, but was now distracted by something, and she could not remember what it was. She had mistakenly begun the meal by serving the chocolate soufflé because she had found that, by misreckoning, it was done when they sat down, and obviously would not wait, whereas the lamb would.

"As a matter of fact," broke in Anna Chadinoff, her points of reference not immediately clear either to her husband or to her daughter, "lamb will wait very nearly indefinitely."

"What did you say, Anna?"

"I said that lamb would wait very nearly indefinitely."

"Do you mean, like the everlasting struggle?"

"What do you mean by that, dear?"

Chadinoff, knowing when the door was finally closed on any possibility of nexus, pronounced the chocolate soufflé quite excellent, and wondered whether they would now be served kippered herring.

No, Anna said. Now there would be lamb. And Chadinoff then understood. Erika understood. God, if he existed, now understood. Erika thought that, really, her parents were quite splendid, but how wonderful it would be to be gone from them for a while: for a long while, she thought that night.

Erika arrived in Paris in the awful, depressed postwar season three years after the war. She was loaded down with letters from her father and mother commending her to the attentions of their numerous friends in the expatriate world. She began dutifully with the first names on the list: Mr. and Mrs. Valerian Sverdlov. Mme. Sverdlov was a niece of Tolstoy; her husband had commanded a czarist cavalry regiment; both had known Erika's parents since childhood and both greeted her warmly once communication was effected.

This proved difficult because although Erika rang the telephone number her father had given her and, after a few days during which there was never an answer, checked it against the telephone book to find it correct, *still* there was no answer. So she sent a letter and got back a prompt invitation to come to tea, which the following day she did. Mr. Sverdlov, quite bald, with a mustache, bad teeth, pink cheeks and twinkling eyes, was always laughing, and he rejoiced at seeing his beloved Chadinoff's daughter, rejoiced at being able to speak in Russian to her, and several times emptied his glass of vodka to celebrate the general celebration. His wife, though more reserved, was also warm. She worked as a tutor in Russian and found now in the postwar world a considerably increased demand for her services. Beginning the following week, Valerian would return to his job as driver of an American Express tourist bus. Erika was faintly surprised to learn this, but then reminded herself that, until a few years ago, her father worked as a concierge and her mother as a dishwasher.

When she alluded to the difficulty in getting through to the Sverdlovs on the telephone, he laughed and laughed and said several times that the French were the *silliest* people in the *whole* world. You see—he adopted a conspiratorial voice—I was a *collaborator!* Yes! I worked for the Germans! One day I traveled with the German Army as far as St. Petersburg. Not *into* St. Petersburg, but as *far* as St. Petersburg—and there—he stood theatrically, and waved his arm forward, "there from the hilltop I could see—my house. My father's house. My grandfather's house. Where your father played with me when we were boys."

But, he said, that was as far as they had got. Russian resistance proved effective and the retreat began. He returned to Paris and resumed his clerical work as translator of Russian war documents and radio communications—it was understood he would work only against the Soviets.

"Now," he said with delight to Erika, who struggled to conceal her chagrin at her father's friend's collaborationist activity but little by little was caught up by his ebullience—"now," he said, "the French know that I was a collaborator. And *they* know that *I* know that *they* know that I was a collaborator. But!"—he stood again and howled with glee, his mustache high over his white, crooked teeth, his wispy hair tousled, cheeks pink with mirth and stimulation—"they cannot prove it. And the reason they cannot prove it is that before the Germans left, I said to Colonel Strassbourg: 'My dear Colonel, you can have very little use for my file in Berlin, so be a good chicken and let me have it.' And he did, and I burned it, right there"—he pointed to the shabby little fireplace with the four pieces of coal warming, or trying to warm, the whole apartment.

"So what do these silly Frenchmen do? They take away my telephone! They do not tell me: 'Mr. Sverdlov, you are a traitor, and we cannot send you to jail, and we cannot send you to the firing squad, so we are going to take away your telephone.' No. They just disconnect it. Everything else is the same. And when I ask about it they just shrug their shoulders and say I must wait!" He laughed at this trivialization of treason, although of course he too, Erika knew, would have used the same arguments her father used about the Nansen passport, so she did not catechize him. She enjoyed him most unabashedly, and he offered to take her the next Monday to Chartres; and, on the bus, where he wore a chauffeur's cap without any apparent self-consciousness, he buoyantly situated her in the seat directly across from him and they chatted as he drove. When, like her parents, he had run out of money, he applied to American Express for a job as a bus driver, stressing his knowledge of French (perfect), German (excellent), English (shaky), and then he qualified his application by saying he would be interested in only a single route: to Chartres. His employer was puzzled until Sverdlov explained that the cathedral at Chartres was the most beautiful sight in the world, more beautiful even than any sight in Russia, and if he was destined to drive a bus every day he might as well drive it to the most beautiful sight in the world.

"Why not?" he exclaimed, his whole face and shoulders rising in interrogation. When after a month the dispatcher told him that that day he would have to drive the bus to the cathedral at Rheims, Sverdlov said that under no circumstances would he go to Rheims—the cathedral there, for all its reputation and pretensions, being simply inadequate. American Express tried suggesting that he was, in fact, under no obligation to join the tourists in the cathedral, but Sverdlov was so affronted by the implied mechanization of his role, American Express quickly retreated, undisposed to discipline the driver who was the favorite of the tourists. By now, even after the war's long interruption, his title to Chartres was secure and no one would question it, he said happily. Later, in a whisper, he told Erika that after seeing the cathedral, he would take her to a little Russian delicatessen where they would have some vodka and some cheese and sausage while the other tourists had their regular lunch.

Erika's reaction, on seeing the cathedral, gratified Sverdlov: she found it was everything Henry Adams said it was, in the book she was assigned to read by one of her art professors at Smith; and other things that Henry Adams had failed to say it was. She asked Sverdlov, whom now she was told to call Valerian Babeyevich, whether he had read Adams' book on Mont St. Michel and Chartres, and he replied that he had not, that he did not want to read about the cathedral, only look at it. Erika mused that her father, who would much prefer reading about a cathedral to seeing it, would scarcely approve of Valerian's attitude: and in the course of the afternoon she discovered that Valerian really knew nothing about her father's career except, vaguely, that he had become a success of sorts in America.

"When he writes me letters"—Valerian laughed, as he tipped his fifth jigger glass of vodka down his throat—"he writes about obscure poets or writers he has discovered, and always he forgets to tell me about Anna and his darling and beautiful daughter."

He looked at his watch and said that they must go back to the bus now, the tourists would be assembling as instructed. He insisted to Erika on paying the bill, which proved painless when the old Russian shopkeeper in turn insisted on refusing payment from his old friend, who had brought that day such an "elegant"—he bowed to Erika— "and beautiful daughter of an old friend."

From the American Express bus terminal it was a short walk to the apartment Erika rented at Rue Montalembert: a bedroom, study/living room/dining room, kitchen, and bath—for thirty-five U.S. dollars per month, on the Left Bank almost but not quite overlooking the river. From there she could walk to the Sorbonne, and did now regularly, even though the weather had turned cold, attending classes in philosophy and the history of art. The classrooms were cold and dirty, the students poorly dressed, and on the faces of many of the boys there was a premature gauntness of expression. Erika noticed

189

a sharp divergence in the attitude of the students. Half, perhaps more than half, diligently took notes on what the instructor said, particularly in the class taught by Jean-Paul Sartre, who when he spoke did so with a precisionist's nonchalance, a quiet and perfect engine of volubility whose words, transcribed, could have formed completed chapters of books, indeed regularly did so. But other students, though they might make a note occasionally, were studiedly skeptical, as if to communicate to the instructor that no presumptive respect was owed either to him or to the words he spoke. During the exchanges these students, when they said anything at all, tended to challenge this or that generality of the teacher, or ask whether, by this inflection, he had meant to say such and such. M. Argoud, who had written a history of art, answered questions, however provocative, neither with indignation nor with servility. If the question was barbed he would ignore those parts of it that were provocative, giving unadorned answers to whatever was left. "Would you not say, M. Argoud, that you slip into confusion when you suggest there are similarities between the theoretical defenses of abstractionism and of primitivism?"

"The similarities to which I alluded are listed in the chapter on Braque in my book."

Next question.

M. Argoud did not care for his students, and did not care if his students cared for him. But he would do what he had contracted to do so that as quickly as possible he might get back to his own work. He broke his rhythm on one occasion to notice Erika, with her tweed skirt, blouse, and sweater, her full bosom—perhaps she reminded him of something Braque had said, or painted, or loved? Erika looked at the teacher, still young, but utterly unconcerned. If he could look ten years younger by snapping his fingers, she thought, he would probably not take the trouble. But to inquire into the authenticity of a Del Sarto in a museum, he had devoted seven months—and came up calmly with the pronouncement that it was a forgery. Erika guessed that, on the whole, M. Argoud would probably prefer coming up with a forgery than with an original: the whole exercise would somehow reinforce his misanthropic inclinations.

Except, of course, for Paul. M. Argoud obviously cared for Paul. Paul's (infrequent) questions were answered in a tone of voice distinctly different. M. Argoud was even seen, on at least one occasion, talking casually with Paul in the cold, high-ceilinged corridor. Since Paul was young and beautiful and intense, Erika wondered whether the relationship was unnatural, but when Paul sat next to her in the cafeteria one day at lunch and they fell to talking she discovered that Paul Massot was François Argoud's half-brother and that they had belonged to the same guerilla unit during the resistance. Both had been tortured in the same cellar at the same time, she would learn weeks later when she and Paul were lovers, and Paul whispered to her early one morning, stroking her breasts with his chin, that if he had known her then, he'd have probably told them everything, done anything, espoused any creed, incurred any risk, performed any treachery, lest they deprive him of her, his Erika, no one else's, ever, ever—his rhythms were matching now the words, and her responses were elatedly fused to his own, as he repeated the word, ever, ever, ever, ever, ever, more excitedly, more quickly, almost shouting now, as she closed her eyes and moaned, then opened them to observe her beautiful Paul, EVER!

Whenever he left her apartment, whether to fetch a book in the library or perform an errand or check the mailbox, there was prolonged discussion. Exactly how long would he be gone? Twelve minutes? That was too long, Erika said, and Paul would agree. And he would say that perhaps if he ran both ways he could manage it in eleven minutes. As often as not, Erika would suggest that the safest way to handle the problem would be for both of them to leave together. His solemn young face would light up with pleasure and, taking her hand, he would open the door, pausing on the stairway, now for a passionate, now for a tender kiss.

Paul Massot's stepfather, the elder Argoud, had died during the war. Since he wasn't shot by the Nazis and did not die in a military prison, he didn't qualify for the Vermork; but he was listed officially as a "casualty" of the war because, suffering from diabetes, he was medically undernourished owing to scarcities that were an undisputed result of the war; so that his impoverished widow, Paul's mother, received a little pension on which Paul now drew a few francs every month to finish the studies interrupted when, at seventeen, he withdrew from the university to devote himself to the resistance.

He had gone then, instinctively, to his austere, normally unapproachable half-brother, older by eight years, with whom he associated during the nearly three years before the American troops, General Leclerc heading the procession, entered Paris. There were long, tedious hours of joint activity. On one occasion, Argoud and Paul were responsible for checking the movements of a Gestapo official. They huddled in a single room across the street with their stopwatches and notebooks, clocking the monster's goings and comings for nearly three months. In the long stretches of inactivity Argoud undertook two missions, the first to teach his half-brother something about the esthetic history of the world: it would prove, before long, a substantial history of the Renaissance. And the second, to convince Paul that the only hope for humanity lay in acknowledging the truths of Marxist analysis and historiography, and in backing the Soviet Union's lonely, and acknowledgedly often brutal efforts to export to the world that which only Russia was experiencing.

Paul knew about Erika's background, and had even read some of the works by Chadinoff, whose fame had come to France. Neither he nor she was perturbed by Chadinoff's reactionary politics. Why should one expect Chadinoff to feel or reason otherwise? Paul said. How natural! If it were *easy* for the world to accept communism, it would have done so by now. The forces aligned in opposition to communism aren't merely those specifically identified by Marx. There are all those other accretions of man: his nostalgia, his fear of the unknown, his conservative temptation to resist change.

"But, Paul, there *are* other things." They were at dinner, in their favorite restaurant where, unless instructed otherwise, the waiter brought them the same appetizer, the same entrées, the same house wine, and the same bill, but no longer any cigarettes (Paul having told Erika she must give up smoking), which came to seventy-five U.S. cents apiece. "There's the suffering in Russia."

"There has been suffering everywhere. Look at the suffering in Germany and Italy. Even in the United States, one hundred years advanced over Russia industrially, they could not manage their Depression. Stalin is not a gentle man, and he has made many mistakes, and will make other mistakes. But unlike the Catholic Church, the Marxists do not claim infallibility for their leader. We claim only that history has imposed a responsibility on him, and we must help him discharge that responsibility. There is no way of getting around the fact, Erika, that millions of Russians fought for Stalin and for their country: and no one disguised from them that they were fighting for communism. Of course it has been bitter and hard. And it will be harder and more bitter if we are to prevent the forces in opposition from gainsaying the effort of all those years, all those lives, because"—he dug into his meatloaf with his knife: he never used a fork—"that is exactly what

194

will happen if, just because the formal fighting is over, we think of ourselves as other than at war."

Erika heard the arguments but could not say, really, that she had listened to them. All through her life she had resisted only that one intellectual challenge, an examination of the ideology that had banished and impoverished her father. She did not, really, want to go into the arguments now, though she would if Paul wanted her to. She would do anything Paul wanted her to. She could not imagine that it was possible to know such joy as she knew, whether at the table listening to him, seeing his straight dark hair fallen over his brow, his sad brown eyes, his pointed and delicate mouth deftly retrieving the morsels of food from the knife, his long tapered fingers, explaining his position to her, sensitive to every sound, every inflection, or in bed during those long bouts of ardor and tranquility. Or sitting next to him, listening to his unprepossessing but acknowledgedly brilliant half-brother. She could admire her father, but she could not ever really *believe* in him. In Paul she believed—entirely. And she knew that she would never betray him. If it should happen, in a final philosophical revelation, that his ideology was wrong, and the contrary of it right, it would matter far less that she had taken the wrong course, than that she had followed him. He was her ideology, her idyll, her lover, her friend, her counselor, her Paul, forever forever forever.

"Do you understand what I'm talking about?"

"I understand what I need to understand. If

you want me to study Marxism, of course I'll study Marxism. And"—she smiled at him—"I'll even win the Marxist Prize if you want me to."

No, he did not want her to study Marxism, said. He would like it if she read Marx, but that didn't matter so much; he, Paul, would tell her everything she needed to know about politics. What he did not want was for her to associate openly with Marxists, because that would put her in the way of unnecessary harassments. The anti-Communist French were mobilizing against the French Communists, and there were divisions already even among men and women who had worked together during the resistance. The Croix de Feu, which drew from the militant wing of the anti-Communist coalition, were talking violence. The forces of American facism were everywhere. There was no need to alert anyone, save his own special friends, to her new political allegiance. He himself had been careful not to enroll in the Party, and not to attend any of its official functions— François, though himself an active Party member, had so counseled him.

And thus it was left, during that golden autumn. One day every week he was away, by himself, pursuing duties which, he told her, he could neither neglect nor explain. One other evening per week he required her to share with his political intimates, who, after the briefest experience with her, were all of them happy that Paul, whose star was so manifestly ascendant, had found so accomplished and lovely a companion. She liked especially Gerard, and when one day he actually stopped smoking long enough to make it

possible to see through the smoke to his wry
face, she was surprised to notice how much he
looked like her own father, though younger of
course. He presided over the meetings, which is
what they really were, and there was a worldiness
but also a spirituality in his analysis of the French
contemporary scene that touched Erika, which
she found wanting in her own father. Gerard was
especially kind to Erika and one day surprised
her by addressing her in a Russian which, though
clearly not native, betrayed a convincing knowledge of Russia, a knowledge the details of which
Erika did not feel free to probe: these were, after
all, clandestine meetings. She did not know Gerard's surname, nor where he lived.

It had proved difficult to locate Gerard, but
finally Erika succeeded in doing so, exactly one
week after the day when, groceries in hand, she
had opened the door, exhilarated at the prospect
of seeing Paul lying there as she so regularly came
on him, dressed only in his undershorts, reading
easily in the dim light. He was there exactly as she
had anticipated, but the book rested flat on his
olive-skinned chest and his head was slightly
turned, by a bullet that had entered his brain.

Erika was released from the hospital just in
time to attend the funeral three days later. Scant
attention was given to the extraordinary shooting
—execution?—of young Paul Massot. Paris was
inured to death and terror, after five years of it.
The detectives came, but eventually they left,
without formal findings. Still white when she

tapped the doorknob of Gerard's apartment, she waited, and Gerard came and, on opening the door, beheld a grown woman ten days after knowing her as a university schoolgirl.

"Who did it?" she asked.

"I don't know," he said.

"You do know"—she looked him in the eyes, and the psychic pressure was greater than the torturer's that nightmare night in 1944. He yielded.

"It was almost certainly the work of the Croix de Feu. Paul was assigned to penetrate the organization." Gerard held out his arms to her but she was past tears, and simply took his extended hand in hers and said goodbye, and told him that if ever he needed her services, he might have them.

13

Rufus and Singer were seated as before. Leaning back slightly in his chair, Rufus began.

"We didn't think it opportune to tell you before, Blackford. The KGB is on to you."

Blackford was astonished and annoyed that he had not been told immediately upon the Agency's learning about it, but he calmed himself that there must be a reason. He found himself defending his professional behavior.

"So help me, I can't figure it out. Where did they pick up the trail? London?"

"We don't know, just plain don't know," Rufus said as though confronting an academic problem. "London, likely. Conceivably in Washington.

Now let me give you some background. You arrived at St. Anselm's just about the time Wintergrin began to get red-hot. On October first, the Soviet ambassador called on the Secretary of State and said, in what was apparently a pretty ugly scene—it was reported right away to the President—that—perhaps you will be pleased to hear *this*, Blackford—said that one of our 'top operatives' had arrived physically at the scene of the Wintergrin operation, 'confirming their suspicion' that the Wintergrin movement had been our enterprise right along. The Secretary of State demanded to know whom they were talking about Their reply: 'The same man you sent to London last year.' Go ahead, the Secretary said. Well, they demanded the United States 'withdraw' the whole Wintergrin operation, or else they would 'rise to the challenge.' He didn't of course specify (a) what he meant by 'withdrawing the operation,' or (b) what he meant by 'rising to the challenge.' The Director, reached by telephone instants after the ambassador left, told the Secretary: Sure, we have somebody at St. Anselm's, and Yes, it happens to be the same guy who did the job in London last year. So though your name was never mentioned by the Russians—by them *or* by us— we concluded—obviously—that they know about you, since there isn't anybody else on our team up there at St. Anselm's.

"Now, we've told them—maybe fifty times? —maybe a hundred times?—that Wintergrin *isn't ours,* that we penetrated the operation not *to help it,* but to assess where it was going and, if possible, to discourage it as reckless. Either they

don't believe us or—much, *much* more likely—
they simply *pretend* they don't believe us. It makes
it easier for them to press their demands. And
you now know what those demands are."

Blackford looked over at Singer. He was
rocking his chair on its hind legs slowly, forward
and back, in unconscious rhythm with the ca-
denced sentences of Rufus, who moved only his
lips.

"Now, we finally agreed to go along on the
proposition that Wintergrin must not come to
power and that the interests of world peace are
better served by neutralizing him before he wins
an election rather than trying to do so later. That
much you know. But we have also been telling
the Russians it isn't any more *our* responsibility
to get rid of him than it is theirs. They keep
coming back at us with the argument that your
presence in St. Anselm's suggests the whole operation is ours. At the *tenth* session with the Secretary Gromyko finally backed down—but only
to the extent of conceding that it was arguably
true that *at this point* we didn't want Wintergrin
to win but only because the Soviets had caught us
and reacted 'as you would expect.' But the idea
—they keep insisting—was ours in embryo, as
witness our incestuous relationship with the Wintergrin enterprise. Then they make their final
point: that as a *mechanical* matter, only *we* can
get inside St. Anselm's and dispose of Wintergrin
smoothly, because only *we* have a trusted agent
within the enclosure. That," Rufus concluded, "is
why Miss Chadinoff's bug is a major development."

"Have you established she's theirs?" Blackford was numb.

"No. We've been working on it on all fronts ever since your call to Singer. It's a tough one. Her background is pure pedigree. Dimitri Chadinoff's daughter: It's as if Joe McCarthy eloped with Priscilla Hiss. The odds are heavily against it. We've sent people to Smith College, to Paris, where she went right after graduating from Smith, to Geneva, Rome, and New York, where she's done translations for various UN agencies, and to Mürren, where her mother and father live. It's too early for all the reports to have come in and of course we may not find anything. Conceivably she's working for Wintergrin—"

"I doubt that," Blackford interrupted. "It isn't possible Wintergrin would treat me the way he does, or tell me the things he tells me if he thought there was any doubt—listen, Rufus, here's something I got from Wintergrin at dinner. *Ulbricht* has reported to Moscow that East Germany would unite against the Russians if their army moved in."

"Very interesting," Rufus said. "Very interesting; and very interesting that Wintergrin told you about it. He shouldn't have done that. Could blow one of his men in East Berlin. Hmm . . . But on the other point: nothing—including Wintergrin's complicity in the tap—should be excluded on the basis of personal hunch. Remember, Wintergrin may not himself have authorized the bug. It could have been done by one of his security people, the fellow Wagner. You said that Hallam Springs says it's a highly professional installation?

"Right."

"Well, the only concrete information we have is this: It *isn't* the Adenauer people. We talked to their top man. They do have somebody trying to work into the St. Anselm situation, but he hasn't yet succeeded. And anyway, their agent isn't Miss Chadinoff."

"Ollenhauer?"

"A technical possibility, but remote. After all, you're hardly an obvious pipeline into the Wintergrin operation. As far as they know, you spend all your time working on the church, and though you have a nice thing going with Wintergrin personally, there are twenty people closer to the Wintergrin political operation whose phones they'd tap before yours.

"No, it's got to be either the Wintergrin people, or the Soviets. And it matters that we find out quickly. Because if it's the Commies, the negotiations between the Secretary and Gromyko change —to our advantage. When next would you probably be seeing her?"

"I'm having dinner with her tonight. Would you like me to strap her into a polygraph, tell her it's a new simultaneous-translation gadget?"

Rufus went on as if there had been no interruption. "There's no way at the moment to establish who she's working for except by the process of elimination. So remember the rule: assume the worst, until something else is proved. We should get reports from the field later today or tomorrow."

Singer Callaway interposed. "There is the direct approach, Rufus. Black could go to Wintergrin and tell him there's a bug in his room, that it leads to Erika's room, and what the hell's going on? Wintergrin calls in Wagner and they either own up, pleading routine security precautions; or else they deny it convincingly, in which case we know Erika is a Soviet agent."

Rufus looked at Singer, disappointment written on his face.

"The disadvantages would appear to me critical. One: What happens then? We are probably at this point better off with Erika Chadinoff in the picture than out. Two: What if Wintergrin's security officer is lying—and he did install the bug? The very fact that you discovered a highly sophisticated bug would suggest to him that you have certain skills alien to those of a construction engineer. Resulting, three, in casting suspicion on you, which is the last thing we can stand.

"No," he concluded, "that's out."

He paused. Oh, God, Blackford thought, we're going into one of those trances. There was nothing to do but wait it out.

It didn't last too long. "Do you remember the Teller-Freeze Bypass, Blackford?"

"Of course."

"It worked in London. A suitable variant could be useful to us here. We need to discover— and we don't have much time—how she is reporting back to her people. If we're lucky enough to find her making contact with a known agent, then it doesn't matter what she says. But if she is passing along information to someone unknown to us, her passing on a special piece of goofy information could help tip us off."

"That's not going to be easy, Chief. I've been using my bugged telephone only to call Colonel Morley. It wouldn't be easy to be kittenish with *him*. And they must all know that Morley isn't a plant. I doubt she's even transcribing my calls to Morley and passing them on. No, whatever I shoot into the Soviet bloodstream won't be through the bug, but in conversations with her. I'll see if I can figure something out, but I don't think this arrangement is a natural for that formula . . . Let me think about it."

"Very well. But think about it fast. Meanwhile, *whoever* is going to undertake the—elimination, if it is to be undertaken"—Rufus was given to direct speech, but certain words he avoided like an undertaker—"plans for it have got to be formulated. We should come up with alternative arrangements. I don't expect you, Blackford, to come up with the definitive plan—that's for Spring and Pulling in consultation with us. But no effective plan can be conceived, let alone brought about, without you."

A day earlier, Blackford would have made a mordant remark. No longer. After this long introspective evening he had come to the conclusion that whatever he elected to do or not do himself, he would refrain from emphasizing his moral superiority over his associates. Either Blackford Oakes would cooperate or Blackford Oakes would not cooperate. He had said yesterday, after the three awful hours with Singer, that he would reserve a final decision on whether he would be willing, as he now termed it, to "trip the wire." He preferred the expression "push the button," which phrase, however, he shrank from both as a cliché and as presumptuous: the buttons, after all, were being pushed in Washington. So, pursuant to his resolution, he spoke now only in professional terms.

"I was a little brusque with the . . . electricians last night. I've already apologized to them. I'll give them the help they need. My principal function—I mean, depending on the final arrangement—has been discharged."

"What do you mean by that?"

"I mean I got them their passes, so they can go in and out of the courtyard. As chapel electricians they get to go anywhere they want. I doubt there'd be any problem if they said they wanted to go right into the castle to look at electrical connections, all that sort of thing. Mention work on St. Anselm's chapel around there and you can do anything you want. So if the 'creative' work is going to be done by Spring and what's-his-name, they've got themselves a pretty free rein. I'm not sure anybody would ask questions if they started constructing an electric chair in Wintergrin's study. What else am I supposed to do?"

Rufus said, "Answer any questions they have. And"—he got up from his chair—"put your own ingenuity at our disposal. You haven't exactly performed as a creative artist."

Blackford decided to say nothing.

He was back at St. Anselm's at four, spent two hours at the chapel, returned to the inn, washed, and killed an hour reading the afternoon papers from Essen, Hamburg, and Munich. Singer had suggested he call at three minutes after eight, ahead of the dinner date, to a special pay phone number in the event there was information from the field.

There was. Erika Chadinoff, the Paris people reported, once had a torrid love affair with a young undercover Communist activist who had been murdered. The culprit was never caught. The deceased's dossier had been carefully examined by M. Raymond de Guest, chief of the political section of the Paris police, who wrote at the time—1948—that in his opinion it was a political vendetta, possibly the work of anti-Communist resistance leaders. There had been four "executions" during that fall for which there was no apparent motive. Two of those killed had been members of the anti-Communist Croix de Feu. (One had been pushed off the first story of the Eiffel Tower at night by a man who thought himself unobserved, but the entire operation had been seen by an amorous young couple whose tender extrication from one another caused a delay in shouting alarm that made chase unfeasible. The other, an excellent swimmer, was mysteriously drowned off Nice. He was wearing contact lenses. But his friends reported that he invariably removed his lenses before going out to swim.) Rome reported that Erika had been briefly in the news in 1949. She was mistress to the fiery young Christian Democrat legislator who in the critical election of 1948 had proposed the illegalization of the Communist Party and very nearly carried the day. He was now in prison, convicted of demanding a kickback from the wages of a translator he had placed with the UN Secretariat. The chief witness, indeed the only witness against him, was the translator herself—Erika Chadinoff. The prosecution had presented checks, made out to Erika by her UN employers but deposited to the account of the defendant, Giovanni Buegos. He swore ignorance of the transactions. Asked how he could account for his swollen bank account, he had replied that eight hundred dollars over six months was not all that conspicuous, and he hadn't even noticed it. Five to seven years. His political movement might as well have been convicted along with him.

"Sounds like what we're looking for, don't you think?"

"Yes. But her *parents!* Did you check out the story that her father suggested she apply for this job?"

"We got someone in to see the old boy—a 'reporter' from the Chicago *Tribune.* Chadinoff likes the *Tribune,* told the reporter he found Colonel McCormick's recent charge that Rhodes scholars are picked with the subversive strategic purpose of effecting an amalgamation between Britain and the U.S. hilarious, but he believes this is a good age to cultivate mutual suspicion. The reporter represented himself as doing a piece on Wintergrin's staff, and obviously his daughter Erika was the best-known member of the staff among the international set. He asked whether M. Chadinoff approved her working for Wintergrin. He said he certainly did approve. So much so that when she told her parents she was going to work for Wintergrin, if necessary as a volunteer, the old boy said if there was no money for her salary, he would stake her."

"Well, that probably does it. She lied to Wintergrin. She told him, and he told me, that the whole thing was her father's idea. So what do we do?"

"What do *you* do? I don't know. I know what we do over here. We're moving all this information to Washington right now. I wouldn't be surprised if the Secretary decides to confront Gromyko with it today."

"In that case she's bound to find out pretty soon that I've blown her cover. Although"—he mused—"the Soviets are even more secretive than you people. Sorry—I mean us people. You didn't tell *me* I was blown until I confronted you with the telephone bug. Maybe they won't tell Erika we know about her. No way of saying. Still, I'd better act fast if there's going to be any element of surprise. I'll let you know how it goes. Same number tomorrow?"

"No." There was a pause as Singer—Blackford could almost see him—turned the pages of his notebook. He read out the new telephone number. "One of us will be in. What are you going to do?"

"I don't know. So long, Singer." In a way he could not account for, Blackford felt better. Perhaps because at least over the next period he would be exerting himself to outwit a Soviet agent, leaving to one side, if only temporarily, the question of how to dispose of the Soviets' most formidable enemy.

She was dressed in blue and wore gold on her ears and around her neck and wrists. There was a trace of red in her light-brown hair and, Blackford thought, a trace of pout in her lips he had not noticed before. Her eyes were a working blue, never still, and she smiled confidently as, putting down the newspaper, he rose, took her hand and affected something of a bow, and said,

"Not bad for a little Nansen girl."

She smiled and they walked out together to Blackford's car, parked across the street.

"Where are we going?"

"I ran into a nice place the other night at Gummersbach. Have you been there?"

"No."

"I think you'll enjoy it."

Driving down the highway he said, "The speech at Bremen went well, I take it?"

"Very well. Did you see the papers?"

"All but the Polish papers. How did they take the declaration of war?"

She laughed. "They were very good sports."

"It does rather give them . . . status, don't you think? Has anyone ever declared war on you?"

"Nobody would dare. Nansen would send the marines and destroy them."

"Nemo me impune lacessit. There, I bet I've said something you can't translate."

Again she laughed. "Silly goose, as they used

210

to say in London. That is the motto of one of the Queen's orders, I forget which. 'No one crosses me with impunity.' *Nemo* means no one, as in Captain Nemo."

"Really, Erika, you are an awful exhibitionist. I should think it would be very difficult for anyone other than Einstein to be married to you. I suppose you know all about relativity?"

"I know everything I need to know about relativity."

"Do you know what E$=$mc^2 means?"

"Yes. Hiroshima."

"What's the difference between Hiroshima and Vorkuta?"

He felt her tighten, and he said to himself, *Cut it out, Oakes. This isn't your show.* Somewhere about four thousand miles away the Secretary of State and the Soviet ambassador are deciding how to handle this one. Cool it. Bang her if you want to, but if you feel like talking politics with her, go take a cold shower.

So he talked about a problem that was vexing him in the chapel and managed to engage her in the problems they were facing in the reconstruction well through the first course of herring and sour cream which—it was late—she ate avidly, injecting enough bright commentary to suggest a genuine interest in the problems he faced. Two hours later they had spoken of her experiences growing up in London, of his brief experience as a schoolboy at Greyburn, of the coincidence of his having been at the same school where Wintergrin spent so many years.

She interjected that she and her parents had

been in London at the same time, leaving right after Pearl Harbor, and Blackford said that he also had left right after Pearl Harbor. When, exactly? And they gasped at the coincidence of their both having sailed aboard the S.S. *Mount Vernon,* and suddenly Blackford remembered the little girl. Could it have been she? Her eyes shone. Of course, the handsome American blond boy with the apple! Really, he hadn't changed so much. It was only eleven years ago. Why had they not seen each other during the voyage? Ah, class distinctions. Erika's face sobered for the moment. She and her parents had traveled in third class. Blackford in tourist class, as they then called the second class, and the barriers between the classes were resolute. So that tall man with the high eyebrows was Dimitri Chadinoff! Off to overpower Harvard University's Russian Literature department! It was all intensely enjoyable, and soon became engrossing. She seemed as anxious as he to exercise her mind and her emotions removed from the epic dimensions of the drama in which she was directly involved. She asked him, when he ordered liqueurs, whether he felt lonely facing so many more months of work in so remote a part of Germany, and he said yes, he was very lonely, and was there anything she could do about it? She let her hand, underneath the table, rest on his knee, and he took it and told her she was very beautiful, and she replied that he was the most beautiful American she had ever seen, and he called for the bill, signaled for Walter and whispered to him and he brought, along with the bill, a bottle of iced champagne wrapped discreetly in

a napkin. In the car they embraced, and he
guided her hand to his excitement and she said in
a whisper, "Quickly, let's go to the inn." He
turned on the radio and, with some difficulty,
drove the half hour while she, caressing him, said
not a word. He told her to go to her room, he
would follow. In ten minutes he was there with
the champagne. She went to him gladly, ardently.
The dim light came in from the bathroom, and
they walked away from its beam to the bed, where
she lay down turning her head away while he un-
tethered himself and came down on her violently,
while she looked him in the face, squeezing him
past pain to pleasure. He breathed with difficulty
and suddenly she was Florence Nightingale dressing his wounds, bringing him back to life from
battle, triumphant in her powers, and now they
were airborne, riding high over St. Anselm's and
the forests of Westphalia, higher, higher, so high
they could see all of Germany and now Poland,
England, Russia, and soon the Atlantic and the
whole world, round and round they sped, the
pleasure ship on the nonstop intergalactic flight
until the moment came for the dive down to
that little twinkling village by the sleepy old castle
of St. Anselm's, just making it in their spaceship,
just in time to their bed, in a delirium of pleasure.
Blackford was wet. Erika tickled him lazily. And
said, hoarsely, that he wouldn't be lonely any
more. That, he said rising, deserves a drink. She
watched him as he uncorked the bottle, the devil-
ishly beautiful young man, and thought yearningly
of Paul, who had been even more beautiful.

14

"Bring him in," he told his aide on the telephone.

The Secretary, a gentleman of tidy memory, calculated that this would be the eleventh meeting with the ambassador on the matter of Wintergrin. And for the first time he felt he could, if not with assurance at least with self-confidence, take the offensive. The door opened and an aide brought in the sourdough Russian who had never been seen to smile. It had been conjectured by a cosmopolitan British journalist—sentenced by his superiors, for gross misbehavior, to three years covering the United Nations, where the Soviet ambassador worked before being reassigned to afflict Washington—that someone had told him,

when a young man, that Stalin disapproved of
smiling as revisionist; and so the ambassador
routinely added this to the other mandates from
Stalin which he faithfully executed, like never
telling the truth.

"Good morning, Mr. Ambassador."

The Secretary rose gravely and, as always,
walked over to the little sofa and sat down next
to his guest, waving the translator in the direction
of a chair in front of them. "Shall we get right to
the point?"

Nothing was better calculated to put the ambassador at ease, inasmuch as his inventory of
badinage was as painful for him to rehearse as for
the listener to hear, and in any case had been de-
pleted after the second visit.

"Now, Mr. Ambassador, the position of your
government right along has been that merely because we had an agent in the Wintergrin entourage, we were presumptively responsible for the
Wintergrin phenomenon."

"That, Mr. Secretary, and the identity of interests of your government and Count Wintergrin."

"Well, if you wish to charge my government
with the heinous offense of desiring that one day
the residents of East Germany should rule themselves, then we are guilty: as is the Human Rights
Covenant of the United Nations, which when it
came up before the Security Council, you did not
veto. But let that pass. It comes now to our attention that *you* have an agent of your own in the
Wintergrin entourage, and that that agent is at
least as well placed as our own."

The translator, who had been with the ambassador for six years now, sensed when he should slow down the rendering of a negotiator's remark, or extend the number of words necessary to convey the message. It seemed a very long time before he put into Russian what the Secretary had just said, and of course the ambassador had that much more time to compose a reply.

"You refer, perhaps, to dissenters in the Wintergrin camp who are opposed to war and fascism?"

"Well, actually, no, I *wasn't* referring to dissenters in the Wintergrin camp who are opposed to war and fascism. I was referring to Miss Erika Chadinoff."

The ambassador elected not to quibble. He knew when to quibble—indeed, could do so for weeks and months on end. To do so now would suggest that his government was keeping him in the dark. In fact, it was—the ambassador had no idea how Stalin would finally respond to a Wintergrin ultimatum if ever it were issued. But on such a matter as the Chadinoff woman it would not do to deny her role. Clearly the CIA was on to her.

"We need to protect our interests, Mr. Secretary."

"Precisely. Now, as to the plan. There is no longer any reason why it should not be executed by your agent rather than by ours."

"Your government bears primary responsibility for Count Wintergrin, and your government must, under the circumstances, take the responsibility of removing him."

The Secretary elected to be frosty, which he could do without strain.

"I shall not spend more time telling you what I told you in our ten previous meetings on the subject, namely that Wintergrin was *not* our enterprise. I will not even go beyond making the obvious historical point that if there were no occupation of East Germany there would be no cause for Wintergrin to ignite. Because of your government's threats we have had, most reluctantly, to acquiesce in a disgraceful enterprise. It clearly matters more to us than to you who should execute that plan. The reasons why it should be our responsibility rather than yours— because we had an agent in the field and you did not—now no longer apply and, accordingly, I invest you with the responsibility."

The ambassador had been in frequent communication with Stalin himself, through Ilyich of the KGB, and knew now how to cope with the hand grenade thrown to him. The directive had come from Stalin himself. He could imagine that Stalin thought it both ingenious and merry, in the sense that Stalin understood merriment.

"I had of course previously relayed to our government the objections you have so persistently made on the point in question. In the light of the current development, I am authorized to suggest a compromise."

"A compromise? How does one compromise on this point?"

"It is suggested that we settle the matter in a way sanctioned by both Russian and American tradition." He reached into his pocket, pulled out a pack of playing cards, and laid them down on the coffee table in front of him. "The low man does the job."

The Secretary's mustache writhed in indignation, contempt, mortification, and settled finally like a bull's horns aimed at his tormentor.

"Mr. Ambassador! Now I have seen everything!"

He rose and paced to his desk, looking up as if pleading at the portrait of John Jay. He could think, at first, only of such a retort as might be appropriate in a western saloon. He closed his eyes as he spoke.

"To begin with, I would need to send the cards to an X-ray technician to inspect." He almost added, "And I would need to search your sleeves." He looked at him out of the corner of his eye, to ascertain his reaction to the supreme diplomatic insult. The ambassador sat as if made of stone, which as a matter of fact, the Secretary thought, he was, really. He paused, wondering whether it would be possible to communicate to him the coarseness of the suggestion. He decided it would not. The diplomat in him took over and he wondered if he might succeed in pushing him further. He would try.

"Mr. Ambassador, if your government is willing to draw cards on the question, then your government is confessing its willingness to do the deed. In that event, what reason is there for you *not* to do it? It serves *your* direct interests, not ours."

"Ah, then, you admit that Wintergrin's enterprise serves your interests!"

The Secretary groaned.

"And besides, you agreed at our sixth session to execute the plan. There is no need, Mr. Secretary, to proceed as if we had not had our previous meetings."

"We agreed to *the plan* on the grounds that your threat, though unspecified, could mean another bloody war. But we have *not yet* agreed to have one of *our* agents carry out the plan."

"Do you wish me to return to my government and advise it that our plan—"

"—your plan—"

"—our plan is rescinded? I am prepared to do so."

The Secretary stopped, thought deeply, and returned to the sofa.

"There isn't much *time*, Mr. Ambassador. The eleventh of November is twelve days away. The efforts to bring Wintergrin down in the polls will begin, as planned, tomorrow. The arrangements for the twelfth, in the event the polls show Wintergrin's probable success, must be laid carefully. *There is no time for further bickering.*"

"Then draw a card, Mr. Secretary."

He'd have given the remaining years of his life to have there and then drawn the two of clubs. But he could not *himself* touch the cards. For reasons of . . . ethics? Pride? He could think of only a single retreat.

"Very well. Let the agents in the field do the card-drawing." There was a certain poetic consistency in this, he thought wearily. And added, "They will in any event need to be introduced to each other formally, since it is agreed that the details of the plan will be approved by your technicians and ours."

"I accept your modification," the ambassador said, reaching down and pocketing the cards. "I shall leave it to you to suggest a meeting place. Of course, not Germany. I would suggest Switzerland. If you will be good enough to advise me the place and the time, we shall deliver Colonel Boris Bolgin, from our London embassy, and Miss Chadinoff. You will supply your agent in the field, and the relevant superior."

The Secretary pressed a buzzer. Instantly his aide appeared.

"Kindly show the ambassador to his car." He rose and shook hands, unsmiling. The translator in his double-breasted black suit waited indecisively. Some diplomats shake a translator's hand always, some never, the Secretary sometimes. The Secretary extended his hand, the translator took it, and they went out.

He went to the red telephone—to report, for perhaps the sixtieth time, the most recent development. The President would talk to no one else about the Wintergrin matter, and with the Secretary he would speak about little else.

221

15

On Tuesday morning, November 2, Blackford advised Overstreet he would be going to Geneva for a few days on romantic leave, that his American girlfriend was there with her parents and that he had grievously neglected her.

Where would he be staying in case anything came up?

Blackford unbraided himself for failing to do his calisthenics as an agent, but he extemporized plausibly. He would be picking up a message at the Hotel Richemond, he said, advising him where the American party was quartered if the Richemond proved, for whatever reason, not to be to the liking of the crotchety father. In any event, he couldn't see that in the next two or three days he would be needed as the work—carpentry mostly, following designs already approved—would be routine. He would be back in plenty of time to submit to the count's weekend inspection trip.

Okay, said Overstreet, and at ten Blackford drove to the airport at Bonn and boarded a Lufthansa Convair to Geneva. From there he went by rail along the lake as far as Montreux, then switched to the MOB line, heading east up the mountainside into the Bernese Oberland. As the little train rose and the Alps descended on him, he found it irresponsible that his thoughts should turn to skiing, which he longed to attempt in the lofty Alps after several winters of rope tows in Vermont during hectic weekends away from Yale.

At the railroad station in Montreux he pick up a hastily produced official tourist brochure describing, in an English obviously torn unwillingly from the German womb, the delights of Alpine life. The Bernese Oberland Tourist Bureau had evidently decided that the area and its inhabitants needed glamorization in order to increase the tourist trade. Accordingly, as the little train chugged up the foothills Blackford read that he would be "passing next by to the grand villa of Charlie Chaplin at Vevey, past the residence of Noel Coward at Les Avants, within sight of the orange-shuttered chalet of David Niven at Château d'Oex." He ruminated that Charlie Chaplin was spending so much time these days avoiding taxation, he must perforce be neglecting the proletarian cause. After Rougemont, the brochure said, he would pass "outside of French-speaking

Switzerland," entering the Bernese Oberland at Saanen. "Go past Saanen to Gstaad," Singer Callaway had told him, because though the Chalet Haltehüs is in Saanen town limits, it's three kilometers up the road and there are no taxis until you get to Gstaad.

Beginning at Château d'Oex even the meadows facing south were covered with snow, and getting off at Gstaad Blackford was amused to see three horse-drawn sleighs available as taxis to passengers leaving the train. He had too far to go for one of these, he reasoned, and so hailed a taxi, a small diesel-Mercedes 180 and, on impulse, asked first to be taken to a ski-rental store. Two blocks from the station, down the single, bustling, Swiss-pretty main street, the car stopped opposite Hermenjat, where he bought curduroy pants and a light windbreaker and rented ski boots, skis, and poles. A skiing map of the area in hand, he followed the route the driver took to Chalet Haltehüs, "on the Saanen road, near Schönreid," Singer had said. Ten minutes later the driver pulled up to a chalet of moderately imposing size, the bottom story covered in off-white stucco, two outdoor wooden staircases leading in a squat V up to the second, clearly the principal story, encased in a cuckoo-clock wood which had probably weathered a hundred Swiss winters. He paid the driver, propped his skis against the stucco wall, walked with his suitcase up the stairs, rang the bell, and was greeted by Rufus.

Blackford, at six foot one, had to duck to clear the door lintel and was surprised by the bright burnished-wood interior. Clearly a refurbished chalet, preserving the original wood panels and beams, but freshly and even luxuriously decorated for winter clients. Rufus took Blackford's trench coat and told him the suite in the first story would be his, that the bedrooms upstairs would be taken by himself and Singer Callaway. "Singer won't be in till later tonight. We agreed there would be only the four of us at the meeting, which"—Rufus looked at his watch—"is fifty-five minutes from now."

Blackford proposed he install himself, put on country clothes, and then rejoin Rufus, which he did five minutes later.

They sat on sofas opposite the unlit fireplace.

"We will get done as quickly as possible the business between yourself and Chadinoff. Then Bolgin and I will stay on and discuss arrangements. It would not be appropriate for you to be present at that discussion. I have a rented car in the garage if you should want to go into Gstaad."

"Rufus, what are the chances the blitz you people have programmed for the next few days will topple Wintergrin in the polls?"

"Impossible to say. Blitz is the word for it. That's what we, and . . . they . . . have prepared. The polls on Thursday put Wintergrin down a little at thirty percent, Adenauer at thirty-six percent. If all goes well, the twelfth of November will pass by uneventfully."

Blackford decided to take advantage of the optimistic note to restress a formal point.

"You realize, Rufus, that I said I'd *cooperate* in the arrangements, but I have never said I'd *do* it . . . myself. I *haven't said that.*"

"I am aware of it."

"Suppose I lose the hangman's draw. What assurance do you have *I* will live up to *your* bargain?"

"I have no such assurance."

"Just so that's clear."

"That discussion is for the evening of November eleventh if the decision then is to consummate the plan."

Blackford let it drop. He found it easier to discuss philosophical matters with Singer than with Rufus. Rufus, he knew from past experience, was given to profound thought. But what wrestling he did he did internally, Blackford supposed. For Rufus ethical dialogue, unless integral to an operation, was digression—worse, distraction. If Rufus were asked to do something he thought unconscionable, what would he do? Blackford wondered. He would probably decide what was unconscionable in the context of the strategic realities, Blackford imagined. But if they did not in his opinion justify the proposal, Rufus would quite simply refuse without giving, let alone elaborating, the reasons. It was not a part of his character to muck about publicly in ambiguities. If at some future Nuremberg Rufus were convicted, he would deserve to die.

"What do we know about Bolgin?"

"Boris Andreyvich Bolgin. Age, fifty-four. Ukrainian. Young career official in the OGPU, sent to Siberia for ten years during the 1933 purge trials, released after Hitler struck, wife and daughter left him, assigned to counterintelligence, fluent in German, at home with English. During the war he served on the eastern front, then intelligence work in Sweden. A friend—if that's the word for it—of Ilyich, head of the KGB; they were classmates at the Academy in Kiev. He is—as you may have learned in London—ostensibly military attaché to the Soviet ambassador. In fact, he is chief KGB agent for western Europe."

"Have you ever met him?"

"No."

"What does he look like?"

Rufus opened his briefcase and pulled out a photograph.

"Grim-looking bastard."

"An expert studying his face might guess he had spent time in Siberia, courting frostbite."

Blackford felt chastened. Rufus left to prepare tea, declining Blackford's offer to help. Blackford looked out the frame window to the Gstaad Valley. The sky was blue in patches; the mountain profiles laced the scene behind Saanen traveling to the west of Gstaad, disappearing in the distance. And to the east was what seemed a different range coming in a few hundred yards in front of the chalet, proceeding north, again as far as the eye could see. Two cows, prodded by an old grizzled farmer with walking stick, came down the road. The bells on their collars sounded dully but distinctly, enticingly. The farmer smoked a pipe.

At least he wasn't dressed in Tyrolean garb, Blackford sighed, wondering how Switzerland managed to look so quintessentially Swiss. Maybe the farmer was the some man who wrote the brochure, moonlighting. Then he spotted the car.

It was coming up the road, and had begun to slow down. He went quickly to the kitchen door.

"They're here."

Rufus walked out with teapot and four cups on a tray. He put it down on the dining table, recessed in a corner of the living room against two windows, and walked to the door, reaching it just as Bolgin and Erika Chadinoff did. He opened it.

"My name is Rufus."

Bolgin walked ahead of Erika, took off his hat and gloves, and said, with a deep bow: "Ah, Rufus, at last. I am Boris Andreyvich Bolgin. And here is Fräulein Erika Chadinoff."

"And this is Mr. Blackford Oakes."

Bolgin unwound a long gray scarf while staring at Oakes, who, wordlessly, took Erika's rough fur coat and Bolgin's, and hung them both on the hooks at the side of the door.

"Ah, Oakes!" Bolgin said, moving toward the dining-room bench toward which Rufus motioned him and rubbing his hands as if he had stepped in from a Siberian cold. "I have looked forward to meeting you. Yes, indeed, I have looked forward to meeting you." Blackford waited tensely. Would Bolgin reveal knowledge of Blackford's activities in London?

No.

"Yes, I have looked forward to meeting you. And, of course, you know Miss Chadinoff. You are," he cackled, "colleagues!" Blackford looked Erika in the face for the first time. She showed no emotion. Why should she? She had known right along what *his* business at St. Anselm's was. And now she knew he had known her true role at St.

Anselm's that night at Gummersbach. So? What did she have to be ashamed of? She hadn't spent the evening artfully criticizing Karl Marx. She had added no private deception to the public—so to speak, the institutional—deception. Her biological attraction to him was unfeigned—indeed, she'd have had to feign the unnatural, otherwise. She had taken her private pleasure with him, during which she was acting other than as an extension of Soviet foreign policy. Bolgin had dispatched a technician to bug Blackford's room, but, listening dutifully once a day to the slender accumulation of the voice-activated tape, she had learned nothing in any way embarrassing to him. She said without a trace of stiffness, "Yes. How are you, Blackford?"

They sat and Rufus poured. Bolgin's chatter was unceasing. Clearly he thought it appropriate to talk for a while about the common concern of the "peace-loving powers," as he persisted in calling them, to avoid the horror of another war. And so he went about the awful, unconscionable gamble Count Wintergrin was taking with the fate of Europe, indeed—Bolgin was using his hands now—the fate "of all the civilized world." Blackford was never more tempted: to dissect that analysis and spit out his contempt for it. But he had rehearsed in his mind how the meeting would probably go, and he could not say he was entirely surprised by Bolgin's prolegomena. At least the CIA did not require Blackford to nod his head in agreement. Perhaps that would come later? In an age of accommodation? But relief came soon. Rufus was having none of it either.

As a matter of fact, even Erika's expression was blank as she sipped her tea and nibbled at a cracker and let Boris Andreyvich go on, and on. But when Bolgin began a story about Soviet heroism in aborting the fascist takeover of Czechoslovakia in 1948, Rufus shot out:

"Colonel Bolgin, we are here to murder a human being not history."

Bolgin reacted instantly to the snap of authority.

"Of course of course of course, my dear Rufus. Of course of course, and you must be oh so tired. Erika and I are rested. We came last night. Indeed, Erika went skiing this afternoon."

Blackford looked up with interest, and allowed himself to say, "Where?"

"On the Hornberg, up the road five kilometers."

"How was it?"

"The snow is fresh. It was . . . fine."

Rufus got up, removed the tea tray, and went to his briefcase.

"Let us be very formal about this, Colonel Bolgin. I purchased these cards in Geneva this morning and you will see that they are still sealed. It is, however, concededly within our resources, as within yours, to doctor a set of cards and make them appear to be new and unused. Do you have any suggestions?"

"Well," said Colonel Bolgin, "in truth I do —not that I mistrust you—on this occasion!" he cackled again. "But as you say, we must be stiff-upper-lip formal." Blackford did not know exactly what kind of formality that was, but waited.

231

Bolgin reached out and picked up one of the three decks, opened the seal, and spread the cards out on the table. Then he shuffled them. Blackford had seen a thorough shuffle or two in his time, but he had never seen anything quite to compare with this. It was mesmerizing. Colonel Bolgin shuffled the cards without comment for the better part of two minutes. Then he lifted the red-and-white checkered tablecloth and rolled it back halfway up the table.

"With your permission, Rufus, I will suggest that the drawing is done underneath the table-cloth. That way neither Fräulein Chadinoff nor Mr. Oakes can study up the back of the card for any"—he laughed again heartily—"identification feature. Is that satisfying?"

Rufus looked at Blackford, who nodded.

Bolgin continued. "Now, the low card loses —that means, does the necessary business. If the same number card is elected we will play by the order of bridge: first—lowest—is clubs, then dia-monds, then hearts, then spades. *D'accord*?" Both Rufus and Blackford nodded.

With a grand gesture of confidence Bolgin invited Rufus to take the pack of cards and place it on the table. Rufus's hand on the table, Bolgin replaced the tablecloth, invited Rufus to spread the cards and then to withdraw his hand.

"Now," he said, "although in the Soviet Un-ion we have the extreme equality between the sexes, shall we follow Western habits and permit the lady to draw first?"

"Go ahead," said Blackford, looking at Erika and uttering a silent prayer. He began saying to himself, "Now I lay me down to sleep . . ." but then recalled the psalm he had translated a week earlier, and jogged his memory to say,

> Mark the perfect man, and behold the upright
> For the end of that man is peace.
> But the transgressions shall be destroyed together:
> The end of the wicked will be cut off.

Erika's face was white, her lips tight. She slipped her hand under the cloth, fingered one card, thought better of it, groped for another. This one she withdrew, her eyes closed. Without looking at it herself, she turned it so that Blackford, sitting opposite, would see it. It was the ten of clubs. There was silence.

Blackford reached under the cloth and yanked out a card. He returned the courtesy to Erika, whose face brightened; and Blackford knew the worst as he slammed down the two of clubs on the table, stood up, and walked to the door.

Outside, on the porch, looking out over Gstaad, he breathed deeply. He was not interrupted. A few moments later Erika came out and spoke to him softly.

"I am going to ski," she said.

"Ski where? It's five-thirty."

"There is a flambeau tonight at the Hornberg."

"What's a flambeau?"

"We go up the funicular between six and

233

seven, eat at the restaurant, and ski down in the moonlight. There are guides. Even 'bloodwagons,' as the English call them, to bring down anyone who has had an accident . . . Will you join me?"

Blackford did not hesitate. "I will join you."

They arrived at Saanenmoser and boarded the funicular sled along with three dozen other revelers. Two schoolgirls, one with golden braids and a golden face, began to yodel as they waited for the funi to fill up. Their voices were high and Alpine clear, and the chattering crowd stopped to listen. Halfway up the mountain the ski guides began a husky counterpoint, alternating with the girls' bel canto, and by the time they reached the top of the mountain all the Swiss were singing, the foreigners shouting bravo after every song —they could not applaud because both hands were needed to maintain balance on the steep, bumpy ride. At the top they dismounted, collected their skis from the stack at the back of the sled, and set out to walk the kilometer grading up to the Hornberg Inn, which was warm and smoky from the huge fireplace and the pipe-smoking of the half-dozen hardy skiers who resided there, interring themselves for the night from the moment the funi began its last regularly scheduled ascent at four-thirty. The flambeaux were scheduled monthly when the moon was right, if the snow also was right.

There were no tables for two, so Erika and Blackford sat opposite each other at a table for eight comprising a Swiss guide and five German skiers. They ordered white wine, a regional

Fendant, and in due course the cheese fondue
was brought out and, from two chafing dishes
filled with Gruyére cheese kept hot by high-in-
tensity alcohol flames underneath, they served
themselves, dunking their bread morsels, skewered
by the long-pronged forks, in the cheese, washing
down the food with wine. An accordion player
hacked away jovially with rollicking Swiss music
and after the fondue was served rallied everyone
to sing together the *"Vo Luzern, gegen Wäggis
zue,"* at the closing chorus of which, arms about
the shoulders of the two people at either side, in
rhythm with the music, the skiers rolled from side
to side, *"Going from Lucerne to Waggis/You
need neither stockings nor shoes/You just swing
to the yodel."* The music and the singing got loud-
er and now the waitresses took orders for kirsch,
coffee, and chocolate. Erika and Blackford ordered *filtre,* kirsch, and Toblerone. Blackford
quaffed the kirsch voluptuously, and Erika was
not far behind. The huge German on Erika's right
asked whether she and her companion would care
to bet: He would undertake to whirl a five-franc
piece within a cereal bowl and keep it going
round and round without collapsing, like the
motorcyclists at the country fairs who in the huge
open barrels zoom about at high speeds sustained
by centrifugal force. Erika and Blackford had
agreed that they would not divulge their knowledge of German, the better to protect themselves
against a cooptive Gemütlichkeit; and so, affecting difficulty in understanding him, Erika finally
came up with a one-franc piece to match the
German's proffered coin. He persevered around

235

the table, collecting from the happily gamey company.

And then he began whirling the bowl. At first the five-franc piece wobbled, but as he increased by subtle movement of the palm the circular velocity of the bowl, concentrating feverishly on the motion of his right hand, the five-franc piece began to spin about in the bowl's perimeter, just beneath the rim. Everyone at the table applauded lustily, whereon, carried away, the German now rose cautiously to his feet, the coin in the bowl still rotating. Now the skiers at surrounding tables joined in applause. Egged on, the German stepped potvaliantly up onto the bench, and the crowd went wild. Then he lifted shakily one leg, like a water-skier shucking off a ski, so that now he was supported by a single leg; and in a final reach for perfection he lifted the bowl high into the air, his right hand maintaining the motion, and stood there like the Statue of Liberty, as everyone cheered and howled. He brought the demonstration to an end by outstretching his left hand and, like a triumphant matador, turning slowly on the balls of his feet to receive the plaudits of the crowd. Then he sat, a huge deposit of self-satisfaction, collected his bets and challenged Blackford to try it. Blackford did, but the coin fell flat after only a second, bringing great happiness and hilarity to the German. Nothing would do but that everyone should try in turn. Happily, everyone else failed, and the German, elated, ordered an extra kirsch for everyone at the table.

The chief guide now stood and said that ev-

ery sixth person would be handed a flambeau and
that the skiers must be careful to keep in line. So,
with the air of pioneers, they trudged out into the
night. The temperature was exhilarating—cold
but not icy. Blackford bent down to help Erika
bind her skis. It fell to neither of them to carry a
lighted torch. After ten minutes of confusion and
merriment the procession was ready and the accordion player, without ski poles, and making
music all the way, began the three-mile ski down
the mountain. They slid down the ghostly snow,
down the wide slopes bordered by pine forests,
through one forest down a winding trail. They
looked like a centipedal firefly as they made their
sinuous way down the mountain, reaching speeds
as fast as thirty miles per hour. Halfway down
there was a check to give the skiers a chance to
rest their ankles. Blackford was grateful that his
seemed in good condition, though he had not
skied in eighteen months. Erika clearly was a
veteran. In the flickering light of the nearby flambeau he saw her face in a new cast. Any latent
dullness was gone. She was girlishly spirited,
flushed with pleasure and relief. They reached the
bottom and cursed the inflexible refusal of the
guides to summon the funi to take them back up
again: The funi operators had long since gone
home. So they walked to Blackford's car, attaching the skis to the harness, and he said, "Where
does one go from here?" She suggested the bar
at Schönreid, the Alpenrose, and there they found
late diners ordering rich meats and the tiny fried
potatoes, and went off to a corner table and told
the waiter they would merely take a bottle of white

wine. They drank this, and talked about everything except what was creeping back into Blackford's mind after the surcease at the Hornberg.
He forced it back out, ordering another bottle of
wine. On impulse he turned to her.

"To take out?"

She hesitated. But then whispered huskily,
"To take out."

In the car he said, "Where are you staying?"

"The Bahnhof at Saanen."

"Sounds to me like my place is better."

"Your place? With that man Rufus across
the hall?"

Blackford explained he had a private apartment on the ground floor.

They drove there and went in. He took her to
the second, empty bedroom, and pointed out the
bath in between, and returned discreetly to his
own room. When he heard the shower turn off,
he waited a moment or two, opened his door and
stepped into the shower, though he hesitated,
fearing to lose the tang of the snow. Then, naked,
he opened her door, and gasped. The lights were
off. But the moon made her body lambent, criss-
crossing it through the narrow frame windows.

He approached her and whispered, "I'd rather do this with you than play cards." Suddenly
he felt again the pain of that afternoon. And, moments later, his mind turned on the legend of the
little boy in Holland sticking his finger in the dike
to hold back the floodwaters. He wasn't using his
finger, he reflected, but however temporarily, the
substitute was working: holding back the floodwaters in his mind. She was Erika, beautiful, warm

Erika born to love and be loved, not to attend to the devil's housekeeping. He? He was what? He was simply the little Dutch boy, holding back the floodwaters. "Look, Ma!" he allowed himself to think. "No hands!"

Erika woke with a start at six-thirty and nudged Blackford.

"I must go quickly."

He went to his room and dressed. She was ready, and silently they went to the car. She indicated the way. At the Bahnhof she kissed him lightly on the cheek and, without a word, left the car, retrieving her skis.

He drove back to Haltehüs and, as he walked into his apartment he looked up at the porch. Singer Callaway was standing there in his bathrobe.

"What do you think this house is, Oakes, a bordello?"

Blackford paused. A grim ditty came to his lips.

Kill a few?
Breed a few!

But it died in his throat and, to Singer, he returned only the required schoolboy fico.

16

Wintergrin called the meeting for 8 P.M. Saturday at the castle. His enterprise was endangered; the three preceding days had been the most damaging of his career. He elected to eat alone before going into the conference room to meet with his associates. Dinner was served in his study: soup, sausage, roast potatoes, salad. A glass was filled with red wine which he did not taste, though he drank the mineral water. Two letters had been placed on top of the mound of clippings from papers from all over Europe. One was sealed, the other opened; two letters Himmelfarb had evidently thought it important to pass along directly.

The first was from the widow of an admiral hanged at Nuremberg. She had a special place in the affection of the German people because it was known she had frequently interceded, at substantial risk to herself and to her husband's position, in behalf of numerous victims-elect of the Fuehrer. Axel had known her since he was a child. Hers was a plea to throw his strength to Adenauer. "Don't you see, Axel, that if you go through with your own plan, you *must* fail? Either you will be killed singly or—just as probably—what is left of freedom here in West Germany will be killed by Soviet troops reacting to your challenge." He did not need to read more (though he did, dutifully), because he had read a thousand such letters in the past months. He wondered, even, whether Audenauer might have been inspiring some of them. But this letter went on to stress an unconventional point: his campaign would be rated by history a brilliant success in any event, as he would have emboldened Audenauer's party to take a far more aggressive line against the Soviets, perhaps even to force, if less dramatically, the issue of reunification.

He put the letter in a basket reserved for correspondence he would himself reply to.

The second letter was still sealed. Unusual because Roland Himmelfarb did not hesitate to open Axel's mail. On looking closely he recognized the seal. And written on the face of the envelope was: "For Count Wintergrin personally." He knew the handwriting of the Queen of England.

"Dear Axel: You can never have doubted that my personal sympathies are with you and your movement. It is clear now, as I reflect on

242

our many conversations during the summer of
1946, that the plans you have crystallized grew
out of an analysis we once ventilated together—
perhaps I presume to believe I might have had a
part in contributing to that analysis. But after listening extensively to the Prime Minister, to our
military advisers, to men you know and trust, I
must advise you that in our solemn judgment the
risks you run are inordinate.

"Could you not, at the last moment, endorse
Adenauer, and transform his own party into
something very much like your own, but—dare I
say it, dear Axel?—just a little more flexible, to
avoid the awful possibility that the precarious
peace we have won will be shattered? No one is
fonder of you, believe me, than I, and I am therefore personally concerned for your personal safe-
ty: but I am prepared to risk pomposity to advise
you that I am imploring you not as your friend
and cousin, but as the Queen of England, to heed
our counsel. My prayers will be with you. Affec-
tionately, Caroline."

He left his half-eaten sausage and reached for
a sheet of writing paper on which he scrawled:
"HM, The Queen. Dear Caroline: If I happen
to be killed at an opportune moment, then by
your reasoning the threat to the peace would have
been eliminated. Does it follow that you desire
me, for reasons of state alone of course, to *be*
killed? You must think through the logic of your
position. Now: I tell you, the Russians *will give
in to my ultimatum*. My victory will *strengthen*,
not weaken, Europe. The men who have been
counseling you were in positions of power when

243

East Germany was lost. And Poland. And Czechoslovakia. And Bulgaria. And Rumania. I spent *five years* dwelling on little else than the arguments you raise now, on the eve of the election. There is nothing new in what you say, not even, I am reassured to note, in the reiteration of expressions of your personal affection, which I return, Ever gratefully, Axel."

He picked up the clippings and walked into the conference room. He scarcely noticed that, for the first time, his intimates rose when he entered. Sitting down at the head of the table he addressed Himmelfarb, his chief of staff; Heinrich Stiller, his communications chief; Kurt Grossmann, his press chief; and Jürgen Wagner, his security chief.

"Well, gentlemen"—Wintergrin's voice was calm, resolute, instantly galvanizing. "It has been a heavy week. The Communists and the Americans would appear to be working as a single team. Would you agree"—he addressed Kurt Grossman —"that the attacks are coordinated?"

"As to timing, I should think yes, definitely," Grossmann began deliberately, analytically. "As to the lines of attack, there appears to be a clear division of responsibility. The Soviet line is almost exclusively: Wintergrin Means WAR." His voice changed. "What is quite extraordinary . . . disgusting . . . is the work clearly inspired by our friends. I mean, when last did the European press think it so horrifying that someone running for office had a . . . natural child?"

"Yes, well, let us attempt to be orderly. The press conference is set for Tuesday. As for little

Rudi, I shall of course admit to siring him, and announce my intention of adopting him."

"What will you say when they ask why you haven't done it before?"

"I shall answer the question."

No one was surprised. It was characteristic. Some of what he intended to say to the press he would reveal to his associates ahead of time. Much he would not. None of his associates knew, before the Frankfurt Convention, what he would say on the matter of a nuclear defense.

"All right," Himmelfarb said, "what about the matter of Russian mobilization?"

"Kurt"—Wintergrin turned to him—"prepare for me excerpts from my speeches in which I cited Russian mobilization as a psy-war threat the Communists would inevitably come up with."

"Did you actually predict a *total* mobilization?"

"No. But in Düsseldorf I mentioned the word 'mobilization' without qualifying it. The fact of the matter is that the Soviet Union is *not* totally mobilizing. You have reports on that, Heinrich? You must draw on all our contacts. It would be fine to show that it is actually a bluff. You know who to be in touch with. In all probability they'll be in touch with us, tomorrow, and Monday."

"What about the statement by Dr. Oppenheimer that it is scientifically impossible for you to have a nuclear weapon at your disposal?"

"I shall cope with Dr. Oppenheimer."

"What about the five million signatures of East Germans denouncing you?"

"I shall point out the coercive nature of the society that produced those signatures."

"What about the vote by the French Parliament disavowing you?"

"That will help, not hurt."

They all laughed.

"All right," Himmelfarb said. "Now the big one. Norway."

Wintergrin turned to Jürgen Wagner, who began his report.

"We have been busy probing the background of Trygve Amundsen. I regret to report that thus far we have established that he was unquestionably a legitimate member of the resistance—did you know him, Count Wintergrin?"

"I never laid eyes on him."

"We nevertheless are convinced that he was engaged in the Vemork operation in which you were engaged."

"That's possible. There were two units of frogmen. Ours went in from the northeast lagoon, the other from the beach. Both groups planted explosives, and as far as our unit knew, both sets of explosives went off. The idea of the two units was of course to hit the ship in the event that one unit was discovered."

Wagner continued. "We have not found him involved in any pro-Soviet political activity. We simply cannot discover at the moment any ideological ties to the Soviet Union."

"Well, what do you propose to do about that . . . liar?" Wintergrin had never been heard to use profanity. "He stands up at a press conference and says he gave me information about the scheduled date of the Allied bombing of the freighter, that I gave that information to the Gestapo, thus permitting Nazi antiaircraft artillery to blast every one of the British bombers out of the air, and he produces a photostat, a forgery, of a Gestapo memorandum recording the details of the meeting with me."

He paused. "If so much of the press hadn't become an echo chamber for *any* anti-Wintergrin story, the Norway allegation wouldn't have appeared except in the satellite publications, unless they had established the legitimacy of the Gestapo document."

"I'm afraid it's being taken quite seriously," Himmelfarb said. "I have telegrams from a half dozen of our critical supporters telling us we've *got* to explode that charge."

"What are you proposing, Jürgen?"

"A trip to Norway, Count Wintergrin, about which I'd rather not say anything more. And, sir, may I see you after the meeting is over?"

"Of course."

He turned again to Grossmann. "I think, Kurt, that after the press meeting Tuesday at Bonn we would do well to organize a big rally, if there is time to do it. I would suggest Frankfurt, at the same Paulskirche. I would then attempt a speech that would reiterate my defenses. Above all, the voters must not now be distracted, demoralized . . ." He smiled. "Anybody got any good news?"

There was silence. Then Grossmann spoke. "Colonel McCormick of the Chicago *Tribune* has endorsed you."

"Well, just so long as Senator McCarthy doesn't endorse me."

"I think we have been able to abort that."

"Anybody else?"

"The Ollenhauer camp is still reeling from the endorsement of you two days ago from Heinrich Regnery. The metalworkers' support was personally courted by both Adenauer and Ollenhauer. Our getting it was a huge plus."

"Well," said Wintergrin, "I suppose it's good to know the enemy probably doesn't have a shot left to fire."

"That's what I want to talk to you about, sir." Wagner said.

Wintergrin rose, told his associates he would be working at his desk most of the evening and would be available to anyone who wanted him.

"Come into my study," he said to Wagner.

They sat down and Axel took another glass of the mineral water, left there after his tray was removed.

"Count Wintergrin, I am moderately well satisfied with the security we have organized for you in your travels—moderately satisfied, not completely satisfied." Wintergrin noticed that young Wagner, undeniably talented and thorough, had even so in the past few weeks contracted a severe case of creeping pomposity.

"The only alternative, Jürgen, would be to arrange to have me give my speeches from the inside of an armored tank."

Wagner ignored the taunt. "I intend, during this last week, to insist on even greater precau-

tions in the assembly halls, and even in the television studios. Do you know the President of the
United States has thirty-two people protecting
him at all times?"

"I am not as unpopular as the President of
the United States"—Wintergrin smiled, having
read about Truman's latest Gallup poll.

"Please, sir, you must cooperate."

"Very well. Make such arrangements as you
deem necessary. But don't put me behind plate
glass when I speak. Is that all?"

"No, sir."

Wintergrin looked hard at him. "Then what
else?"

"We must do something about internal security."

"What do you mean?"

"There really hasn't been a sufficient check
on the people who have access to you. I asked
the sentry the other day for a head count. An
average of fifty-five people came in and out of
the courtyard every day last week, even with our
sentry system which denied passage to"—Wagner
pulled out his neatly kept notebook—"one hundred and six people, including a delegation of
ladies who called themselves 'Daughters of the
American Revolution.' Apparently the American
revolutionaries dress well, according to the sergeant. Who *needs* to come into the courtyard?
Your family and aides, of course; suppliers for
the merchants; the mailmen; messengers. Now,
most of those in this category don't enter the
palace, but some do. And anyone posing plausi-

bly as a supplier could situate himself so as to work mischief from someplace within the courtyard."

"I don't know that I even have the technical authority to close it off to suppliers. I forget, do I own the courtyard?"

"Legally you do. Legally you own the land on which the shops are situated. Two hundred years ago they were leased, on a yearly rental payment of one mark, which is regularly collected by the bursar, preserving your technical rights."

"What do you propose I do? Drop the bread and cheese for the villagers from an airplane?"

"Sir, we must escort all merchants to where they are going, and back out. We have the manpower to do it with the help of the Freiwilligen. All packages and mail for the castle should be left with the sentry."

"All right. But call a meeting of the courtyard—after all, there are only twenty—present the problem, and ask for their cooperation. I am hoping for one hundred per cent of the St. Anselm's courtyard vote. Is that all?"

"No, sir. There is the reconstruction gang. This afternoon I counted *eight* people working in the chapel."

"Good. I wish it were eighteen. Or eighty. *Nothing* must slow down the work on the chapel . . . . Don't worry, Jürgen. I know Blackford Oakes well and I trust him."

"Why should you?"

Axel said nothing for a moment. Jürgen resumed:

"He brings in Americans, Italians; this morning I signed a pass for a Portuguese—"

"Ah yes, the mosaicist. Oakes talked to me about him. Said to be better than anybody in Italy. Or, at least, anybody available."

"But we don't have proper security checks on them, any of them. We don't even have a proper security check on Oakes."

"What kind of check would you propose we do?"

"I do not propose a check. If Oakes were, say, a CIA agent, they would have arranged a pretty good cover for him, probably something we couldn't penetrate. You should require that all work on the chapel be suspended until after the election."

"Impossible. Out of the question."

"One week? Why? The Americans aren't going to be so angry they'd cancel the project."

"Nothing is to interrupt the work on the chapel. Jürgen, I do not mean to be less than appreciative, but it is not unusual that, when charged with security, one becomes—overcautious. Let me leave it this way: I trust Oakes personally; besides which, and do not ask me to elaborate, I believe he is . . . ideologically useful to me."

"Sir, the two superpowers are determined to stop you. God knows they've made that plain in the last few days. Why shouldn't they be willing to do so . . . right here?"

Wintergrin paused and leaned back in his chair. He looked suddenly older, judicious. He examined the hard young face of Jürgen Wagner, just young enough to have escaped service when the war broke out. And lucky enough to have had a French godmother across the Alsatian border who spirited him in to escape service in the war when, in 1943, he reached seventeen. He lived at the lonely farmhouse as her retarded son. It had been a long, long act, and Wintergrin wondered at the weight of such an imposture on someone of that age. During that period, passing month after month hiding from the Nazis and from the collaborators, Wagner had become nervously conscious of security, and intellectually interested in the subject. So that, on returning to Germany and showing no special aptitudes in academic work, he had gone to the police academy in Heidelberg, then quit to take on private assignments in security. He was plodding, literal, fearless, and exceedingly suspicious. Wintergrin felt it necessary not to discourage him, but now felt it necessary to curb him.

"Jürgen, what you say is not outside the range of possibility. But it is very unlikely, and I have no alternative than to assume that that which is grossly unlikely will not happen. Otherwise I would not dare have breakfast with my own mother. And anyway, the logic of your suspicion leads to the fatalistic conclusion that if they insist on my scalp, they'll have it."

"They wanted Hitler's scalp, and they didn't get it."

"Hitler controlled Germany. I do not." He rose.

Wagner said, "Do I have your permission, then, at least to tighten security in the chapel?"

252

"Yes. But don't get under Oakes's feet."

Wagner nodded his head, and left, without saying goodnight.

He raged with resentment and frustration. He did not, to begin with, like Oakes, and he persuaded himself, over and over again, that there were no personal reasons for this dislike—though it was true he was put off by the young American's savoir faire, his easygoing relationship with the count, whom he addressed as "Axel"! He resented Oakes's obtrusive good looks, his fine physical build, his fluency in German, his manifest mastery of the work in the chapel. He thought it odd that someone of Oakes's background and training would be devoting so much time to the rebuilding of a chapel which, however splendid, was a minor concern of a very busy world and, *a fortiori,* of a very gifted young engineer. But he forced himself to lay the matter of Oakes to one side. Right now he had mostly Norway on his mind. Later in the week he would make a close inspection of the chapel, after everyone had left for the day.

17

Trygve Amundsen got off the commuter train
and walked with his companion toward his little
office on slightly seedy Klingenberg, where he
struggled to make a living as an importer of foreign automobile parts. At the door his companion
told him he would be by to pick him up and escort him home at exactly five. He would meanwhile be across the street, by the designated telephone, if his advice or his services were needed.
Amundsen nodded, and reminded him pleasantly
that he, Amundsen, had been decorated for bravery in the resistance and was not exactly defense-
less. The office was locked, so he took out his key.

The door opened directly on the main business room with its long counter, the order forms

and catalogues and bulletins from France, Germany, Italy, the United States, Sweden, strewn about. He was surprised that Ingemar was not there. It was nine-thirty, and his young assistant was to have begun the monthly inventory check at nine. He picked up the telephone from Ingemar's empty desk on the far side of the counter and dialed his home number, intending to reproach him most directly—Ingemar had been married only a month ago and Amundsen was disposed to be indulgent; but the honeymoon was over. Ingemar's wife answered. "I have been calling you at the office every few minutes, Mr. Amundsen. This morning at six, Ingemar's mother's doctor called from Beitstad. Ingemar's mother took very ill last night. They fear it is a stroke, so Ingemar left on the nine o'clock plane for Trondheim. But he is booked to come back tonight if all is well with his mother. He asked me to apologize to you."

"Well, hardly his fault," Amundsen said, just the least bit reluctantly, hung up the telephone, and looked up into his own office door and into the barrel of a .44 automatic. At the same time, from behind, he felt steel on his neck and the man behind him said:

"Put your hands behind your back, Amundsen. And hear this: As far as I'm concerned, I'd rather kill you than get from you what we are here to get from you, so I beg you to give me the opportunity."

Amundsen moved back his hands, which were then handcuffed with professional dispatch, and he was shoved into his own office, onto the

256

couch where he would seat special buyers when they came to him.

The same man said: "You had two appointments this morning. Your assistant thoughtfully wrote down their telephone numbers. We telephoned to say you were called away for the day. In fact, your absence may prove to be permanent. Your buddy across the street doesn't expect to see you till five. Ingemar is north on a wild-goose chase. A small sign outside the door says 'Closed for the Day.' We will not be interrupted."

Amundsen said nothing. The two men had made no effort to disguise themselves. The one who was doing the talking he recognized without difficulty. Dana Neilson. He too had been in the resistance. On two occasions they had worked briefly together. Like Amundsen, he was about thirty years old. Unlike Amundsen, Neilson was still lean; he was strong-jawed, with a splotchy face that showed the ravages of frostbite, and dark-red curly hair. His companion was younger, intense; his pistol, to which he had now affixed a silencer, was aimed once again at Amundsen's head, from which it never moved.

Neilson sat down at Amundsen's desk and tilted back the chair, looking across the room at Amundsen, sitting on the couch, his arms behind him, his eyes on the floor, his once flat stomach paunching over his belt.

"There is no time, Amundsen, as you must realize. So where are we? Your business is very nearly bankrupt, your wife is tubercular, your son is with his grandparents. You badly needed money. You did not know Axel Wintergrin, so what you did to him you did impersonally. That makes it a little easier to swallow—I suppose. But I *did* know Axel Wintergrin. He saved my life at Vemork, and he very nearly gave his life on more than one occasion to help my country. Incidentally, your country too, Amundsen. But we are here now to extricate ourselves from this mess you got us into." He got up and walked to the end of the room, leaning now against the door.

Amundsen did not move his head or his eyes to follow him.

"First let me tell you what we *don't* require of you, and that is your exposure as a fraud-for-hire. That's *your* problem, and if you live, you can live with it.

"The story will be as follows: An unidentified man telephoned you ten days ago and said that unless you cooperated with him he would kill either your wife or your son, and moreover would kill them sooner or later if you turned to the police for help.

"He told you the story you were instructed to carry to the press. And he sent you by mail the forged page from the Gestapo records, with the story that you had snatched it from Gestapo Headquarters when you participated in the assault on V-Day.

"Since then you have had a bad bout of conscience, and you asked a former friend in the resistance—that's me—for help. I did some sleuthing in the ideological underground and got a lead on the man who phoned you—that's Hans, sitting over there. I 'almost nailed him,' but he slipped through my fingers on a flight to Paris. I will have given a complete description of him to the police. I have that description here. It will coincide with the flight out of Oslo to Paris at two P.M. today, which Hans here plans to take. No ideological clues. It does not serve our interests to link this operation either to the CIA or to the Communists, or to Wintergrin's political enemies in Germany.

"The money, however much it was, and wherever it is, you get to keep. I wouldn't worry about your contact moving in on you. I intend to take you to the north country right now, and there you will hold a secluded press conference tomorrow before three invited and highly respected journalists so as to disguise your whereabouts until Hans here is 'run down.' Your wife and son will be under protective surveillance 'till November fifteenth. The German elections are a week from tomorrow, after which whatever the damage in Germany it will have been done, and you'll be safe. You have my word that if you need protection in the future, I and my friends—and Wintergrin's friends—will give it."

Amundsen spoke for the first time.

"The man outside. You are aware he is from the police?"

"Of course. His name is Olaf Erlingssen, and he works out of the Bogstadveien Police Station."

"Is he supposed to believe all this?"

"You know him better than we do. But we have plans for Hans to leave a meaty enough trail to make the police believe he is a central figure."

"I suppose I should ask: the alternative?"

"We will kill you right here, at noon when

those bells up there go off. And, this afternoon, four members of the resistance—including Dr. Rosenkrantz—will go as a delegation to the press and give our opinion that Wintergrin has been gravely libeled, that you were mixed up in an intricate international power play, and that maybe you got your just deserts."

Amundsen's jaw jutted out and he lowered his head. He thought about his wrecked life and wondered fleetingly whether he mightn't just as well accept the bullet, which he had not an instant's hesitation believing would enter his skull at the stroke of noon. But he thought then of the pale face of Margrit, who the day before had said to him with that sadness that always overpowered him: Would he truly wait for her, even if the cure required a whole year? And he had answered huskily that he would, that he would wait however long it took.

"Very well," he said.

18

Over the weekend tension heightened. The announcement on Saturday that Wintergrin would hold a full-scale press conference in Bonn on Tuesday at eleven created a rendezvous on the international calendar. All Monday the television crews were at work. Finally Kurt Grossmann announced that facilities would need to be pooled and a drawing was held to decide whose cameras would be permitted into the 150-seat chamber, admission to which had been solicited on behalf of three hundred reporters, cameramen, and photographers. That morning, *Die Welt* had said editorially that Count Wintergrin's answers to the myriad questions, personal as well as political, would influence many voters still on the fence. "A people have the right to know their leaders. Some of the questions that will be put to Count Wintergrin are concededly extrapolitical, but the fate of Germany is a total concern. We need to know not only the policies of our leaders but something about their habits, their morals. The country is entitled to ask, and weigh the answers to, any question that might throw a light on the character of a man who seeks to guide that nation toward what some see as perdition, others as the first step toward a reunified republic."

Blackford Oakes read the editorial that morning and wondered whether its author had apprenticed in the New York *Times*. What makes them all sound so orotund? he wondered. Perhaps the editorial writers' anonymity.

He would be watching of course—over the television, at the Anselmsklaus in the courtyard. Overstreet and Conditti had said they too wanted to watch, and asked Black if he would translate for them. Erika had taken her staff to Bonn so as to go to work instantly after the press conference. She could not translate Wintergrin's answers to the questions ahead because he declined to write his answers out or, for that matter, even to give out the substance of most of them. Blackford knew that the rational thing was to hope that the press conference would go poorly for him, causing a precipitous drop in Wintergrin's standing in the polls. But he could not quite bring himself to root for the successful victimization of Wintergrin by that great psy-war machine the new cartel had put together.

By Tuesday morning, under the battering of the weekend's events, Wintergrin's rating took a dive. He was down to twenty-six per cent, with Adenauer holding firm at thirty-six per cent. Blackford knew—a fatalistic intuition told him so—that that tenpoint spread, which was a Safe Conduct pass for Wintergrin from November 11 to old age, would contract. But by how much? He dared to hope the spread would stay big enough to relieve him of his awful assignment. After all, that there was *movement* over the weekend— Wintergrin down eight points in five days—confirmed that his standing was volatile and that there was in fact something of an expertise in the manipulation of public opinion. Blackford switched on the power at the fuse box, walked over to the stool and bent over the chromoscope, manipulated the levers, and lost himself in concentration on the hues that filtered through six different tinctures of blue glass. Sliding the right-hand lever forward, he could see how the blue he had come up with would appear at dusk on a sunny day, on a cloudy day, at high noon on a sunny day. His researches persuaded him that the legendary Gerard must have experimented with different lights in different locations, before specifying the final, perfect composition. He was still sitting on the stool, bent over the viewing port, when he was interrupted by Overstreet, raising his voice to be heard over the machine's whir.

"It's ten to eleven. Shouldn't we go?"

Blackford raised his head and walked back to the wall to switch off the machine.

At the Anselmsklaus the saloon was crowded. Every villager and off-duty sentry was on hand, there being no other television sets around save for one in the castle, before which Countess Wintergrin, entirely alone, sat after the butler had tuned the set and pronounced it ready. Thirty-five people pressed about the bar and listened, in the minutes before Wintergrin would make his appearance, to a commentator discussing the gravity of the questions that would be put to the candidate of the Reunification Party.

In Bonn, in the little office outside the large reception room, Wintergrin looked at fresh clippings supplied by Heinrich Stiller. He reached out to capture the full flavor of the assault—the particulars he knew well enough—and as he dropped one clipping after another neatly to one side after reading it, his face was without expression, though once or twice he fastened, and then unfastened, the lower buttons on his jacket. He looked very young, gentle, unassuming—and determined. Since the program would be broadcast live on television, at two minutes to eleven Grossmann, who had come in from the platform, addressed the scattered staff and began the countdown.

"TWO MINUTES. God what a mob, Axel. They're sitting on the radiators. It's hot as hell. You'll have to face a little to the right. The lights on the left are blinding. ONE MINUTE THIRTY SECONDS. Hot as *hell! I*'ve tried to open some windows. Siegfried Schlamm is sitting right in front of you. He's looking real mean. Looking natural. ONE MINUTE. Did you see *Der Spiegel* gave him a big raise? He was offered a job by the Cologne-Düsseldorf-Bonn group. I think you can count on his getting in the first question. I'll *have* to recognize him. Adenauer had a press conference this morning THIRTY SECONDS and said he thought it quite possible that you would pull out of the race, leaving the leadership of—get this— quote our common cause unquote in quote more seasoned hands unquote. He's playing that FIFTEEN SECONDS 'seasoned hands' stuff so much you would think he went to school with FIVE SECONDS Moses. Good luck, Axel." Kurt Grossmann opened the door and, following him, Axel Wintergrin went out on the stage and walked directly to the podium. Grossmann edged Wintergrin gently to one side and took the microphone himself:

"Ladies and gentlemen; Count Wintergrin will not be making a prepared statement. As most of you are aware, he will be delivering an address tonight in Frankfurt. The floor is therefore open to questions."

Unlike most public figures, Wintergrin did not like to recognize a raised hand himself. He felt this practice objectionable on two counts. First, he could be accused of favoritism—of neglecting one hand in favor of another that had been raised earlier. Second, he disliked the schoolmasterish symbolism—humiliating, he had always thought, to the press's image and to its august function. The suppression of a free press, he had frequently said, made Hitler possible. So Grossmann took the responsibility and, in resigned recognition of the anticipated initiative by

Schlamm (who had raised his hand before Grossmann even began talking), he nodded to him, and twenty other raised hands went down.

"Count Wintergrin, it was alleged last Thursday in the *Daily Mirror* that you have a son living in London. Indeed his name was given, and his alleged mother with whom he is living was identified. Do you have a comment on this?"

"Yes," said Wintergrin. "I have available, for those of you who feel the matter germane, photo copies of a letter from the lawyer of my son's mother dated January 12, 1948, and a second letter from that lawyer dated approximately one year later. In the first he acknowledges in behalf of the boy's mother my willingness to adopt him, but advises that his client desires to defer any action on the matter until the baby is a little older.

"The second letter, written sometime after the Heidelberg Manifesto, advises me that the child's mother wished to put off renaming the child until political matters in Germany quieted down. One week after receiving the letter I executed a notarized will naming him as my heir. Copies of the will are also here. The boy's mother is married, and if she permits him to come here when the situation is stabilized, my heir will return, I trust, to a united Germany." Grossmann's timing was deft. Without a second's hesitation he recognized the next questioner in the rear, the representative of *Die Welt*.

"Count Wintergrin, the French Chamber of Deputies voted on Friday, by a count of three hundred and forty-one to eighty-two, its disapproval of your program."

"Of course. That will take a moment or two to analyze. In the first place, it is altogether natural that Frenchmen should be less anxious than Germans to reunify Germany. I don't think it's reasonable to expect that other countries will be willing to face sacrifice on the same scale as the beneficiary country seeking to recover its own nationhood, and the freedom of its own countrymen. On the other hand, I could not in good conscience ask my fellow Germans to make sacrifices that exceeded those made by so many Frenchmen to liberate their own country during the past war. General de Gaulle said while in London that if Frenchmen had to fight for a century to free their country, they would be prepared to do so. Unlike those great French leaders who summoned the French to war for the liberation of their country, *I* am not summoning anyone to war, inasmuch as I do not believe war necessary merely to assert a right so universally respected. I do say that we must be prepared to fight *if necessary*: but that is in no sense new. Under the NATO agreement, practically all the nations of western Europe are pledged to fight if necessary to preserve their freedom and indeed each other's. It is only distinctive about my platform that I believe that our brothers in East Germany should enjoy the same rights and protections we enjoy in West Germany and others enjoy in Italy, France, Scandivania, the Low Countries, and Great Britain. I am quite certain that when reunification comes, the French Chamber will rejoice in the same spirit as freedom-loving people throughout the world rejoiced when Frenchmen were liberated."

"Jesus Christ!" Blackford said to Overstreet. "Good God almighty! How're they going to stop that guy! He just managed to make the frogs look good while disemboweling them!" The Germans in the saloon were cheering.

In the press room Grossmann once again turned quickly to the next questioner, who stood by a television crew.

"Count Wintergrin, how do you account for the five million East German signatures urging us to vote against you and your party?"

"You are perhaps familiar, Herr Klaus, with the threat made to ex-President Theodore Roosevelt during the period of American neutrality in the First World War. The German ambassador advised the former President that if America joined the war on the side of the Allied powers, one million German-Americans would rise up against their government. Mr. Roosevelt observed that in America there were more than one million lampposts. By the same token, there are five million lampposts in East Germany, with which to intimidate the population. I do not doubt that a totalitarian government can deliver signatures behind any petition whatever. What is perhaps remarkable is that only five million signatures were presented. As you know, the Soviet Union has a great penchant for unanimity. East Germans went to the polls only one year ago, and delivered ninety-nine point four per cent of the vote for Herr Ulbricht."

There was a rustle of papers, and then the Reuters man was recognized.

"Count Wintergrin, the Norwegian Trygve Amundsen last Wednesday revealed . . . perhaps I should say, alleged . . . that during the time you were in the resistance in Norway you were in fact working secretly for the Nazis. He produced a document which purports to describe a meeting between you and"—the Reuters man was examining his notes—"a Captain Hessler, on July 4, 1944, at which you advised Captain Hessler of the date of a bombing run planned by the British against the heavy-water installation at Vemork, on July 7. The records indeed show that the British initiated such a raid on that day and that the surprising intensity of antiaircraft fire resulted in the devastation of the British squadron."

The reporters stirred. Wintergrin paused for a moment. Then he reached into his pocket and brought out a folded piece of paper which he placed on the podium.

"I was of course aware the matter would be brought up, and am glad that the matter can be clarified.

"One: I have never laid eyes on Trygve Amundsen, though I acknowledge that he was a member of the resistance.

"Two: I never met, heard of, or was interrogated by, Captain Hessler. He was not one of the Gestapo officials who tortured me at Oslo during the spring of that year.

269

"Three: As we meet here, Mr. Amundsen is meeting with members of the press in Norway. He is issuing the following statement and will answer questions about it put to him by the press. I shall read it, if I may:

" 'On October 30, I received a telephone call in my office from a stranger. He advised me that unless I cooperated with him in a certain matter, either my son, or my wife, would be slaughtered. My wife is very ill and in a tuberculosis sanatorium. My six-year-old son is with his grandparents. He told me that if any report were made to the police, my wife or my son would similarly be executed. He then told me that I must be prepared to testify that Count Axel Wintergrin was a double agent during the period of the resistance, and that when I took part in the final raid on the Gestapo headquarters in Oslo I retrieved a memorandum documenting a conversation between Captain Hessler and Count Wintergrin in which Wintergrin betrayed the British Air Force. I received in the morning mail the next day the page from the Nazi journal. I proceeded to make the public accusation.

" 'Since doing so, members of the resistance —my former colleagues—who fought alongside Count Wintergrin and were personal witnesses to his bravery, approached me and promised to supply protection against the threatener. Measures were taken over the weekend that succeeded in tracing the telephone caller—who narrowly escaped the country. The Norwegian police and Interpol have been notified and are on the alert to arrest him for the crime of threatened murder and extortion. I heartily apologize of course to Count Wintergrin, but also to the German people. Signed, Trygve Amundsen.' "

Blackford signaled the waiter, and ordered a drink. "Poor mixed-up guy," he thought. "So. Work your way out of every trap, and what do you do? You commit suicide."

Everyone now was ordering beer. And, at the press hall, the applause was spontaneous, even heartfelt. The press manifestly felt dirty at having been so easily led to the diffusion of a sordid and apparently baseless accusation. Rather than let the applause continue, Wintergrin signaled quickly to Grossmann to recognize the next questioner, but the Reuters man insisted on a follow-up question.

"Have you speculated, Count Wintergrin, on who is the probable client of the man on the telephone?"

"Yes," Wintergrin said, "yes, I have."

There was silence.

The Reuters man said, "Well?"

Everyone laughed. Wintergrin looked uncomfortable.

"I should think it most probable," he said, "that the enterprise, clearly motivated to discredit me, was the handiwork of the same party or parties who produced five million votes alleging that East Germans prefer servitude to liberty. The two libels are cognate—"

"What does 'cognate' mean?" Overstreet whispered to Blackford.

Blackford interrupted his own running translation.

271

"Related, sort of. Shhh."

"But," the Reuters correspondent persevered, "it isn't only the Communists who seek to discredit you, is it? The majority of the French Parliament, for instance, are not Communists."

"Of course not. And although I would hope for encouragement by every German, I can hardly expect the vote of every German, and would never for a moment suggest that those who oppose me are in any sense sympathetic to Communism. What I am saying is that the Norwegian enterprise is typically totalitarian in its total disregard of truth, fair play, and the appropriate sense of restraint. It is for that reason that I have speculated —*your* word—on the probable sponsor of the project."

Grossman now interrupted: "Next question?"

The next questioner was Erik von Königsberg, the grand old man of German journalism, imprisoned throughout the Nazi years.

"Count Wintergrin, on Thursday the Russians announced a general mobilization. It would appear that they are preparing for the contingency of a victory by you, in which case they would use all their armed might to crush you, your party, West Germany, and conceivably the rest of Europe while they are at it. May I have your comments on that?"

"Yes, of course, Herr Königsberg.

"In Heidelberg, on September 28, I said in my address: 'Inevitably the Russians will threaten to block with their whole military might any move to liberate East Germany.' In Cologne on October

4, I said: 'The Soviet Union will make great objections, no doubt including ostentatious mobilization of its forces.' In Stuttgart on October 11, I said: 'Germans must not permit themselves to falter under threats of force from the Soviet Union, precisely calculated to deter us from our path.'

"Now, I am aware that to predict that something will happen, which I did, does not make its happening any the less significant.

"But bear in mind the following. In the present situation, the Soviet Union theoretically does not need to mobilize in order for its armies to reach the English Channel. It has one hundred and seventy-five divisions along the eastern front, five times the number of NATO's, and a similarly disproportionate number of tanks and support aircraft.

"The Soviet Union is kept at bay by a combination of factors, among them the atomic deterrent, postwar economic exhaustion, and the difficulty the Soviet Union would have in administering conquered territories of people who are enjoying their freedoms after the long nightmare of Nazi rule and Nazi occupation.

"Now, here is a concrete piece of intelligence: Since the Soviets' theatrical summons to mobilization: one, *no reserves have in fact been called up;* two, *no fresh orders have been issued to the reserves;* three, *no administrative centers have been established for the processing of recruits.* In other words, save for the announcement itself, exactly nothing has happened. The Soviet Union is not satisfied to coerce the East Germans.

It desires to influence the election in West Germany."

The press began talking all at once, and Grossmann gaveled for silence.

"You will want to know how I have that information. I cannot tell you. I can tell you this, however, that on investigating it, to the extent that you have your own sources, you will find it to be true.

"Now"—Wintergrin did not want to slow the momentum and wait for what he knew would be the next question—"on the matter of an atomic defense, since the topic is raised over and over again. I am aware that Dr. Oppenheimer has said that it is a 'scientific impossibility' for me to have come up with the bomb. I wish to repeat here: I do not threaten the bomb except against anyone who is prepared to annihilate Germans seeking their own freedom. I have no intention of inflicting violence on, or making war against, the Soviet Union. I am simply advising the German people that I am a practical man, with no taste for windmills. Although I believe in the end in the supremacy of the spirit—witness the valiant struggle of the Israelis to survive against such heavy odds—I also believe in the necessity of making only *credible* assertions. In economic strength this country is already third in the world, so soon after our devastation. We are a nation of fifty million people. Our factories can give us the conventional tools of war. And the bomb—should it come to that? I am free to say only this, that it is true—Dr. Oppenheimer is correct—as of now it is scientifically impossible for Germans to have developed an atom bomb. But it does not follow that we cannot have *acquired* an atom bomb. That is my answer to Dr. Oppenheimer. And"—now he was clearly addressing the television audience—"my message to the German people is: Don't let any of the distractions with which you have been assaulted during the last week deter you from what is your clear resolve. *Until we free our brothers we are continuing victims of an ignoble past.*"

There was a cacophony of sounds. Commotion, reporters struggling to get out, applause, here and there a whistle: the sounds of excitement. Wintergrin raised his hand deferentially, turned, and walked out of the room. The camera went back to the network host.

In Washington the same two men sat wearily by the same kitchen table in the same empty house in Georgetown where, a month earlier, they had set into motion the plan to neutralize Count Wintergrin. It was six twenty-five in the morning.

The Director rose and turned off the impressive short-wave speaker that had brought in the press conference, simultaneously translated exclusively for this audience of two men by an intercepting technician in an electronic warren a mile away.

There was a long silence.

"Pelzerhaken. So that's where the warheads ended up," the Director sighed. "Well, at least it's no longer a mystery. And thank God the Soviets have never got on to it. Though, come to think of it, if we hadn't already decided on the

275

other . . . plan, it mightn't have been a bad idea to let 'em know Wintergrin's people had got hold of those bombs."

The reference was to the B-36 bomber which, with its four atom bombs, went down on maneuvers eighteen months earlier close by the East German border, near the mouth of the Lü-beck estuary off Pelzerhaken in North Germany. CIA divers with the latest equipment had got there in three days. But when, on the tenth day, they came finally on the carcass of the plane, the bombs were gone. Not a word about the missing aircraft, let alone about the missing bombs, had leaked. It was the most heavily guarded secret of the season. It was assumed by the Pentagon and CIA that the Soviets had got there first with one of their omnipresent patrol boats out of nearby Rostock and spirited away the vicious, precious cargo; but the President decided against accosting them with it. And decided also against advising the NATO powers about the incident for fear of a sundering scandal. In Soviet hands the bombs were merely redundant. In the hands of Winter-grin they were something else.

The Secretary spoke. "If Wintergrin goes, we've still got to get our hands on the bombs. We can assume from what he's been saying that a scientist—maybe more than one—is in on the act, how you set off the goddam things, that kind of business. Why not comb the list of his sup-porters among German scientists and see if any of them hangs around the Lübeck area? It must have been local German divers-of-opportunity, prob-ably sportsmen, who pulled them up. God knows how they got from Pelzerhaken to Wintergrin. Will it ever end?"

The Director was silent.

The Secretary's voice brightened as he turned to another subject. Sarcasm was his crutch, his staff of life, his very best friend, come now, at twilight on execution eve, to his rescue; the first service, at 6:30 A.M., it would perform for its master in a long, long day of servitude. The Secretary rose and, walking to the stove for the coffeepot, said in his . . . public voice: "I say, Allen, that was a *great* performance your people managed in Norway."

"Yes," the Director said. "I was sure that would impress you."

"Once a member of the resistance, always a member of the resistance. I rather wish that particular member of the resistance, your pal Amundsen, had been a casualty of the occupation."

"We didn't have much time."

"Right, right. I suppose with *more* time, we might have contrived for Wintergrin to get *seventy-five per cent* of the vote."

"Assuming he went on to the polls."

"I had not thought to make that macabre distinction. Of course, now that he has proved so successful, he will end up not receiving *any* votes, now that we have—I believe necessarily—succumbed to Soviet blackmail. But as a point of technical interest, have you looked into the question whether his name on the ballot can be struck, on the grounds that he has . . . departed this vale of tears?"

"Between November twelfth and November

fifteenth? I haven't, to tell you the truth. I see what you mean. Theoretically he could, so to speak, win posthumously."

"I suppose. But no, his vote will collapse, necessarily . . . I must say, Allen, he *is* an impressive young man."

"Fatally impressive."

"No puns. Remember, we made that covenant at Potsdam."

"I wish that was the only covenant we had made at Potsdam."

"Yes, he really is something. Are you a betting man?"

"Depends whether one of my agents can inform me what's going to happen. Or make it happen. What do you have in mind?"

"This is Tuesday the ninth. We'll have the critical poll the day after tomorrow. I bet it will show Wintergrin even with Adenauer."

"I decline the bet."

"Have some more coffee, Allen."

"I don't want any more coffee." He rose and walked, pensive, to the door. As an afterthought he murmured, "Thanks anyway."

19

Jürgen Wagner said goodnight to Heinrich Stiller
and Kurt Grossmann when, at about ten, they left
their desks and, assuming he would decline—he
always did—invited Wagner perfunctorily to join
them for a nightcap. He would stay at his desk,
he said with maybe a hint of self-righteousness,
for another hour or two—he had a number of
reports to read.

He waited an hour until he was certain Stiller
and Grossmann had left the courtyard. Sometimes they paused across the way at the Anselmsklaus for their beer or brandy, instead of going
on to the bar at the inn. He opened his drawer,
brought out his .32 automatic, snug in its holster,
and buckled it on his belt. He fished out a large

flashlight from the closet and his overcoat from the rack. Saying a curt goodnight to the palace sentry, he walked out into the courtyard and down toward the chapel. The Anselmsklaus closed nowadays at eleven, Wagner's security arrangements having put a crimp on outside patronage. There were only the sleepy second-story lights from some of the living quarters of the residents of St. Anselm's, at the southern end of the courtyard, to interrupt the darkness. The chapel on the east end was dark. He looked about cautiously. There was no one lingering outside, in that black and cold; only mounds of dimly perceived building materials. He went to the door, which was unlocked (how typical! *Typical!* To leave the chapel unlocked. Typically American, and quintessentially Oakes, with his easygoing approach to all things. And the bother he had gone to to secure a duplicate key to the chapel door!). He pushed it open. In the narthex he stumbled. He flashed his light down and saw a half-empty case of white Tafelwein. His breath, crossing the ray of light, produced billows of fog in the cold. Wagner did not really believe people should drink *alcohol* under any circumstances. To drink at work was unthinkable. But it did not surprise him that the "chapel crowd," as he regularly referred to the workmen under the American Oakes, should take wine with their midday meal—and tipple at God knows what other hours! He stepped around the wine.

Next he saw coils of heavy wire, over there a mound of bricks, everywhere sacks of mortar. Beginning his methodical clockwise tour, he

280

walked past the first of the reconstructed columns up the northern aisle, past the heavy lathe that caused the whine heard halfway down the courtyard. He buttoned the throat button of his overcoat and set out to do what he had come to do: make a systematic inspection of the chapel.

At the north end of the transept he came on Oakes's little enclosed office. Wagner opened the unlocked door and shone his light about the desk, the filing cabinets, the long table with the stacks of blueprints, sketches, photographs. In the deep left-hand drawer of the desk, opposite the typewriter, there were papers and correspondence that betrayed personal—highly personal?—notations. These he began examining in laborious detail. Knowing no English, he copied meticulously into his notebook marginalia, presumably in Oakes's hand, scratched out on letters, most of them from Bonn—perhaps they would provide a clue. He would confide in Erika tomorrow, and ask her to go over them.

An hour later he had worked his way past the choir stalls, behind the altar, back to the south transept where the formidable chromoscope was rooted, and along the south aisle to within a few yards of the narthex and the entrance door. He stepped into a cavity in which a recessed confessional had stood and, climbing out, grazed against yet another heavy tarpaulin. A little wearily he tucked up the apron to look at the contents. Instead of the habitual naked building materials, he saw a wooden box of sorts, half as tall as himself, equally wide and deep. He was surprised to find it padlocked, further surprised to note that the lock was substantial. His light traveled to the hinges, but these were buried inside the wood—there was nothing to unscrew. Moving the tarpaulin off the large box, he edged around to examine the possibilities of rear entry. But the wood was solid. He tapped his flashlight against it. It wasn't as heavy in the rear as on the other three sides.

He walked resolutely across to the tools he had passed, neatly laid out on improvised shelves. Running his light back and forth he selected a hand drill and a small saw. Fifteen minutes later, after drilling enough contiguous holes to allow the point of the saw to enter, he was neatly incising a square five inches by five inches, which he jimmied out, permitting him to train the light into the box.

There were bundles of electrical wire, an assortment of what looked like converters, or adapters—several boxes of them—and, still visible before the surrounding materials choked off the light, an instrument that appeared to have an aerial appended to it. He inserted his arm through the little hole and drew the device gently out.

He studied it. Some sort of radio, since it had an aerial and a speaker. Conceivably a listening station? For instructions?

From whom?

He gripped the radio and slowly, carefully, drew out the aerial. He propped the radio against the back of the box, and the steam from his breath hindered for a moment his inspection of the dials. One switch was clearly the On/Off switch, so he turned it on, heard a click, and a gratifying hum. Then nothing. He would try turning up the volume. He put his finger on the knob and turned it gradually clockwise. Still no reception. He continued to turn, and at the end of the cycle there was a click, as if the knob had reached the end and would be locked there. But it bounced back. So he turned it again, and again, and again, causing a click-click-click.

BUZZ. BUZZ-BUZZ-BUZZ. Blackford sprang from his bed and dove into his clothes closet, whence the unmistakable signal had unmistakably issued. He bent over his set and instinctively raised it to his lips so that he could reply to the signaler. But he paused. To *what* signaler? Only Hallam Spring and Bruce Pulling had access to the counterpart set in the chapel, reserved for extraordinary communications between them, and they had all said goodnight to one another at the bar a half hour earlier, all three heading for bed. The box. With the instruments. And the other things . . . In less than three minutes, wearing a sweater and corduroy pants over his pajamas, he was in his car, his flashlight beside him. Approaching the courtyard he forced himself to be calm, and gestured nonchalantly at the night sentry who, recognizing him, waved him past. He doused the headlights and slid the car up under the old tree, thirty yards from the doorway to the chapel. Stepping out he realized how cold it had become. Now all the lights of the courtyard were out save a dim undifferentiated illumination that hung over the sentry boxes at the palace, and by the sentry he had just passed. He grabbed his light and walked slowly, noiselessly, to the door of the chapel. He stopped and listened. A faint noise within. He concentrated. What was it? The sound came in strokes of irregular interval, and the tones were not equally pitched. One stroke sounded squeaky; and then he knew that the man inside was sawing wood. The same man who had just now used the radio. Why, having apparently gained access to the box, was he now sawing wood?

The sawing stopped. Oakes concentrated his thoughts furiously. *In the box was all the equipment Spring and Pulling had brought to permit them to adapt to the requirements of any situation.* Most of the material was consistent with the general inventory an electrician would need on rebuilding a chapel—wiring, voltmeters, generators, the radio—explosives? He thought quickly: What might be the excuse for a variety of explosives at St. Anselm's chapel? He knew now that he was at the mercy of an intangible: the intelligence and the degree of suspicion of whoever was examining the box. He feared the worst. Routine inspection would not be conducted at this hour, or with such tenacity. His heart was pounding as he forced himself painfully to think through the alternatives. His mind closed on them. And all of them required that he open the door lest the man inside should leave the chapel and—become the proximate cause of a third world war, for God's sake! Blackford flashed on the light, swung open the door, closed it shut behind him, and said in a loud tone aiming the light at the box, "Who's there?"

Wagner came out from behind the box, a

bundle of dynamite sticks in his hands. Blinded by the shaft of light, he could not see Blackford, but recognized his voice. His own flashlight thrust forward, Wagner walked two steps toward Blackford, dropped the dynamite and, his free hand wrestling to unbutton his overcoat, let out a long fierce yell. *HOOOOWWWWWAAAWWOOW-WW!* Wagner's flashlight waved wildly as with his other hand he thrust for his pistol. In the darting shafts of light, Black saw the wine case, grabbed a bottle by the neck and with the massed strength of his whole body thrust it fiercely up at Wagner's Adam's apple, exactly as he had been trained to do at the gymnasium in Arlington. Wagner fell back, lifeless, dead. Blackford, sweating through the cold, dragged the tarpaulin over him, pushing under it the hand with the pistol grip locked firmly in it. He grabbed the bottle of wine, smashed the cork end across a pile of bricks, shielded the ragged edge with his thumb and second finger providing a nipple and, struggling to imitate the goulish frightened scream he had just heard, repeated it again, *HOOOOOOWWWWA-AAWWOOOWWWWW!* He walked quickly to the north end to his study, turned on the light and shouted one more time. He was halfway through the shout when the door burst open and the two sentries, lights flashing, automatic weapons pointed, descended on him. Blackford looked at them and took a long swallow from the bottle of wine. Lowering his voice, he began again to wail.

"I am so sad, my friends, I am so sad! Here" —he aimed the wine bottle drunkenly at the empty glass on his desk—"here, have some wine. I was in bed, my friends, right in bed, right . . . ready . . . when she—no explanation, mind you, not a word of explanation—what did I do to her, you may be thinking? I did *nothing* to her. *Ooooh.*"

"Quiet! Herr Oakes! You will waken the castle itself."

"Nothing! I did nothing to her, and she ups and leaves me. I run after her—practically in my pajamas!—but she has disappeared, and I can think now only of my work to distract me, but I cannot disguise my grief!"

"You had better go home and get some sleep, Herr Oakes," said the older of the two men, offering to give him a hand. Blackford drained the wine bottle and agreed that perhaps this was advisable, slurring his words. And then he turned and said to the senior sentry:

"Do you suppose she might have changed her mind? Come back to my room?"

The young guard muttered to his companion in rapid, idiomatic German that if she did, she would not take much satisfaction from Herr Oakes in this condition.

Blackford began slowly to walk out, clutching the bottle, though it was empty now, and chattering ceaselessly as he teetered past the door, grabbing it for balance.

At the car to which the guards escorted him the senior guard said, "Do you want me to drive you to the inn, Herr Oakes?" Blackford took mock offense, stiffened as if he were a general conducting an inspection tour, stepped into the driver's seat, stripped the gear, lurched the car in reverse, and then, after several forward spasms, the car began to move, and Blackford waved regally, driving off.

He knocked softly on Hallam Spring's door. In a minute it was open and Blackford, still breathing heavily, let himself in.

"Get Pulling," he whispered.

Spring went to the adjacent room through the connecting door and in a moment came back with Bruce Pulling, looking apprehensive but, like Spring, wholly alert.

Blackford sat on the couch and made motions requesting a scratch pad. Spring snatched one from the desk, giving it to Oakes with a pencil.

Blackford wrote, *Is this room clean?*

Spring read the pad and broke silence. "Yes," he said in a normal tone of voice. "We sweep it every couple of days. Go ahead, but keep your voice down anyway."

"I just came from the chapel. I killed Jürgen Wagner. He sawed his way into the provisions box. When I came in he had a bundle of dynamite in his hand. He had sawed open the back of the box and pulled out the walkie-talkie and, screwing around with it, buzzed my unit. I got the signal and tore over there. I got there, I figure, just after he finished sawing a big section out of the rear, so I went in. He let out a godawful scream, so I gave it to him in the throat with a wine bottle. Just in time. When he went down he had a pistol in his hand."

"How'd you get out?" Spring reverted to a whisper.

"I yelled and screamed where Jürgen left off. Pretended I was drunk—no sweat with the sentries, who heard the yowling and ran in. Now: You two have got to get there in the morning ahead of Overstreet and the gang. They check in at eight. How long do you figure it would take to put the body in the box or in a tarpaulin, clean up whatever is suspicious, and load it on the half-ton?"

"Not long," Spring said. "Figure an hour to be safe."

"Okay. The faster you can do it the better. It wouldn't look good driving the half-ton in there too early. So—get there at seven. Now, what's the point in keeping the gear in the box you know you're not going to need, no matter what? . . . For God's sake, Bruce, will you stop taking notes on that fucking pad? Can't you memorize: *Seven A.M., remove corpse, remove TNT?*"

Hallam ignored the blast, motioning Pulling to put away the pad. "No point. Bruce and I were talking about that yesterday when we finished sizing up the job. But we figured a supply of explosives in a chapel being rebuilt is less suspicious than a supply of explosives in a sleepy medieval inn, if somebody stumbled into them."

"Well, somebody did, and came out shooting. Get them out. Take them to Bonn with you in the morning and deposit them with Sergeant

Gold. We don't know what they're going to start searching when Wagner stays lost. Now on that problem. He'll fit in the box if you take out the junk and put it in the tarpaulin. But you'll have to nail back the section Wagner sawed off."

"What do we do with the box?" Pulling asked.

"The long-term objective is to keep it from being discovered, ever. The immediate objective is to keep it from being discovered before the elections."

"That's one week. What kind of . . . condition is he in?"

"The neck will be black where the trachea was fractured. But there's no blood. I'll tell you what. I'll check this out with my guy in Bonn, but let's assume it'll go this way: Take it in the box to Gold at Engineers, and have them put in for a coffin. I'll suggest we fly him out with papers as a U.S. Army casualty, and bury him at Arlington or someplace. My people will attend to the paperwork, you get him into a coffin as soon as possible and remove all identifying material."

"When do we get the final word?"

"Oh what, the coffin?"

"No. The elimination."

"Tomorrow. When I come back from Bonn I'll have it. Now, I'll be getting to the chapel tomorrow at the usual hour. Have the truck loaded up, but don't bring it out past the sentries until the working gang is in. If there is any reason to call me, don't use the walkie-talkie. Ring me in *this* room—give me your extra room key, Hallam. Erika's bug is out, but I don't trust her or Bolgin.

289

I'll be in this room between seven and eight. Then I'll head for the chapel.

"Goodnight," he said.

Back in his room, he undressed, showered, and put on fresh pajamas. His dreams were tormenting, confused. He was at Yale, entering an examination room without having read any of the books, but when he reached for them they quicksilvered their way through his fingers. He was in Washington, surreptitiously dropping the addresses of the safe houses to the Soviet ambassador, when a hand clapped him on the shoulder: it was J. Edgar Hoover. He was in Buckingham Palace at a ball when suddenly his trousers slipped down, and he was wearing no underwear. Suddenly he was the Dutch boy back at the dike. He looked down, to find that Holland was being kept from flooding by—a wine bottle pressed into the dike. Now he was taking Holy Orders in a reconstituted chapel at St. Anselm's, and felt peace at last, and slept.

20

At a quarter to eight the phone rang in Spring's room and Blackford picked it up.

"Everything is going well. Anything at your end?"

"No, I'll be there in a little while. So long."

He walked out and looked more intently than usual to see who, if anyone, might be looking at him. The street had only normal traffic, mostly Volkswagens and Fiats and bicycles, carrying the people of St. Anselm's to their shops and offices and to the leather factory and distillery. Blackford walked across the street to the Westfalenkrug and ordered coffee. He looked about again at the three or four figures usually there at that hour and was satisfied no one was covering him. He bought the morning paper and read an account of Axel Wintergrin's speech the afternoon before at Stuttgart, of the crowds, the ovation. Paper in hand, he walked casually back to the pay phone. He was grateful for the German propensity to massiveness. The telephone closet was virtually soundproof. Having carefully rehearsed his message, he rang the number for Singer Callaway.

"Hello, Singer. How are you? Good. I got bad news from home. Montenegro broke his leg. Jockey's fault, same guy I trained. They're taking the remains to Corpus Christi; be there in a couple of hours, I guess, local time. But anyway, I'll be seeing you on schedule. Anything for me?" Blackford had communicated: *I killed Jürgen Wagner and his corpse is being taken to our drop at the Corps of Engineers and will arrive in a couple of hours.*

There was tension in Callaway's voice.

"No, nothing. Great then, I'll be seeing you."

At the courtyard everything appeared normal, though he noticed that the sentry looked at him a little impishly. No doubt the story of the evening's debauch had made the rounds and the morning shift knew all about the vinous behavior of Blackford Oakes the night before. Or was he deluding himself? He managed with his eye something an innocent outsider would dismiss as a tic, but an insider would take as a genial wink. The sentry winked back, and Blackford moved into the parking area. As he left the car he was approached by Kurt Grossmann.

"Have you seen Jürgen Wagner, Blackford?"

"No. At least, not since yesterday afternoon. What's up?"

"Stiller and I were with him until ten last night. He wasn't at the seven-thirty staff meeting this morning. We checked the inn. He's not there and didn't spend the night there."

"You don't suppose our Jürgen has been revelling?"

"He'd have had to revel with Mother Margaret"—the reference was to the 300-pound barmaid at the Anselmsklaus—"because the sentries don't have him checked out of the courtyard. That means he spent the night here—occasionally he does, usually on the couch in the banquet hall. Well, just checking. If the sentry made a mistake, he sure picked the wrong guy to make a mistake about. Wagner will have his ass when he shows up. See you."

Blackford took his advantage.

"Oh, Kurt, is the count still planning to be here tomorrow?"

"Yes, during the day. He's here now, and going tonight to Hamburg, back late, then Freiburg tomorrow night. Monday night there's the big final rally in West Berlin—that's the one we're really going to need Wagner for!—then back here Tuesday to vote, and listen to the returns. The TP people begged him to set up shop in larger quarters Tuesday night, so we're going back to Königshof in Bonn."

"Good," Blackford said. "He may want to see me tomorrow." He waved and walked to the chapel. The half-ton truck was parked, as it so

293

often was, just outside the church door, and Blackford, without turning his head, managed to scrutinize the inside of the truck as he passed by. The box was well forward. Behind it was assorted material, including a large cardboard barrel filled with papers and crating materials sticking up from its mouth. He walked inside, up the aisle and left to his office, beckoning to Hallam Spring. He shut the door and sat down at his desk.

"I got the word to Bonn. They'll be expecting you. Take the truck just the way it is. Any problems?"

"We had a hell of a time trying to lift the box into the truck. Finally ramped it up on a board. But it was loaded away well before Overstreet and the gang got here."

"Did the sentries question you coming in?"

"Only the usual."

"Okay, take off."

Blackford walked out to the courtyard from which he could follow with his eyes the truck to the sentry post. The guards waved it on its way.

Inside he went to the fatal spot and dropped his pen. He bent down as if looking for it, and scrutinized the area. There was nothing. He got up and walked to where Overstreet was expostulating with a German carpenter. After reconciling them, he addressed Overstreet:

"I'll be leaving for Bonn after lunch. I've requisitioned a couple of extra electric heaters. Hallam has set it up so that we can handle the extra load. Maybe I'll be able to bring them back from Bonn after I do my own business."

"Sooner the better," said Overstreet, rubbing his arms for circulation.

Blackford went to the office and spent five joyous hours in the womb of amoral science, checking inclines, templates, cut lines, the mechanical preliminaries to the art of stained glass; he never loved science, with all its engrossing, bloodless concerns, more. Then, carrying a cheese sandwich in a hard roll in a paper bag, he walked to his car and set out for Bonn.

In Westphalia the meadows stay obstinately green into November, and the tall poplars give up their leaves grudgingly. The air was sweet and cold, and he marveled that he was never out of sight of the most distinctive characteristic of that countryside, the sharp spire of a church, reaching surefootedly, knowing confidently its station in life, higher than any surrounding building. The barns, for the most part painted a rich brown red, looked as if they had been retouched to withstand the coming of winter. On the highway, though not yet transformed into the autobahn under construction, the drivers took their cars at speeds for which, in the general consumers' abandon after the war, Europeans had become celebrated. Blackford let them pass, regretting it when the telltale signs of urban concentration began.

During the drive he prayed. *Lord, let the German people spare the life of Thy servant Axel by rejecting him in the popularity polls.* Blackford had never desired anything so much. He tried praying to St. Anselm. *Dear St. Anselm: Intercede in behalf of the lord of St. Anselm's. You, who proved the existence of God, help prevent others from playing the role of God. . . .* The sandwich untouched, he parked the car three blocks from Rufus's flat, which he reached at the designated minute, 5:03.

The moment he walked into the room, he knew.

He had *always* known. Known right from the beginning. An Axel Wintergrin *could not be permitted to live* in this world. That wasn't the way he would put it to Rufus, but that was the way it was. When he looked at their faces he could tell by a kind of human refraction that he must have turned very pale. Quietly, lest his stomach turn, or his head feel giddy, he sat down on the couch and addressed Rufus.

"We go?"

"We go."

"How bad is it? I mean how . . ."

"The poll we tabulated at two shows Axel Wintergrin with thirty-seven per cent of the vote, four points *ahead* of Adenauer, and only seven ahead of Ollenhauer. So—we are to go ahead."

From now on for Rufus it was all business. "Have you definitely established he will be there tomorrow?"

"Yes, I asked this morning."

"Are you certain you can get him into the chapel?"

"Hell, Rufus, how can I be *certain?* All I can tell you is he's never refused to come before; he's made maybe fifty trips to the chapel in the last three months. But certain, shit. I mean suppose before he gets there the Russians declare war or something?"

"Tomorrow is the one day the Russians definitely won't declare war."

Blackford changed the subject. He would have talked about the World Series to stay away from the one remaining question he knew Rufus had to ask him. "Did you get Wagner taken care of?"

"Yeah," Singer said. "He's lying in a coffin in the warehouse, with the American flag over it and an honor guard. He'll fly out tonight on the regular milk run. We pulled an emergency set of papers we keep here. He'll be buried tomorrow."

"Where? . . . What the hell. What do I care *where* he's buried? " Blackford raised his hand. "Don't tell me. Thank God he's a bachelor. From now on, Rufus, promise to make me kill only bachelors, okay? I've developed a taste for killing bachelors."

Rufus observed him sharply. He understood. But Rufus did not make room for imponderables. He needed to probe Blackford's emotional state, and proposed to stay with him until he had done so. There was always the alternative plan, but it was far riskier. This plan, centering on Oakes, was sound, he felt. He, Rufus, must see it through. That, Rufus permitted himself a moment's introspection, was what his life had come to mean to him. The thinking gets done: and then action consistent with that thinking is taken. Otherwise thought is vapid, meaningless, frivolous.

"I'm sorry about Wagner. Tell us about it."

Blackford recounted the story.

Rufus was pensive. One of his silences ensued. And, finally:

"Was Wagner close to anybody? Is there anybody with whom he might have shared whatever suspicions took him to the chapel in the first place?"

"He wasn't close to anyone I know of. But he was devoted to his job, terribly thorough. More thorough than the poor bastard Wintergrin could really stand. I don't know if he ever confided any suspicions to Wintergrin."

"Might he have kept a log, or notebook, in which he wrote that he intended to inspect the chapel?"

"I don't know," Blackford said, reproaching himself for not having wondered about that possibility.

"If he did, and if the last entry in it says he's going off to check the chapel, we could be in trouble when the sentries are quizzed about your late appearance there."

Rufus went on: "Did Spring or Pulling find a notebook on him?"

"I don't know," Blackford said, feeling like a schoolboy.

Rufus looked at Singer, who without further ado picked up the telephone and dialed a number.

"Sergeant Gold, Singer here. Do you have the personal belongs of Corporal Selznick?"

"I have them in the safe."

"Did you examine them?"

"Yes."

"Was there a notebook?"

"Not exactly. A scratch pad. And the notes on it were all in English. Besides that, there was just his wallet, identification, a little money."

"No address book, or notebook other than the scratch pad? . . . Right . . . Right. I tell you what. Get that stuff out of the safe and bring it around in a sealed envelope. Leave it with Frau Augstein. Thanks."

Black reported his conversation with Kurt Grossmann, which suggested that, at least as of eight that morning, they hadn't got around to looking about suspiciously for clues on his desk. Then he said—

"I tell you what we *could* do. We could ask Erika to look on Wagner's desk. Her desk is about ten feet away, and she's not going to Hamburg, because Axel's giving the same talk there he gave at Stuttgart."

He and Singer looked at Rufus. Rufus was thinking again.

Finally he looked at his watch. It was nearing six. "No, we won't call her now. If they decide to examine the desk, they will already have reviewed its contents. If they have not reached that point of apprehension or suspicion, they probably won't until tomorrow, or—who knows? —even the day after tomorrow. To call Erika without having arranged a code is dangerous. Look her up tonight, Black, and get her to go to work early and look then in Wagner's desk. If there is anything there that suggests the chapel was his destination last night, get it from her and destroy it, and tell her to leave everything else intact. Sooner or later they will get around to it. It is fortunate that the missing man happens to be the man who would be directing the investigation if he were around. We have to assume that the trail will not lead to you, Black, or that if it does, there will be nothing like enough evidence to indict you. Your behavior in the chapel was concededly bizarre, but to prove on the basis of it that you killed Wagner is more than anybody could handle. People don't move with great speed in these matters. And from tomorrow at about four the concerns of the Wintergrin people will be over other matters. But now of course is the time to plan for all contingencies. If Erika informs you tomorrow morning that the desk *has* been searched, I would *still* think it safe to assume you would not be questioned during the day—certainly nothing resembling formal action would be initiated. But if tomorrow you should be approached, then after the elimination"—he says it now without pausing, Blackford noticed—"you will need to be careful. It might prove necessary to go home, but only if the police start showing an interest in you. Otherwise you are to stay in St. Anselm's until the spring at least."

Rufus turned suddenly to Singer.

"Shall we have a glass of sherry?"

He hadn't said anything so libertine even on the critical evening in London, Blackford thought. Blackford had regained his color, but his eyes were darker, furtive, and Rufus could not descry their meaning. Singer poured, and Rufus then said it, using exactly the words Blackford *knew* he would use. Blackford knew that, if only to make it hard for himself, Rufus would use the most provocative formulation, tushery and all:

"Are you prepared to do your duty, Blackford?"

Blackford put down his glass.

"Rufus, I don't want to be argumentative. But are you aware that I was never told on joining this outfit that I would be expected to kill people in cold blood? Let alone the leading anti-Communist in Europe?"

"This organization is structured to deal with contingencies. Are you saying we should have—could have—recruited people disposed to deal with *this* contingency, and trained them to do so? Where would we find them? Just what would we tell them? How would we train them? You aren't *required* to do it even now. But I *am* required to lay it on the line. The fact is the commander-in-chief of your government, his principal foreign affairs adviser, and the director of the intelligence agency devoted to protecting American interests —our sovereignty, our freedom—by nonmilitary means; these men, drawing on all their resources —yes, moral resources included—*feel that the situation is critical:* that this single man's activities are about to put the lives and liberties of whole peoples on the line. They despise, as I do, the government that has given us this ultimatum. They cannot even know, for certain, whether that threat is bluff. But they agreed, finally, that responsible statesmanship forbade taking so awful a risk—consider it"—Rufus managed to say it so that it sounded fresh, and awful—*"conceivably, the risk of millions of people dead*. They negotiated as hard as I have ever known our people to negotiate."

"Harder than at Yalta and Potsdam?" Black interrupted.

Rufus let it pass. "Yes, harder than at Yalta and Potsdam. At every level. And finally, even on a little point, a point that was trivial to Stalin, but important to us: the matter of who should pull the lever. Here was the high point of Stalin's sadism, and the low point in our humiliation. *It doesn't matter to him. It does matter to us.* The best we got was the concession we played out in Switzerland; and you, and the United States, lost.

"So I put it this way, Blackford. You are the front-line agent of the commander-in-chief. You have been involved in the evolution of the plan. And it was you who drew the card. In doing so— never mind your reservations, which I admit you registered—you made, your protestations notwithstanding, a contract. If you decide now to refuse, we will have to try to maneuver without you. But if we should fail, you may be directly responsible for suffering on a terrible scale. Certainly you will be responsible—I speak now of what *has* happened, not of what will, or might, happen—for murder. For the murder of Jürgen Wagner. Because if the plan for tomorrow does not go forward, then what you did to Wagner was impermissible. If you follow through tomorrow, then last night you acted as a soldier. If tomorrow you refuse to consummate the plan, then last night you murdered."

Blackford recoiled at the word. He paused a long time, and refilled his sherry glass. The room was silent. Then he said,

"Let's get on with the details."

21

He called Erika from Bonn and asked if she would have a late drink with him. Yes, she said, but she too would be working late. It occurred to Blackford that that was fine. "I've got to go to the chapel for a minute, so I'll pick you up at your office. How's that? About ten?"

As he drove he forced away the main theme, concentrating on the notation. *He would much prefer going over Wagner's desk himself,* without asking Erika to do so and giving her, unnecessarily, the story on Wagner. (Why should she—they —have and enjoy that extra mug shot of criminal America?) He pondered how he might physically manage it, and turned on the radio. The lead bulletin was of a joint declaration between the lame-duck President of the United States and his successor, declaring that any military aggression by the Soviet Union against West Germany would be met with the full force of NATO's troops. "Neither the President nor the President-elect mentioned any possible use of atomic defenses," the commentator said, "and there was no immediate reaction in Moscow, where a general mobilization was ordered a week ago." The commentator went on to review the day's profuse endorsements by labor union leaders and newspapers of the candidacy of Axel Wintergrin. Blackford snapped off the radio.

At dinner with Singer Callaway in Rufus's apartment he had thought back on their dinner together the preceding January, when neither spoke of the next day's enterprise. Tonight they did. Resisting moral speculation, they talked only about the plan, so thoroughly rehearsed now since the idea of how to kill Axel Wintergrin came to Hallam Spring. At a long meeting with Rufus, Callaway, and Blackford in Bonn, ten days earlier, Spring and Pulling had read from their portfolio of choices.

Spring provided the narrative, Pulling the technical interpolations, leafing through his copious notebooks for details. The requirement—that it should be accepted as an accidental death—clearly contracted the possibilities, and palpably depressed Bruce Pulling with his affinity for explosives, which are uneasily assigned to detonate accidentally. Pulling argued the plausibility of an avalanche destroying Wintergrin's caravan descending from the courtyard, and he was in-

dustrious enough to document a natural phenomenon of similar nature in 1755—"perhaps related
to the earthquake in Lisbon," he suggested, hope-
fully. Blackford asked whether it was a concomi-
tant part of the plan that a diversionary earthquake in Lisbon should be engineered on November 12, and Pulling, returning to the notes,
said, No, he didn't think that necessary. There
was a Poison Plan (mother's mushrooms), a Car-
bon Monoxide Plan (old exhaust pipes in the
hermetically enclosed Daimler), an Incendiary
Plan (he would perish in his bedroom from the
smoke before the flames consumed the castle).
The mode decided on, and checked out as agreed
with Bolgin in Switzerland, was what they came
to call the Scope Plan.

The division of responsibility was straight-
forward. Blackford must contrive to deliver Axel
Wintergrin to the chromoscope. As always, Wintergrin would sit down, bend over until his forehead touched the face plate, and stand by to adjust the waist-level levers rooted on opposite sides
of the chromoscope. Blackford would then turn
on the current at the switchboard. A few seconds
would go by while the count fiddled with the
adjustments. "Then you gotta do *your* part,"
Spring said to Blackford.

Blackford's "part" would sit in the pocket of
his jacket. A cigarette-package-sized transmitter.
On depressing the switch a module tucked into
the chromoscope would be activated.

"The way I worked it out," Hallam Spring
had explained at the midnight session to Rufus,
Singer Callaway, and Blackford, Pulling at his

side doodling on a notepad, "is this. We're better off electrocuting the subject sometime after the power is turned on. Otherwise it has the feeling of an . . . execution. I could fix up the module with a computer circuit to go off when the subject moves the light lever on the right of the box the nth time, say the fifth—or the fiftieth, for that matter. But that would require monitoring the use of the chromoscope before the subject used it and counting exactly how many times it's used before the subject comes in, and I figure *that's* no good. The alternative is to detonate by a portable transmitter. It's a solid-state-receiver module, works like one of those garage-door deals, door goes up when you push the little transmitter button in your car.

"The chromoscope is wooden, so it's easy to insulate. I'll substitute a plastic linkage for the light lever, instead of the metal linkage inside the casing now, and lead a wire right to the metal handle. Another wire will lead up to the metal face port. I'd suggest Blackford wait maybe five, six seconds, to augment the impression that something went screwy inside the box, rather than have the one-to-one electrical effect of a guy turning a switch, then POW!

"Now when the house current, two hundred and twenty volts, is released, the subject's right hand will clamp onto the lever with the grip of a pit bull (reflex action), and contortion will force the head harder onto the face plate as the two hundred and twenty volts flow from the hand up the arm through the heart into the head and face. This will stop the heart. No ands, ifs or buts.

308

"The second function of the internal module is the incendiary one. It will go off at the same moment the electricity is sent to the right-hand lever and the face plate. The same current source will go into an igniter core, a block of magnesium (or chemical mixture—I'll decide between the two), either one capable of intense heat for enough time so that the fire will spread through the box and destroy the module and the insides of the machine. I can even rig it so the heat/fire source could spatter pieces around to accelerate the fire within the box.

"Here's something else I'll do. Wrap with rubber tape the heat/fire source, and that will produce plenty of 'burning wire' smell. Nothing to it. Window dressing. But people expect electrical fires to smell like something burning."

And he finished with easygoing pride. "You like?"

Blackford asked Singer Callaway how Spring and Pulling would stand up under questioning.

"They're trained agents. They won't budge. As for the plan, we ran it through the lab in Maryland. It checks out. There shouldn't be any problem. They can peer into the bowels of the scope all they want to. They won't find anything. A crazy accident."

"After I fry him, am I supposed to register the conventional emotions? Or do you have a special emotion reserved for me?"

"Cut it, Blacky, nobody likes this business. You're to be both dismayed and unbelieving.

Electricity isn't your specialty, but you have never been given any reason to believe the scope was dangerous. You might yell a little at Conditti—his dad invented the thing. An accident is an accident."

Singer then rehearsed Blackford in emergency instructions to be followed in the hideous event of a snafu. Blackford knew Rufus well enough to wonder whether Blackford's own elimination might be an integral part of the deal, and he voiced the suspicion.

"I give you my word it isn't."

"I believe you, Singer, but I wouldn't have much trouble dismantling that assurance if I were Rufus. You could be under instructions to give me your word."

"Well, Black, if you believe that, then you shouldn't ask me in the first place, because *ex hypothesi* I can't satisfy you."

"Maybe I ought to tell you that a letter is waiting someplace to be sent to my lawyer if I'm not around to stop it? Shall I tell you that, Singer?"

"*Are* you telling me that?"

"No. I'm just wondering whether I *should* say that, even if I hadn't actually taken the precaution."

"This is getting a little complicated, Black."

"Yeah, let's drop it." And, a moment later, "I'd better get moving. I've got to check with Erika later on tonight."

"There's one thing more, Blacky." Singer walked over to his briefcase, twiddled the combination lock, and drew out a pouchful of pipe tobacco. He reached inside and pulled out a metal-gray case. "The transmitter. Two switches: 'Battery On,' and 'Depress.' It's been tested." He reinserted it into the pouch, and handed it to Blackford.

"Will I see you again, Singer?"

"I don't know, Blacky. If all goes well, they may pull me out right away. *You* have to stick around."

"If I'm alive, Singer. And if I'm alive—"

"Yes?"

"I'm going to stay here until the chapel is finished. Put in that word for me. Okay?"

"The chapel will take another year, maybe."

"In that case I'll stay here another year."

"I understand." He rose, reached for Blackford's coat, helped him on with it, and led him to the door, where he shook his hand warmly.

Blackford pulled into the courtyard, parked, and told the sentry at the palace he was expected by Erika Chadinoff. In the old dining hall he saw Erika at work with her Polish assistant on a manuscript. He went by her, waved silently so as not to interrupt her while giving instructions, sat down at Jürgen Wagner's desk and reached for the phone.

Erika had paused, so he sang out to her: "Got to put in a call—I forgot my mother's birthday. Do you mind?"

"No, go ahead. I can quit anytime, but there's always work to do."

In the swivel chair he pivoted his back to

Erika, dialed the long-distance operator, and gave his mother's number in London, inverting the last two digits. "Make that a collect call from Blackford Oakes. O-a-k-e-s. O for Otto, A for Adalbert, K for Kaiser, E for Emil, S for Sophie."

His eyes combed the desk furiously. Unfamiliar with it, he did not know whether the neatness suggested it had already been inspected, or whether great neatness was the way of Jürgen Wagner. As if looking for a piece of paper, he opened the right-hand drawer and fussed with its contents. Here were two slender notebooks. The contents of the desk had presumably not been sequestered. The receiver still in his hand, even though the operator had said she would call back, he maneuvered to open the first notebook. He saw names and disbursements. The second listed contacts in different cities. As if failing to find what he was looking for, he opened the drawer on the left side. It was the stationery drawer. He thought it wise to scoop up a sheet of paper to scribble on. He felt a bulge under the pile of paper, probed it, and came up with a trim leather diary, small enough to fit in the pocket of his suit. He would read it that night.

"She's not in? All right, operator, cancel the call. I'll ring in the morning. Thank you." He made a notation on the paper and stuffed it in his pocket.

He pivoted the chair back to face Erika. "All set?"

"All set."

They drove in their own cars to the inn. It occurred to Blackford that, diary safely in hand, he had no official business left to discuss with Erika. So—they might just as well have a drink, he thought.

But seated in the saloon she began "Did you know Jürgen Wagner was missing?"

"Yes. Kurt told me this morning. Do you have any reason to suspect he has a line on you? Or me?"

"No. But I know he didn't like you, and a few days ago he suggested to Wintergrin that he suspend all activity in the chapel until after the election. Roland told me—Axel told him, and said he had vetoed Wagner's suggestion."

"Well," said Blackford, "maybe he's defected!"

She did not want to play. "I sent in a report on his disappearance."

Blackford nodded. "Maybe I'll do the same thing."

She looked at him under the light. He was dressed in a blue blazer, gray flannel pants, and a narrow regimental tie. Probably what he wore as a sophomore at Yale, she thought correctly. The fingers of his right hand were fiddling with his wine glass. His head was slightly bent, the light above his head drew out the blond in his hair, and she sensed the distraction in his pale, slender, almost childlike features. He was perhaps projecting the role his fingers would play tomorrow? Might as well wade into it.

"Bolgin raised a point. If Axel's feet are off the floor when he sits down on the stool, there wouldn't be a ground."

"Crap."

313

"Does that mean you don't want to talk about it?"

"It means it's unlikely Bolgin has thought about anything more comprehensively than we have, especially anything that elementary. The scope itself provides the ground. He could be tap dancing on it and still he'd be a goner. Don't worry about it."

"You're doing the only thing, Black"—she reached out her hand. "I know your feelings about him and his movement. I understand your feelings about him personally. But he is an anachronism. I mean, look at that place. Count Axel von Euchen Wintergrin indeed! Private castle. Private chapel. Lord of the manor stuff. This isn't Graustark."

"Better Graustark than your little Siberian resorts."

"Let's not get into that again. The point is he projected himself as the leader of an insurrectionary movement that's moved us toward a great war, and everyone who matters has agreed he's got to go, it's that simple."

He looked up at her. What could have made her, at twenty-three, so talented, and so . . . *dumb*.

"For the record, Erika, everybody who matters *didn't* agree he's got to go. *Our* people agreed to the elimination"—here he was, himself using that word!—"because *you* gave *us* no alternative. That's the official view of it. God knows it isn't *my* view of it. I'd have told Gromyko to go straight to hell, which is where he's going in due course anyway."

"I'm glad you're not President of the United States."

"And I wish *you* were Secretary of the Central Committee of the Communist Party. I'd like to hear *you* issue orders to kill someone in cold blood. You're taking refuge in the concept of Higher Authority—"

She interrupted him. "Aren't you?"

He breathed deeply. "Erika," he said patiently, "I didn't mean to be provocative. But your organizational discipline is for the purpose of imposing the will of one man—the will of one ideology, if you insist—on others. *Our* organization is defensive in nature. Its aim is to defeat your aggressive intentions. The acceptance of discipline in the one enterprise isn't the equivalent of the acceptance of discipline in the other enterprise. I accept the need for discipline. I am troubled only by my human revulsion at the discrete enterprise we're engaged in, and by an awful feeling that the West is aborting a great historical opportunity. But please, don't say that Goering following Hitler's orders is the equivalent of Montgomery following Churchill's orders. You begin by the dissimilarities between Churchill and Hitler. That factor wrecks all derivative analogies."

"Stalin has his weaknesses, but he also has his great strengths." Erika thought it imprudent to continue the argument.

"Yeah, he eats people. But it's very good for the blood. And the muscle tissue. And the complexion."

"Come on, Blackford."

But he had risen, leaving money for the drinks.

"Sorry, Erika. I'm bad company tonight."

She got up. "Never mind. I understand. And"—she tapped him lightly on the hand; if she had said to him "good luck," he thought, he might just hit her—"remember, perhaps not next week or next year even, but one day you'll see that cooperation between our two movements is the right thing."

He said nothing, but leaned over, in the European manner, and brushed his lips on her right hand, rubbing her determined fingers thoughtfully.

22

On Friday, November 12, the temperature was muggy-cool, the morning light gray, the southerly wind bringing in the depressing, unseasonal föhn that sleazes over Europe with dumpy barometric pressures that enervate and depress (in Munich the doctors decline nonemergency surgery during a föhn). Blackford, at twenty-six, was immune to vicissitudes in the weather. He enjoyed the sun, but more often than not, if otherwise absorbed, didn't really notice whether it was shining. Today he was unaware of the weather, having taken no notice of it since waking at the summons from his alarm after a hectic sleep; though at last, his mind was made up.

He dressed carefully. The costume was the

same, the light-brown corduroy pants, the light-blue shirt and beige sweater, but his motions were more deliberate than usual, and as he shaved he looked at his reflected face for the first time he could remember other than to satisfy himself that he had successfully shaved. He noticed that his cheeks were obtrusively pale, his hair lifeless, his lips dry. So he slapped his face to see if the color would return, and thought suddenly of Lady Macbeth, and wondered wildly whether he would be pale forever. He gave up his self-inspection after a few seconds, reaching no conclusion about his face other than that it interested him not at all.

He stared briefly at the hot rolls and butter, drank a half cup of black coffee, and walked across the street to the pay telephone.

There was no need, really, to call Singer. The rules of the agency were: Communicate upstairs as infrequently as is efficient. The rule of thumb is to communicate disturbing news, not reassuring news. He had only reassuring news. Wagner's diary did indeed make mention of the chapel, under a heading of "Areas and Persons to Be Investigated." Wagner had drawn lines down the column up to the chapel, suggesting that investigations had been completed to that point but not including it. But now Wagner's diary no longer existed. It had been cremated in the little fireplace in Blackford's room, and no copy could reasonably be assumed to survive it.

All this he told Singer Callaway, using the code, but really why he called—he knew, and Singer knew—was on the miraculous chance that

Washington had suddenly thought better of the plan, granting a reprieve.

He didn't put the question directly, but he did ask whether he shouldn't telephone Singer later in the day—he was pleading, actually, for an opportunity to make yet another appeal—"in the event you had anything to report." Singer replied slowly, and a little sternly, that no change in plans was conceivable at this late moment, that in the incredible event that such a change should be ordered, he, Blackford, could count on his old friend, Singer, to communicate to him, in time, an interdictory message. So Blackford rehitched himself to the work wheel.

He spent the first half hour with Overstreet, who pronounced the restructuring of the chapel's trussed roof complete, the timbers and crossmembers sound and stalwart. The carpenters were busy now on the choir stalls, the lathe whining away at the kiln-dried wood under the watchful eye of Conditti, transmuting it into the subtle arabesques of an unknown master.

"You know the count's coming in this afternoon to check the glass?"

"That's Conditti's department."

"Yeah, I know. But after he's through looking at the glass, why don't we show him the first meter or so of the choir stall, to see what he thinks of it?"

"Why not? He'd *better* think well of it. We've only got one of the best woodworkers in Europe doing it."

"What did you say?"

Overstreet raised his voice to be heard over

the lathe, and repeated himself. Blackford nodded, and walked over to the chromoscope, beckoning Conditti to join him.

"Wintergrin's coming in to check the blue this afternoon. Let me have a look at it."

Conditti laid out the sample crystals in the frame, tightened it, and inserted it in the chamber at knee level. Blackford leaned over, looked into the viewing port, and put his hands on the control levers.

"Okay. Light her up."

Conditti pulled the switch and Blackford found himself looking into a deep blue, rich, dark, but translucent. With his right hand he slowly decreased the intensity of the beam. The blue got darker, and, finally, opaque. Under the frame was the lettering 1-B-5.

"Next," Blackford said and Conditti clicked the second frame into position. This blue, 2-B-6, was noticeably lighter.

"I'll try 'em side by side."

Blackford turned the zoom, control permitting all six blues, substantially reduced in size, to be seen at once. He fiddled with the light intensifier and let his eyes travel back and forth from the lightest blue to the darkest, straining to evaluate not only translucence but richness. Viollet-le-Duc, in the *Dictionary of French Architecture*, holds that "the first condition for an artist in glass is to know how to manage blue. The blue is the light in windows, and light has value only by opposition." So Blackford instructed Conditti to arrange on the tray a border of yellows, purples, greens, in identical sequence, to surround each blue, so that the eye could judge the composition. Conditti went to work and Blackford went to his office.

Outside there was hubbub as the campaign caravan returned after the evening at Hamburg. There was no window in Blackford's office, the makeshift ceiling of which began under the north rose, so he could only imagine the scene he had seen so often—Wintergrin jumping out of the car, a weary but exhilarated staff filing out with papers, briefcases, overnight bags. Only four more days . . . What must it be like at the campaign headquarters of Adenauer and Ollenhauer? he wondered.

He felt hungry and asked Overstreet and Conditti if they would join him for soup at the Anselmsklaus. They agreed, and Conditti pulled a bottle of the Tafelwein from the case by the door. He usually brought his own wine and sandwich, ordering soup and coffee from the restaurant. Spring and Pulling, sitting on workbenches, were already eating their box lunches and sipping Coca-Colas. They acknowledged Blackford's perfunctory greeting and went back to their sandwiches, accompanied by the tap of American jazz coming in over their portable radio from the U.S. Armed Forces radio station in Frankfurt.

At the table Blackford asked, "If the count wants a target date, is it too early to give it to him?"

His mouth full, Overstreet nevertheless managed to say, "Figure late summer, early fall"—he swallowed and took a glass of wine—"if we can get enough people on the glass. But with the scope, we can code the colors once and for all, and won't have to bring 'em in one by one to test. The lancet windows won't be any trouble, we'll have that glass in a month. It's going better than I expected."

Blackford nodded.

Conditti asked, "If the old boy becomes chancellor, I understand we might just have to suspend this here project, won't we?"

"Who told you that?" Blackford spoke sharply.

"Well, everybody talks about mobilization and war, that sort of thing. I assume if this place is going to become a battlefield, they aren't going to want American workers underfoot. At least not *this* American worker. I was too young for the last war, and I plan to be too old for the next one."

"Don't you understand," Blackford heard himself almost shouting, "the Russians are bluffing. They've got no *intention* of overrunning Germany. It would be suicidal in the long run, and maybe even in the short run." Conditti and Overstreet were startled by Blackford's vehemence. They had thought him unconcerned with such matters. His next words were reassuring to their image of him.

"At least I don't think they would"—his voice trailed off, as if he had lost interest in the subject.

At three-thirty, a secretary from Count Wintergrin's office came to the chapel to confirm that he would be ready for his appointment at four o'clock promptly.

"I'll come by and pick him up," Blackford said.

"That won't be necessary."

"I have to leave something with Miss Chadinoff," Blackford said, pointing vaguely to a flowerpot at the corner of his desk.

"Very well," she said smiling. "We'll see you later. Do you think the count can finish his inspection within an hour? He has other appointments."

"I think we can be finished by then," Blackford said.

At three forty-five he walked out of his office and approached Conditti, who was working on the mosaic Tree of Jesse. "When the count comes in, Arturo, no need to stop your own work. I can handle the crystals."

Putting on his windbreaker he stepped outside and headed up the courtyard, the little flowerpot in hand. The sentry admitted him and he walked sure-footedly into the dining area to Erika's desk. Her Polish assistant was seated at the next desk down, earplugs on, typing out a translation. He pulled up a chair next to her and set down the flowerpot on her desk.

"Erika," Blackford said in a whisper. "Listen to me carefully." His outward expression, as he slouched in the chair, was relaxed—he had a minute before going in to fetch the count.

"Yes," she said, the smile suddenly gone.

"I'm not going to do it."

"What do you mean, you're not going to do it!"

"Quiet!" he whispered. Then, "Look, we don't have time, so just listen, don't argue. *I* am not going to fire that transmitter. Nothing you or anybody else can do is going to make me. You've joined Axel on his chapel visits from time to time. Well, join him on this one. And then *you* do it if you want to." He pulled the little metal case out of his pocket. "There are two switches." He clicked one. "There, the battery's on. The second switch is that one, recessed to prevent its going off accidentally." Erika stared at the case which Blackford held below the surface of the desk. "The plan is to depress that button about five seconds after the chromoscope is turned on. Then dispose of the damned thing first chance you get. Here's your chance to strike a blow for organizational discipline," said Blackford, dropping the transmitter case discreetly into Erika's open purse. "I'll be a good assistant. I'll put him through his paces. But if the plan goes forward, it'll be because *you* depressed the switch."

She turned to him, unbelieving, trembling, scared, speechless.

Blackford got up. "The show is in your hands. If you don't fire the thing, nobody does, and the plan will abort. Fire it, and maybe you'll be secretly decorated by Stalin. Maybe by my government. Who knows? They could be working up a joint award."

She got up and with her lips made a spitting sound, grabbed her coat with trembling hand, and went out into the corridor. Blackford knocked at the door of Wintergrin's study and Axel opened it himself, the eager light in his eye he inevitably brought to business in the chapel and, in the past few weeks, to visits with Blackford.

"All ready, Blackford. All ready." He pulled a raincoat off a hook and strode out, an arm around Blackford's shoulder, followed by the leech-like Wolfgang. At the vestibule were Erika and Roland. "Come on," he said. "Let's all go and see the progress."

They sat out across the courtyard. Axel engaged Blackford in rapid conversation. "The crowds last night! There was no mistaking their purpose. *No mistaking it.* Their mind has been made up. A few months ago they were excited. Today they are determined. It will come to pass, Blackford, you wait and see."

Blackford had to look away. He could not have spoken at that moment.

He did not have to, because Axel went on. "There was a woman there who stopped me on the way out. She has a mother and two brothers in Leipzig. One of the brothers has been sent to an eastern camp. The mother is in prison for delivering a letter to a friend, a letter from a prisoner to his mother. The woman said she and her family have been praying for me every day since the Frankfurt Convention. And let me make a prediction. On November sixteenth, an intermediary will call on me with the intelligence that the Ulbricht government wishes to negotiate. That's more, Blackford, than a mere hunch. But let's talk about the chapel. About the enduring things."

They reached the door and entered the chapel. The workmen paid no attention to their august but familiar visitor. The visitors walked up the aisle and turned right at the transept. Wintergrin glanced at the chromoscope. "Ah yes, our friend here is proving useful, isn't it? What Meister Gerard could have done with one of these!"

"Yes"—Blackford forced himself to say something—"the flexibility is certainly there."

Wintergrin went rapidly to the operator's position, sitting at the stool, bending over, and reaching for the controls. Roland Himmelfarb was looking casually about the chapel to gauge the progress in a more general way. Blackford looked up at Erika. She was ten yards removed from the switch box, staring resolutely at Oakes. He followed her eyes to the switch box. On an adjacent hook she had hung—her handbag. Her eyes pierced his. Erika Chadinoff was not going to do it. The voice of Count Wintergrin, a little impatient, sang out. "I say, I'm ready, Oakes." Blackford walked to the switch box. Wintergrin, head bent down, hands on the dull-gray levers, went on.

"Maybe this time we'll get it, eh Blackford? The original St. Anselm's blue. Sometimes even at midday I close my eyes and see those blues, the north rose. Everything is more authentic in the mind's eye."

"All ready, Axel," Blackford said huskily and, staring at the hanging handbag, the clasp open, he pulled down the switch, closing his eyes. He counted to himself—one—two—could Erika have left the handbag, but kept the transmitter?—three—four—he opened his eyes and stared into the half-open bag, and spotted the dull-steel corner of the transmitter. Axel was saved! But he continued as if by inertia counting—five—six— seven- -his heart pounded under the pressure of conflicting emotions- -eight—nine—ten--a blast shook the heavy machine, followed by firecracker-style explosions within it, and a searing human moan. Rufus had made contingency arrangements, Blackford knew instantly.

He yelled and yanked off the main switch. Himmelfarb shouted and ran over to Axel, seizing him by the shoulders. "Oh my God! Oh my God! Oh my God!" Wolfgang hurled himself at the machine and pounded his fists on it. Workmen from all sides rushed to help. They stretched out Axel Wintergrin gently on the ground. Himmelfarb yelled at Erika, "Get a doctor! Get a doctor!" She ran out, pausing only to snatch her purse. Roland leaned his ear against Wintergrin's heart.

"There's no sound there," he said, "no sound," he said again, sobbing convulsively until the doctors came, and the ambulance and the guards, taking them both away.

23

Blackford spent the next chaotic hours in the chapel, mostly with Overstreet and Conditti, trying to answer questions for which they had no answers Conditti was heard to say over and over again that his father's chromoscope had never before caused injury, let alone death. He had instantly attacked the charred hulk with screwdrivers and wrenches to examine the blackened interior, but despaired finally to reconstruct the cause of the accident. The electrician at St. Anselm's, conscripted to duty by the magistrate, stared at the remains and professed his inability to explain what had gone wrong, mumbling that it should be shipped to the laboratory at Düsseldorf. "It's like the wreckage of an airplane," he kept repeating to everyone who approached him. Conditti asked Hallam Spring if he could help with the analysis, and Spring traced the electrical cables from the chromoscope to the fuse box behind it, and from there back to the central power source. The wires had standard insulation. Clearly, he surmised, defective insulation inside the box contrived to electrocute Wintergrin, and the short circuit had then caused a fire in the box.

All these deductions were arrived at within the hour, but for three hours more they repeated it, to themselves, to each other, to relays of representatives of Count Wintergrin's staff, to reporters crowded outside (the magistrate forbade them entry into the chapel, posting two guards). There was a press conference of sorts, held at the porch of the chapel, with Overstreet and Conditti answering questions, then the electrician from St. Anselm's, then the magistrate. In the turmoil, there was a sudden silence when Countess Wintergrin, dressed in black, a Bible in hand, walked slowly, unaccompanied, up the steps to the porch. The crowd made silent way for her, resuming their dogged interrogatories only after she had disappeared into the narthex.

She walked slowly but without hesitation up the aisle, observed only by the Portuguese mosaicist, who sat upright on a chair beside his mounds of colored chips, saying a rosary. The countess turned toward the chromoscope but said nothing to Overstreet or Conditti, standing by it, or to the local electrician, on his back wrestling with the wires extruded like spaghetti from the bottom of the machine. She turned to the north side and walked to the open office of Blackford Oakes He was there sitting at his desk, grime and sweat on his face, talking in a rapid and suddenly dislocated German over the telephone to a reporter who had had the ingenuity to come up with the number.

On seeing her he rose and, without comment, hung the receiver on the hook.

The countess, a tight smile on her lips, addressed him.

"Are you satisfied, Mr. Oakes?"

Her atrophied smile was not without a strange understanding. Without giving Blackford time to reply, she turned and walked in measured gait to the half-constructed altar, before which she knelt, bowing her head, her lips moving for a few abject seconds. She rose then, retracted her steps, head slightly bowed. Once again the crowd fell silent as she moved through it and began her way up the cobblestone courtyard one hundred meters to her castle.

Blackford reached his bedroom at ten. All the world, or so it seemed, was at the inn. A half-dozen reporters attempted to reach him, and now he was neither answering the phone nor acknowledging knocks on the door. "I should have insisted on counting your balls. Thank God Rufus saw through you— Spring." Blackford stared at the note, and tossed in finally into the toilet. He tried lying down on his bed, but he could not uncock any muscle in his mind or body. At eleven he got up and knelt to pick up a sheet of paper slipped under the door, only after concluding that otherwise the man pounding on the door would knock it down. The note read: "It is Wolfgang here, to give you protection." He opened the door to the huge frame of Axel Wintergrin's personal bodyguard.

Wordlessly, Wolfgang reached into his back pocket and brought out a weathered black wallet. From it with fumbling fingers Wolfgang took out a piece of blue writing paper, folded. He handed it to Blackford, who opened and read it. Blackford turned white and felt his knees weaken. He murmured to Wolfgang to sit down and went to the bathroom, locking the door. There he was ill. He ran the water to dull the sound of his heaving. After a while gasping for breath, he sat on the toilet seat and stared again at the note. Could he, oh God, be misunderstanding it? He whispered the German words slowly, as if teaching them to a class: *"Wolfgang: Falls mir irgend etwas zustösst* (If anything happens to me), *sofort Herrn Oakes benachrichtigen* (please report to Herr Oakes). *Er könnte Hilfe benötigen* (He may need help). *Gib ihm diesen Zettel* (Give him this note). *Das genügt* (He will understand)." It was signed, *"AW."*

He looked up at the date. October 16. He pulled the engagement book out of his pocket. On October 15 they had dinner at Gummersbach. He struggled to recall exactly the words Axel had used. *"I could never escape the West, if the de-*

cision were made." He had been right. He could never escape the West, let alone the West combined with the East. All he could do was hope that, through Blackford, his urgent and hopeful analysis would be relayed to Washington, and his life, and mission, spared. Blackford felt he must weep. But there was pounding on the door.

"Are you all right, Herr Oakes?" Blackford dried his eyes, washed his face, and opened the door.

"You are very white, Herr Oakes. Shall I bring you medicine?"

"No, Wolfgang. I wish to go back to the chapel. Kindly escort me there without my being seen by the press."

"Wait here, Herr Oakes. I will return with a plan."

Blackford winced at the word.

"I'll wait. Knock softly four times."

In fifteen minutes he heard the knock, opened the door, and was handed a hat and, with a certain diffidence, a mustache.

"It was Count Wintergrin's. He used it when he wished to travel incognito. It was in my safekeeping. I am sure he would want you to have it."

Wordlessly Blackford brought it to his upper lip. He put on the hat and, head tilted slightly down, followed Wolfgang out, away from the lobby teeming with the jabbering reporters and the blaring television, through the kitchen into the cold air of Westphalia. He signaled to Wolfgang to follow him. On reaching his car, he motioned Wolfgang to the driver's seat. "Less chance of detection that way."

Wolfgang drove skillfully to the fork and up the mountain road. He stopped automatically at the sentry gate and with his headlights illuminated the home-painted sign: ABSOLUTELY NO VISITORS. The sentry flashed a light on his face and paid no attention to the mustachioed stranger sitting by him. "Ah, Wolfgang. Is there any news? Do they know the cause of the accident?"

"They do not know the cause of the accident, Werner, and maybe they will never know."

"A terrible day for St. Anselm's, Wolfgang."

"A terrible day for Germany, Werner."

The car slid forward. "Where do you wish me to stop, Herr Oakes?"

"It doesn't matter. I shall be going to the chapel for a few minutes. Please wait for me." Blackford sensed that Wolfgang would take satisfaction from being given orders, all the better if they entailed physical discomfort which, in Wolfgang's mind, would be a measure of expiation for his failure to keep Count Wintergrin alive. "Of course, Herr Oakes, but first I shall see that you enter the chapel."

This required safe passage past two sentries posted outside with strict instructions to prevent noncourtyard-folk—Schlosshofleute—from access to the chapel.

Blackford had removed his mustache and Wolfgang nodded authoritatively to the sentries.

"Anybody in there?" he asked.

"Only the lady translator," one guard replied, motioning Oakes in.

Blackford stopped. He thought of retreating. But what, after all, was he pursuing on this morbid mission, if not a kind of full exposure? He'd have all the more willingly entered the chapel if warned it was tenanted by the whole detachment of Wintergrin's Freiwillige Schutzwehr, thirsting for victims and vengance.

He took, without explanation, Wolfgang's flashlight and walked in.

There was no light, not even from a flashlight. Only the cigarette ember from the aisle, where the box had stood that carried out the body of Jürgen Wagner.

Blackford stopped.

He stood by her, leaning against a column.

She said, "Why did you do that?"

"Because, after a lot of thought, a distinction crystallized in my mind."

"A distinction between a contract entered into with capitalists and with Communists?"

"I wouldn't put it that way, but you can. A contract to do the wrong thing."

"But then, after all, you did it." In the dark Erika could not see the astonishment on his face. Instantly he understood. She thought he had, finally, reached his hand into the purse and touched off the electrocution. He would let her think it, he decided quickly.

"I suppose you think you would have been less guilty because you didn't push the button."

"I wouldn't have been less guilty under the law. But I needed to assert my will. We are all—increasingly—automatons, Erika, and you are one willingly because it is a part of your creed. But even you broke. Even you." And, he thought to himself, we have the all-seeing, all-knowing Rufus to thank for--his death and—the survival of European freedom?

"I don't know what they will do to me if you tell them what happened. They"—he moved his flashlight vaguely east, toward Moscow—"will never know that you were prepared to let the mission fail. I understood the necessity of what happened today, and even the necessity of my co-operation. But I needed to cut out for myself a tiny little area in which I was free to move. The freedom of a prisoner, in a cell six feet by six feet, to move to one or another corner of the room. The gesture was important for me, and all the more so now, knowing that it was important to you.

"But I have something else to tell you, Erika."

"There's nothing more to say."

"Yes there is.

"He knew. *He* guessed I was an agent. He guessed what might be my mission. And he arranged that I should know this--through Wolfgang." He passed over the letter, and shone the light beam down on it. And, then, away from Erika's eyes, because he sensed, by her silence, her emotions.

"He was a good man," she said with strain.

"He was the finest man I ever knew," Blackford said. And then, hoarsely, "If there's anybody left like him, we must meet again to . . . eliminate him."

They moved toward the door and Blackford

stumbled. The beam of the flashlight pointed to the case of Conditti's wine. reduced to two bottles. He leaned down, thinking to pull one out and suggest one for the road, but decided against it.

Epilogue

"Every year"—Roland Himmelfarb complained
to his young companion who, though only sixteen, insisted that this time he would participate in
the arrangements—"it becomes harder and harder
to make out the list. Tomorrow will be *chaotic*.
Quite *chaotic!* By placing chairs behind the altar
we have made room for exactly twenty-two more
people. Twenty-two! My own wife Heidi is seated
in one of the confessionals!" Himmelfarb relaxed
for a moment, and grinned at his long-legged,
slim-faced, lightly freckled assistant. "If you have
any sins on your conscience, Rudi, *that* will be
the time to recite them: Heidi is very forgiving,
as long as it's not me."

The lanky boy, absorbed in grouping the

three-by-five cards on the large table in front of
him, did not turn his face. His chin was as yet
without trace of a beard, his flaxen hair, a fading
blond, touching lightly on his beige sweater, his
features tilted toward his work, on which he concentrated. Without lifting his head he smiled and
replied, with a trace of an English accent, "Herr
Himmelfarb has always been very kind to take all
this trouble and responsibility."

Roland Himmelfarb, owner-manager of St.
Anselm's cement factory, only eight years old but
already the largest in Westphalia, made no acknowledgment.

"My, how they agitate for an invitation. The
chancellor's office has made six separate requests.
I felt like saying: 'The only seat left in the chapel is for the chancellor himself.' But *he* wouldn't
come—no. Not even the Berlin Wall will bring
him. Not even on the tenth anniversary. Maybe it's
because of the Berlin Wall!" Himmelfarb's voice
trailed off. Now he was talking to himself. He
wondered what Axel would have done about the
Berlin Wall. But then there would have been no
Berlin Wall. He turned again to Rudi.

"But the party leaders, oh *they* are all coming. Afraid not to. Haven't missed a year. It's the
foreign diplomats who—mostly—do not dare. A
few do. Always the Spanish ambassador. And"—
he chuckled—"in 1956 the Hungarian ambassador—what timing!—entered St. Anselm's as an
accredited ambassador, and left St. Anselm's forty-five minutes later as an ex-ambassador! Axel—
your father—would have been amused. Look at
those letters"—he pointed to the table in the old

refectory. "Over ten thousand this year. Had to make a public announcement—in September, while you were at Greyburn—telling all applicants to go to their own churches at four P.M. on November twelfth, or listen on radio to our services. What they all keep asking for is television, but your father would *never* have permitted television in the chapel. Imagine what the television lights would do to the stained glass! After all that trouble in reproducing the glass. After that"—his voice faltered—"that—machine, for duplicating the glass. Well, the machine did its work. It killed your father. But . . . it took your father's blood, his light, his spirit, and put them in that glass. It restored St. Anselm's. No question about that. Some say"—he whispered now—"some old-timers say the reconstituted chapel is more beautiful even than it was before!" For the first time Rudi had turned from the cards and, eyes wide open, was looking into Roland Himmelfarb's face, the boy's father's intelligence lighting the eyes, and setting the lips. Himmelfarb went on.

"I never saw it before the war, Rudi, but I agree. Because nothing is more beautiful than St. Anselm's. The Americans spared no expense, Rudi. They were here eighteen months after the accident, and at the opening in 1954 the critics—as they say in your Latin service, *una voce dicentes*—with one voice, Rudi, they acclaim it. You are—technically—the sole owner of one of the most perfect, most beautiful twelfth-century chapels in Europe."

Rudi, who was arranging cards by code as Himmelfarb spoke, said: "Is Schwarzei-Mein an ambassador?" Roland took the card from the boy's hand and, wheeling left on his revolving desk-chair, reached for a directory on his reference shelf.

"Schwarzei-Mein . . . Dieter . . . Yes. Ambassador-designate to Italy. He'll have to be seated in the Red Section. Any room left?"—he returned the card to Rudi.

"Yes. You forget, Herr Himmelfarb, that Prince Richard broke his leg skiing yesterday. That opened up a seat." Rudi handed him another card. Himmelfarb looked at it.

"Yes. I don't know this gentleman. Except that he is an American. The request that we admit him came from—the chancellor's chief of staff. A direct call to me. He has only called me twice in all these years. Once to request, bashfully, a ticket for his daughter, who had a picture of your father hung over her bed at school and announced she would run away unless she could attend our Te Deum in 1956, I think it was— much to her father's vexation. And this time he told me he could not give me the name of the gentleman, who must be anonymous. But I accepted—in good faith (Herr Wittfogel is our friend)—his request. This is the card. Herr Mayer.' Could be anybody; any nationality. He is *not* to be seated in the Red Section with the diplomats. And of course not with family and friends in the Blue, or old comrades in Yellow, or press in Green. Put him in White—'Other Categories.' Ten years ago, Rudi, I'd have thirsted to know exactly who he is. Now I care only if he is in the market for cement. All there was before was spilled on

November 12, 1952. But maybe all my energy, all Germany's energy, is stored somewhere, perpetually, like the energy in that stained glass. Maybe it will flow out of there one day. But if it does I hope it will be on a Tuesday or Thursday, because on the other days I am traveling with my concrete salesmen."

At exactly four the next afternoon the bells of St. Anselm's church began ringing, and in the courtyard the procession formed. It was led by the Archbishop of Paderborn, who was preceded by six altar boys in white surplices and red cassocks and followed by six priests. They began their stately way up the porch, into the narthex up the nave to the altar. The day bright, the air crisp, and the courtyard teeming with several thousand people who, from loudspeakers hoisted at a half-dozen locations on the castle and on the storefronts opposite, heard the bells melt into the organ tones that silenced the crowd, transfixing it in the sorrow tones of Bach's *Kom süsser Tod*. They could hear, the chorale ended, the choir, the voices of men, women and boys singing choruses written over two hundred years earlier at Leipzig, as by a composer who knew not only the organic sorrows of the human condition but presaged those of his own parish in East Germany destined to live under protracted human tyranny. Inside, just north of the last pillar before the transept, Blackford Oakes was seated. He listened to the choir and the organ, and closed his eyes. It was, in his memory, ten years ago. To the left, diagonally across the transept filled now by celebrities, some seated with heads slightly bowed, some kneeling, he saw his office door wide open. Through it he saw the papers, the files, the apparent chaos—though, in fact, everything had been in its place—because from that clerical and architectural pandemonium the chapel had been reborn, in beauty and rectitude. Just ahead of him on the right the chromoscope had squatted. The chromoscope. Blackford shut his eyes tighter, as he had done at all the other anniversary masses—this was the fourth, out of ten, he had been able to attend. But the tighter he shut them the more livid the stigmata of death. The knife-switch to the right under the explosive colors of the south rose. Blackford, his eyes still shut, allowed the vision to track back down to the narthex, past the grubby aisle where the big box covered by tarpaulin had lain, to the corner where Conditti kept his case of lethal wine bottles.

The chorale ended, the voices stopping in perfect, blissful unison. And Blackford opened his eyes on the dazzling perfection of the colored glass that showered its chromatic unity on him, a shaft of color from behind, and in front of him the even light, resplendent beyond the October deadline Meister Gerard had warned of, the entire nave and altar sections frozen in stained-glass beauty as the brilliant silence struck and the bishop, swinging the censer, roused the choir yet again, and, the Dies Irae begun, the monks, seated in the choir stalls beyond the rood screen, so finely chiseled and varnished, responded in the Gregorian mode. The tradition was observed that there would be brief readings from Scripture, but no homily. The old priest who had been ordained in that chapel before Hitler came to power read of the eternal wells of grace for the good of the meek of heart, and all the chapel resonated, an echo chamber for the words of beauty and hope. Blackford wondered, as he had wondered before, how he could last through the ceremony; but, as before, he looked about him with awe, knowing he would never again accomplish anything to match the re-creation, at age twenty-six, of this mausoleum of hope.

It was in that proprietary sweep of *his* chapel (that was his most private vanity, though sometimes in a redistributionist excess he would think of it as his and Meister Gerard's chapel) that he spotted the man sitting at the east end of the pew, one row ahead of him. Blackford had laid eyes on him only once before—at the White House, he thought back, when Blackford was a young, anonymous escort to the pretty girl he eventually married. Allen Dulles had grown much much older in eleven years, but he was unmistakably himself. And, seated where he was, removed from the dignitaries' section, clearly he had not given his identity, else he'd have been placed, even though retired as Director of Central Intelligence, in the transept with the notables.

Blackford was inclined to ignore him as, the solemn pontifical mass ended, the congregation filed out, the boys' voices hitting the high notes in the exultant harmonies of a final chorale.

But it was not his way. Blackford observed him. No one in the throng was there to escort him, or even to notice him. The old man made his way silently, unobtrusively, through the som-

345

ber crowd, turned to watch the recessional out of the chapel. Again the altar boys and the archbishop, followed by the priests. These now were followed by the monks, and after them, walking by himself, head erect, angular limbs in uneasy rhythm with the clergy, dressed in a morning coat that made him look like an emissary from Eton College, the sun catching his light hair as he stepped down from the porch, was Count Rudolph Wintergrin, followed at a modest distance by a cluster of family and friends. His bearing was manly, but not martial; his step firm, but not obstreperous. There was a resolution and a tenderness there— —the unique blend of his father; and as he looked at him Blackford's eyes were moist. But he turned quickly and had no difficulty in relocating his quarry, who, all alone, was making his way to the parking area, just short of the castle where fifty cars, with special passes on their windshields, squatted around the tall, leafless elm trees.

Blackford waited until the old man unlocked the door at the driver's end and entered his car. He knocked on the window opposite and, surprised, but without hesitation, the old man reached over and tripped open the door handle. Blackford opened the door, got in, and closed it. Instinct led Allen Dulles, from his end, to open his door slightly. Sitting with his hands on the steering wheel, he turned his head.

Blackford did not extend his hand. He said, simply, "I'm Blackford Oakes."

"I see." Allen Dulles did not go through the formality of introducing himself.

There was a pause.

"Well, Mr. Dulles, did we do the right thing in 1952?"

"Mr. Oakes, the question you ask I do not permit. Not under *any* circumstances."

"Why not?"

"Because in this world, if you let them, the ambiguists will kill you."

"The ambiguists, as you call them, were dead right about Count Wintergrin."

"You are asking me to break my rule."

"Excuse me, sir, but is your goddamned rule more important than Wintergrin and his cause?"

"Actually," said Dulles, "it is. Or if you prefer, put it this way, Oakes: I have no alternative than to believe it is. And I hope you will understand, because if you do it will be easier; if you do not, you are still too inexperienced to discuss these matters with me."

"I don't want it to be easier for me." Oakes turned now to look directly at the man whose will had governed Blackford's own for ten years. He found himself raising his voice—something he never did. *"Wintergrin was the great hope for the West. The great opportunity. The incarnation of Western hope.* You made me . . ." He stopped, already ashamed of a formulation that stripped him of his manhood. Nobody *forced* Blackford to lead Axel to the execution chamber. He changed, as quickly as possible, the arrangement. "You lost the great chance."

Dulles was now aroused. He lit his pipe with jagged movements of his hands.

"I believe you are right. I believe Wintergrin

was right. The Russians—I believe—would not in fact have moved. But do you want to know something. I *don't* believe, Oakes?" His voice was strained.

Blackford was silent.

"I *don't* believe the lesson to draw is that we *must not* act because, in acting, we may *prove* to be wrong. And *I* know"—his eyes turned to meet Blackford's—"*that you know that Axel Wintergrin thought so too.*"

For ten years Blackford had wondered if Adjunct Professor of Russian Erika Chadinoff of the University of Geneva had confided to anyone the contents of Axel's note, and, if so, to whom. Dulles hadn't told him in so many words. But Blackford knew now whom Erika had finally turned to, whom she was talking to. That much, at least, had been accomplished by their awful experience.

There was nothing more to say. Impulsively, Blackford extended his hand, and Dulles took it.

Notes and acknowledgments

I am indebted to many friends who read the manuscript and gave me valuable suggestions. I desist from giving their names lest they should be thought responsible for any surviving imperfections, assuming there are any. But I must mention gratefully the laborious reading given to the book, and the splendid advice, of my old friend Sophie Wilkins, and my brother F. Reid Buckley. Mr. Alfred Aya of San Francisco is the gifted—and clearly dangerous—electrical architect, to whom I owe my thanks. Mr. Samuel S. Vaughan, president of Doubleday Publishing Company, has got to be the best editor in the world, as well as—running away—the most amiable. Joseph Isola, as usual, read the galleys with patience and precision. And my very special thanks to Countess Nona von Oeynhausen, who not only read the manuscript but took me to Westphalia, over hill and dale, poking in and out of castles and eateries and antique chapels, providing me with whatever insight into the German question is here.

W.F.B.

*Stamford, Connecticut
January 1978*